Butterfly 2

ALSO BY ASHLEY ANTOINETTE

Butterfly

2

ASHLEY ANTOINETTE

ST. MARTIN'S
GRIFFIN
New York

First published in the United States by St. Martin's Griffin, an imprint of St. Martin's Publishing Group

BUTTERFLY 2. Copyright © 2020 by Ashley Antoinette. All rights reserved. Printed in the United States of America. For information, address St. Martin's Publishing Group, 120 Broadway, New York, NY 10271.

www.stmartins.com

Designed by Omar Chapa

The Library of Congress Cataloging-in-Publication Data is available upon request.

ISBN 978-1-250-13638-1 (trade paperback)
ISBN 978-1-250-13639-8 (ebook)

Our books may be purchased in bulk for promotional, educational, or business use. Please contact your local bookseller or the Macmillan Corporate and Premium Sales Department at 800-221-7945, extension 5442, or by email at MacmillanSpecialMarkets@macmillan.com.

First Edition: 2020

10 9 8 7 6 5 4 3 2 1

Playlist

"Jupiter Love" by Trey Songz

"Claim" by dvsn

"Complicated" by Nivea

"Kissin' On My Tattoos" by August Alsina

"Take My Time" by Enchanting

"I Keep It To Myself" by Monica

"Show Love" by Kiana Ledé

"With You" by Drake ft. PARTYNEXTDOOR

"Suffocate" by J. Holiday

"Sippin' On Some Syrup" by Three 6 Mafia

"7 Rings" by Ariana Grande

"Understand Me" by TXS

"Circle" by Marques Houston

"You" by Jacquees

"Sorry" by 6lack

"U Should've Known Better" by Monica

"Footsteps" by Kehlani ft. Musiq Soulchild

"They Don't Know" by Jon B.

"Grateful" by Mahalia

"Won't Waste Your Time" by Jacquees

"Street Symphony" by Monica

"Destroyed" by TXS

"Where Did We Go Wrong" by Dondria

"Remind Her" by Eric Bellinger ft. RJ

"Wicked Games" by Kiana Ledé

"Loyalty" by Ann Marie ft. Vedo

"Deep" by Summer Walker

"Think About It (Don't Call My Crib)" by Donell Jones

"Wasted" by Summer Walker

"Different" by Tink

"How Could You" by Mario

"Tru Shit" by Jacob Latimore ft.
Trevor Jackson

"Can I" by Kiana Ledé

"Never The Right Time" by Janine

"Karma" by Summer Walker

"U Say" by The Bonfyre ft. 6lack

"Sleeping with the Enemy" by Sydney
Renae

"Coming Home" by Casanova ft.
Chris Brown

"What You Did" by Mahalia ft. Ella
Mai

"Wasted Love" by Jhené Aiko

"Take Me Serious" by Devvon Terrell

"All Her Love" by Donell Jones

"I'm There" by Summer Walker

"Change Me" by Justin Bieber

"You Do" by dvsn

"Come Here" by Sabrina Claudio

"Unstable" by Janine

"Promise" by Jagged Edge

"All I Ever Think About" by
Chrisette Michele

"Over and Over" by Sky

"Everything is Yours" by Kehlani

"I Wanna Be" by Chris Brown

"Easy (Unplugged)" by DaniLeigh

"Too Deep" by dvsn

"Fantasy" by Alina Baraz &
Galimatias

"Distraction" by Kehlani

"Focus on You" by Vedo

"Finesse" by Drake

"Keep Calm" by dvsn

"Lovely" by Billie Eilish ft. Khalid

"Notebook" by Chrisette Michele

"Mean What You Say" by Eric
Bellinger

"Be the One" by Sinéad Harnett

"Nobody Else" by Summer Walker

"Who's" by Jacquees

"Come With Me" by Sammie

"If You Hate Me" by Kiana Ledé

Prologue

The fog was dense as Messiah maneuvered his car through the state park. The sun had barely risen. Orange and purple painted the sky as life began to awaken. He gripped the steering wheel with one hand and kept his other on the pistol in his lap. He knew there was no point in carrying it. He wouldn't use it. Not on this day. Not on this man. He had tried before to curl a trigger on this target but had failed. He wasn't stupid enough to make the attempt again. He saw the red taillights to a silver F-150 and then saw Ethic as the driver's door opened. Stern and moody, Ethic appeared as he always did. Intolerant. Intimidating. He went to the bed of the truck and released the gate. He began to unload buckets and fishing poles, and bait from the back.

"This shit, man," Messiah mumbled as he pulled in behind the truck. Messiah knew better than to exit the car with his pistol. He stored it under his seat and climbed out, slamming the door.

"It's 6 a.m. man. We couldn't do this at no better time?" Messiah asked as he frowned.

"Fish bite best at dawn," Ethic stated.

Messiah hated the skeptical eye Ethic looked at him with. It was a new light. Ethic had never looked at him with such mistrust two years ago. It made Messiah feel like he wore his betrayal on his forehead. A scarlet letter of disdain that he feared he would never be able to shake.

"Grab that bait," Ethic instructed.

Messiah snatched up the bucket and followed Ethic down the dock to the boat that sat tied to the end.

"You bought a boat?" Messiah asked.

"For Alani. She wanted one. Something to take the kids out on. She picked this mu'fucka out and it just sits, so I took up fishing to justify the expense," Ethic said as he climbed aboard. It was a beautiful vessel with a bar, two berths for sleeping, and living space beneath.

"You'll do anything for her, huh, O.G.?" Messiah asked.

"Whatever she asks, whenever she asks. That's my job. To anticipate her needs before she even knows she needs something. I'm her man so that's my role. She'll never want for anything with me, not even attention, not even time. The money is cool but the things I can't buy she appreciates most. It's why I buy her everything else too, cuz she don't give a fuck about it."

Messiah didn't know what to say. He hoped to have something like that one day. Even his hope for it was progress because there was a time when Messiah didn't want that type of connection with another human being at all. Now he craved it. Now he yearned for it. With Mo. Damn how Messiah Williams wanted to buy Morgan Atkins a boat.

Ethic got in the captain's seat and the motor came alive, chopping up the water beneath them. They didn't speak as Ethic sailed away from the shore. Messiah took a seat at the aft, leaning over onto his knees, hands rubbing as he held his head low. He was lost, completely drowned in his own thoughts. He didn't even realize how far out they had gotten until he heard Ethic cut the engine.

He looked around as Ethic lowered the anchor.

"You know why we came out here?" Ethic asked.

Messiah bit into his bottom lip and nodded. "You're trying to decide if I'm going to stay out here," he answered. He had known the moment he had seen the boat. They could have fished from the bridge. Ethic had taken him out for tranquility. It was a perfect morning to commit a murder and the lake was a suitable resting place. Messiah was on thin ice. He knew it and still he willingly joined Ethic on this early morning boat ride. It would either be his funeral procession or his walk of redemption. Ethic would decide which. There was no avoiding it.

"You're well? You feeling a'ight?" Ethic broke the silence as he turned his chair to face Messiah.

"I'm breathing," Messiah answered. "For now."

An awkward silence. Then a scoff of acknowledgment from Ethic and more silence as Ethic stood. He grabbed the poles and the bucket of bait before going to the edge of the boat. He sat, feet thrown casually over the side as he cast a reel into the dark waters below.

"Grab a stick, let me teach you how to catch your meal, Messiah."

Messiah grabbed a fishing pole and sat beside Ethic about a yard away.

"Alani is my meal. She fills me, nourishes me. I had to hunt her because a real woman knows how to evade you. They know how to maintain some control in their lives. It's a must they retain some governance over themselves. So, I had to figure out how to get her to think that submitting to me was a choice and not dominance. If she thought I was trying to conquer her she would buck. She would go against what I wanted and the role I needed her to fill. So I hunted that. I caught that. Her heart you know? Hit every target with precision. Her heart. Her body. Her mind. Showed her a nigga could be her suitor. I proved to her over and over again that I could keep her safe, not just physically, but mentally and emotionally. By the time she even realized the game she was mine. Now she can't live without a nigga, can't breathe without me, don't sleep right without me, body don't react to nobody but me. I caught my meal. She fed me. Put everything in my belly that was needed to make me feel like a man and that pussy my nigga . . ." Ethic shook his head and Messiah snickered. Ethic didn't share details like that and Messiah hiked his brows in surprise.

"Word?" Messiah asked.

Messiah was surprised when he saw a coy grin pull at the corners of Ethic's lips. He nodded. "I'ma lucky man, young."

"I never would have fucking thought."

"You never will think about that. I'll pluck the sense from your fucking head before I ever let you look at her and think anything of the fucking sorts," Ethic snickered.

Messiah grinned.

"You got to lay bait for Mo that's so tempting she can't do shit else but bite," Ethic said. "You got to feel good to her Messiah. You got to feel safe for her. You got to look nourishing. You want her to submit and open every part of her. You got to secure her. Throw out your bait to catch a queen. A queen is gon' pick the safest kingdom. Your bait is the kingdom you build. The last name you're offering. The history behind it . . ."

Messiah's chest locked. It protested inside him.

"I can't help who I am. She'll never want that. Blood to the nigga that rocked her entire world. She won't love that. She don't want no parts of me. Mizan . . ."

"Wasn't your brother," Ethic interrupted.

Messiah's heart stilled. All his waters ran dry. His throat closed, his blood thickened, his stomach hollowed. Ethic's words attacked him, exploding in his mind like a mental bomb. The headache and heartache they caused felt cruel because no way could the words be true.

"I wish that was bond, O.G. but . . ."

"When have you ever known me to say anything just to say it? He's not your blood. He was Bookie's lover maybe. I don't know man. The shit is so fucking twisted. Your father had some preferences, some demons." Ethic paused, trying to choose his words carefully for Messiah's sake because while Mizan was no longer attached to Messiah, Bookie was. Bookie had changed him, had hurt him.

"Don't call that nigga my daddy. He ain't that. He didn't raise shit. I see how you are with Eazy. How you guide him, teach him, even when he do something wrong and you got to get in his ass you're stern but you easy with homie too. You walk real light on his heart even when you got to be the bad guy. I see that between you and him. That's fatherhood. That's the only way of being a father I will ever acknowledge. What he did . . . who he was . . . that shit ain't . . ." Messiah stopped speaking and lowered his head, shaking it in shame.

"Some niggas just got the devil in 'em. What he did to you and young boys before you. I'm sorry about that. I know it turned you cold. You never really had a chance Messiah, and if I had known earlier . . . if you had told me. I mean if I had even the smallest clue of what was happening, I would have eliminated that nigga. I would have hit him in the middle and bled that nigga slow." Ethic said the words so casually that they sent chills down Messiah's spine. He knew it wasn't an empty threat. There was no need to be loud when you meant what you said. Messiah was surprised Ethic had spoken the words at all. So often a threat was eliminated without warning because Ethic didn't grandstand. He was a murderer. Plain and simple.

"I couldn't tell nobody that," Messiah stated. "Not even you. Especially not you."

"I believe he did the same to Mizan, but the abuse turned into something else. Something sick. Some fucking Stockholm shit that I don't think anyone can ever understand because the only people who can explain it are no longer breathing. They were twisted but I have proof that Mizan was not your blood. You're not related to the man that ruined Mo's childhood and it don't matter that Bookie was yours biologically. I chose you a long time ago Messiah. I don't know if you're like my son or my brother or a little bit of both but you're mine. The shit you did cut deep. I ain't slept right since the night you told me who you were. Ain't breathed right. I lost something that day. Mo lost everything that day but you not being Mizan's brother. That'll mean something to her. It'll give you a chance. You only gon' get one shot with her though. I won't let you mess her over again. You got to come right. You got to have your shit together Messiah, none of that half-assed little boy shit you carrying around on the inside. You couldn't help your past. Couldn't control it. Couldn't do anything to stop the chaos. You can control what happens next though. You're not that little boy anymore. You understand?"

Messiah nodded and sniffed away the overwhelming emotion that watered his eyes. He flicked his nose than squeezed the bridge of it.

Ethic stared out at the water as Messiah tried to control the onslaught of trauma that plagued him.

"You cross me again and I won't hesitate," Ethic stated. "You even breathe wrong and . . ."

Messiah's grief was palpable, and Ethic stopped the threat because he realized Messiah knew what was at stake. He put a hand on Messiah's shoulder. He gave it a hard squeeze and then handed him the fishing pole.

"Fuck I'm supposed to do with this, big homie? Wifey done turned you into an old ass man," Messiah said.

Ethic chuckled and nodded as he reached into a jacket pocket retrieving an expertly rolled blunt. "Old as fuck and she probably gon' bitch up a storm when she smells this shit on me, but the least I can do is blow one with you."

"I mean, she can make an exception considering I got cancer and all," Messiah said as Ethic sparked the blunt.

"That might be the only thing that stop her from putting me on the couch," Ethic snickered.

Messiah watched Ethic pull the smoke into his lungs, cheeks puffing, and then he blew it into the air. He passed the blunt.

"Shit must be nice," Messiah said as he hit the weed. "I want that. With Mo. Shorty Doo Wop could put me on the couch every night as long as she let me come home."

"I need you to keep your distance Messiah. You can't pop up on her without warning. I need to talk to her first. Mo's fragile. She can't take a lot. You focus on getting you together and I'll figure out how to let her know you're back. Hell, that you're alive at all. She went through a hard time when you left. You've got to be careful with the way you come back into her life."

"I just want to be here man. Whatever it takes."

Messiah passed the blunt back to Ethic and Ethic nodded as if he were settling things in his head.

"I love you kid. No more fuck ups," Ethic stated.

Messiah's eyes burned. To have forgiveness and love after what he'd done. He hadn't expected to receive that much. It was a gift he had never received. A gift he didn't deserve. He couldn't even respond with words because he was afraid he would lose it. The sudden tug on his line startled him, distracting him. A friendly shift of focus from God right when it was needed . . . right when the vulnerability was making two of His most difficult children uncomfortable. A fish had taken the bait.

"Oh, shit what I do?" Messiah asked.

"Start reeling," Ethic said. Messiah stood, slightly panicked as he pulled in the fish.

"Yo' this mu'fucka ain't coming up!" Messiah shouted. It was one of very few times in his life that felt carefree. It felt easy. Like nothing outside of this interaction mattered. Like Ethic was indeed his father and as long as he had him, he knew he would be okay. Ethic would never know how much he meant to Messiah because Messiah would never tell him. Messiah whirled the fishing pole until a small fish came flopping out of the water.

"Yo' this little mu'fucka got heart," Messiah said, holding up the end of the line.

Ethic hollered as he stood to his feet.

"Throw it back, man. Sometimes you catch something just to let it go. When it's for you, you'll know it. That ain't our catch."

1

Ahmeek sat in the car listening to the hum of his engine as it ticked to a stop. Crickets serenaded the night air. The green numbers on his console read 11:24 p.m. It had taken him two hours to get to her and he had been sitting there, engrossed in thought, for half an hour longer. He knew she was waiting but his conscience had him glued to his seat. His heart thundered in his chest as he finessed his beard, mind zoned out as his thoughts swarmed him. He rested against the head rest. He had to take a beat. He had to pause. To think. He was in deep. He was drowning in Morgan Atkins and neither of them wanted to be saved. They hadn't even taken a moment to come up for air. What they were doing was reckless. His heart was involved. Hers had been from the start and he didn't want to fumble, his or hers. He didn't want to ugly up something that had been beautiful thus far. He felt like turning around because once he got out the car he would have to take it all the way. She had called him. Requested his presence in the middle of the night. There was only one thing she could have wanted, but now he questioned if he should oblige. Conflict swirled in his chest. He saw her legs first as she descended the steps. Heels at midnight, silk boy shorts, and the tiniest silk spaghetti strap negligee. The color was the same as her skin. He could barely tell that she had anything on at all.

"Damn," he whispered. Morgan Atkins was beautiful. Ass for days, thighs that trembled, and full breasts that bounced with every step. Flashes of his lips around her areola as he palmed them entered his mind. They had just done this. She had just called him for rescue days before and he had dropped everything, to get to her, to save her. He had explored her depths just hours ago, not even a full day had passed and already she needed him again. It scared him. This was becoming a need. It was becoming serious and his heart pounded. He had witnessed this pull. He had seen Messiah get lost in it. Like a black hole Morgan had sucked him in. Now he understood. Now, that it was him, now that his mind was telling him to cut the shit off, but his heart was laughing at the request, he got it. She was irresistible. He was gangster, but she was godly. She called the shots. She was the coach and she was making him put up a thousand shots. Ahmeek was a fucking shooter. Three points, all net. Her franchise player. His dick jumped. Ahmeek couldn't do anything but shake his head and appreciate the sight as she folded her arms across her chest, forcing the mounds of her flesh to peak as she walked to his side of the car. She pulled open the door.

"Are you going to sit out here all night?"

He switched off the ignition and turned sideways, placing his feet to the concrete and leaning elbows to knees. He snapped his eyes closed. Air filled his lungs. One hand against his strong thigh he braced himself before looking up. He knew when he looked at her she would hypnotize him. Morgan Atkins stood in front of him.

"Did they give you a hard time at the gate?" she asked. She

was fucking phenomenal. Long hair curly and slightly damp from the shower she'd taken, face bare, eyes as dark as night.

"Nah, they didn't," he answered.

"Are you giving yourself a hard time?" she asked. He bit his bottom lip and nodded, hanging his head. His turmoil hung on his shoulders. The guilt of his attraction to her weighed on him, but she had called and when the queen summoned, you answered.

"You're fucking me up, Mo. I'm trying here." Morgan placed a hand on the top of his head and he placed a hand to her stomach, fingers balling the fabric of her tiny camisole in his hands as she traced the pattern of his waves. "You know where you're going to end up, so let's just stop feeling guilty about it," she whispered.

"You got to understand love . . ." he pushed and shook his head. "The shit I wanna do . . ."

"We've already done," she reminded.

"Nah, love. New shit. More shit. Meek shit."

Morgan's entire body came alive. Her face turned red. She had heard the stories. Him fucking bitches until they lost their minds. That stalk a nigga dick. That bust his windows out his car dick. That put his tags in your name dick. That let him flip your income tax return dick. She wanted it, wanted it so bad that her nipples tightened, screaming for attention. Mo grabbed one hand with both of hers and pulled him to his feet, backpedaling until he stood and followed her. His stomach hollowed. His head was all over the place. Morgan and Ahmeek. Nobody could have predicted this. If anyone had ever suggested it he would have smacked the shit out niggas, but here he was. Here they were, and it was more than sex. It was more than physical.

"You have to be careful with that girl, Meekie. It's not right. It's not wrong either. It just is. The two of you are in denial if you

think this is friendship. This is love and the stakes are high. You be extremely careful with how you handle this with her. She's been broken before. Women don't come back the same and someone's going to end up hurt."

His mother's words rang in his mind. It was the warning that made him think maybe, just maybe this wasn't such a great idea.

"I don't plan on doing no hurting Ma," he had said.

"You need to worry about her hurting you. She's not one of them little jump-offs you used to running around here with. She got the leverage son. She's going to eat you alive."

They were both silent as he followed her up the stairs. The way her body reacted to movement was incredible. Little Morgan wasn't quite little Morgan anymore. She had filled out, mentally and physically and she had ordered him up like she was picking up the phone to request a meal. She wanted dick, extra-large, with a side of finesse. Morgan was amazing. She took all of him. She didn't run. Women ran from him, when he hit the bottom they bolted. Morgan took it and called his name. Her sultry voice, screaming that shit like she was in another world. He shook his head. Maybe his mother was right. She was going to eat him alive because he couldn't get her off his mind. The sway of her hips led him to her door. Candles lit. Vanilla scent. They filled the apartment.

"Have a seat, Ahmeek," she said. Her voice was sugary, full of seduction as she pulled a chair out for him, positioning it right in front of her mirrored wall.

Girl you know that you're the shit when you're walking with them heels on . . .

Morgan tiptoed over to him and stood between his wide legs. For the entire first verse she appreciated herself, swaying her hips, rolling her waist, and lifting her hands then pulling her own hair before swinging it wildly. Morgan was a show woman, the very best kind. She reached into his pocket to retrieve his phone, powering it off and tossing it to the couch. He was hers. No phone calls would be interrupting them. When that bridge hit Morgan lowered slowly into his lap.

I think it's time we take a trip to the bedddd

Her hands wrapped around his neck, then up the back of his head and over the top of his waves as she surfed on him, riding wood so hard that the seat of her shorts soaked.

She stood and turned. Her eyes closed when she felt his teeth on her ass. He peeled her shorts away and licked the entire crease of her ass. Morgan quivered as her face crushed, like the can you put in the recycle machine. She was destroyed. Lust recycled the moan that slipped from her mouth. One hand to the small of her back bent her over. Her hamstrings pulled as she placed her hands on the floor. Ahmeek parted her, lips spreading, opening her like she was a double-sided refrigerator and he was looking for something to eat. His favorite dish. Her. He dove in nose first, moving his head side to side, nestling deep then pulling her clit into his mouth. He used so much pressure that his cheeks collapsed, dimpling, as he feasted on her.

"Meekie," she gasped as her face pinched.

"Mmmm," he groaned, planting both hands on her ass and pulling back to admire her body as he squeezed then rotated it. So much fucking ass in the palms of his hands. His dick ached he wanted it so bad. "My God, love. This shit . . ."

He didn't even want to take the time to undress. He reached in his joggers and gripped himself, lowering them just enough to pull her down onto him.

Morgan danced, hands in front of her, snapping, eyes closed, swagging. Lip trapped between her teeth, moaning.

"You the shit, love. Fuccccck." He couldn't even control the shit that came out his mouth. Morgan was in a zone. She had called him over with this very thing in mind. Morgan had caught a groove. She kept the beat, a little off, always a little off as her head nodded, and her hips hit circles. She switched direction, rocking on him so hard the back legs of the chair lifted every time she rolled forward.

"Ssss," he sucked in air between his teeth as he gripped her hips. His toes curled. Morgan was working him. Putting in overtime. A double shift on a holiday so she was getting time and a half. She rolled her body left and snapped, those fingers keeping the beat.

Forward. Snap. Right. Snap. Left. Snap.

I think it's time we take a trip to the bedddd . . .

He pushed her ass up a little, so he could see her sliding on then off. He licked his lip and bit down. She glossed him so well. "This pussy is amazing love. Shit's ridiculous," he groaned. He leaned forward and planted teeth in the slight roll that gathered when she grinded against him. "Fuck, Mo."

She popped that thang to the beat, lifting all the way to the tip of him, squatting on the dick, thighs burning, back sweating, hair swinging, heart pounding. Nobody moved like Mo. She made everything art. Like she did everything to music. A lap dance, the most sensual kind, only he didn't have to pay to play. He had free access, like a thirty-day trial, and he wondered if it was temporary, if he'd have to figure out how to keep coming back. Switching emails every time the shit expired so he could get it again and again. Fuck it, he was signing up.

Auto-pay every month so he could have it whenever he liked. Some shit was just a necessity.

"Meekie baby, I'm cumming," she gasped.

"Yup," he admired as she creamed all over him. She was making a mess. "Ohh shit."

He exploded, and he physically picked Morgan up to avoid shooting up her club. "Damn, love. I'ma put a baby in you. You got to chill," he groaned. "Fuck." Ahmeek was a man who could fuck all night, but Morgan had broken him down in minutes. She was that good. He'd have to make up for it on round two because there was no holding back what was coming out of him.

Morgan lifted and Ahmeek grabbed her hand before she could walk away. She looked at him.

"This shit is fucked up," he said.

"I know," she answered. One hand held her lower back, the other gripped one side of her face. "I know. If it has to feel a little bad to feel this good, I'll take that. I'm never letting go of this. Not ever."

"What time you on, Mo?" Ahmeek whispered. The words didn't even feel like his own. Now he was the one asking about status? Fucking then wondering what it meant? Many women had posed the exact same question to him after an amazing night. Oh, how the tables had turned. Morgan and the ride she had given him on the magic Morgan bus, had him searching for clarity. He felt like a whole bitch.

There was vulnerability hidden behind his tough exterior. Gangster ass. Hood ass. Murder Meek had been touched. Morgan had gotten to him . . . touched him right where his ribs be at. Anxiety caused tension in her. He felt her apprehension. "Leave that nigga. I got you. I got the twins. Fuck with me, Morgan. For real. No games. No apologizing for it."

"You don't want that," she whispered. "You think you do, but you don't. It's a lot, Ahmeek. It's not always like this. It's not fun. It's responsibility. We haven't even been out together yet. Me leaving with you after a night of clubbing doesn't count."

"So, let me take you out. We had plans. *You* altered them," he snickered. "Skating on Friday. Your request. I prefer something a little more grown man, but I'm with it, love. I'm not tucking you away. I don't want to come through at night and leave in the morning. The shadows and shit. It's not how I prefer to do this, not with you."

She blushed and turned her head. "You want to show me off," she whispered.

He snickered, licking those lips. "You pretty as fuck, Mo, but it ain't about the stunt. I just don't want you to feel like you're a secret. You hide shit that you're embarrassed about. Time's up for your nigga though. You ain't his no more."

She kissed him and Ahmeek loved it. Bitches and their lips. It wasn't his thing. He and the crew had joked often that you couldn't trust women. That you never knew where the lips of women had been. The three roughest men in the city had all fallen victim. Morgan had taken out two of them. Aria had handled the third. He felt like a sucker as he groaned, getting lost in the taste of her. The delicacy of her. He'd heard stories of Justine Atkins, even more stories of Raven Atkins, but damn, Morgan Atkins elevated the bloodline. She would be a legend. The fucking queen that launched a thousand ships because Ahmeek would go to war for her.

I think it's time we take a trip to the bedddd

He carried her to the bedroom and tossed her on the bed. She laughed as she bounced, and he stepped out of his clothes. He placed knuckles to the bed as he climbed on top of her.

"What you do to a nigga ain't normal, Morgan," he said.

"Morgan, huh?" she said, biting his bottom lip.

"That's what your mama named you, nigga," he said. He was inside her and they just lay there.

"That ain't what my man named me, though," she whispered. "My man calls me Love so get it right next time."

He smiled, and Morgan shook her head. That smile that was so rare made her heart flutter. He stroked her, and she gasped. "Your man, huh?" he asked.

She nodded, eyes closed, as she moaned. "Mmm, yes, Meekie. You're mine."

He was so deep, and it felt so good that Morgan was elevated . . . high . . . there were stars on the ceiling. He was a beast and Morgan couldn't slay him. He left her exhausted. Legs quaking as they wrapped around his waist. Clit sore because when he was done he sucked on it all night. She was spent. She could barely keep her eyes open by the time they were done. Three orgasms each before they realized any more would be gluttony. She laid on top of him, leg strewn over his body as he wrapped her with one arm. The sound of his heartbeat lulled her to sleep. This man was hers and she was terrified of what it meant because the last time she had given her heart to a man like Ahmeek she hadn't come out of the situation the same. The last thing Mo wanted to do was give someone the chance to hurt her again.

I've got to be careful with this.

2

Morgan awoke first and the level of comfort she felt when she looked at Ahmeek made a warmth spread through her heart. She smiled, turning on her back and lifting dreamy eyes to the ceiling. She placed both hands over her face and shook her head in disbelief. She opened her fingers to peek through them, just to get a glimpse of him. She had to stop the giddy titter from waking him. She had never felt like this before. She had been in love. She had been crazy in love before. Messiah had connected to her soul in ways that made them one, but with him the emotions were so heightened that it felt risky. It gave her anxiety to be with Messiah. She had lived for that heart pounding thrill ride. Loving Messiah was like riding a rollercoaster. The thrill she had experienced with him was the same thrill she felt when she used to climb on the back of his motorcycle. Nothing made her heart race like those late-night rides. No one made her heart race like Messiah Williams. She couldn't ever take that away from him. He lit her soul on fire. Ahmeek Harris was like a big body Benz. The ride was smoother. It felt like luxury. Ahmeek felt safe.

Her phone went off and Morgan reached for the night stand, unplugging the phone from the charger to silence it before it awakened him. She wanted him to sleep. She wanted him to stay . Morgan wanted to be up under him as long as possible before the day's demands pulled them apart.

BASH
Open the door.

Her heart stalled. Morgan climbed out of bed, hurriedly throwing on her silk kimono robe, and trying her hardest not to awaken Ahmeek. Her heart pounded, and her legs felt like they would give out as she pulled the door to her bedroom closed. She damn near ran to the front door. She opened it slightly.

"Hey, what are you doing here?" she asked.

Bash frowned and put a hand to the door. Morgan pushed back. "I'm not feeling well, Bash. I know we have some things to talk about . . ."

"Like you running off with a nigga in the middle of your Free Press interview? Yeah we got some things to discuss, Mo. What's up with you?" he asked. "Which one of them are you fucking?"

"What?" Morgan asked.

"You ran off with one of Messiah's friends. Which one?" he asked. "Ahmeek, right?"

Bash pushed against the door again. "What you doing? Let me in. You gon' make me talk through the door?" He pushed into the apartment and towered over her. "You embarrassed yourself and my family. You do the most asinine shit! We were good in London! I take you out the ghetto and you—"

"The ghetto?! I grew up in a million-dollar house! What are you talking about?" Morgan protested.

"I'm talking about how you were one way in London and we come back here and you're a completely different girl, Mo. What the fuck is up? You're wearing my ring and hopping on motorcycles with bums who won't be more than the neighborhood thug."

"He's not a thug." She knew she was dick-whipped because she didn't even mean to defend him. The accusation that the man in her bed was nothing more than a statistic pissed her off however.

"Don't defend your side nigga to me!" Bash shouted, pointing a stern finger at her. His face burned with aggression.

"He's not a side nigga!" There she went again with her defending. How could someone so important to her be a side anything? Ahmeek Harris was the main dish, the turkey on Thanksgiving, and if he was a side, he was Macaroni and Cheese because that's what everyone loved the most on the holiday anyway.

"I can't do this right now. Please, I promise. We'll talk but just leave. My head is pounding, and I just don't want to fight." She walked to the door and held it open.

"You're serious right now?" Bash asked. "I'm not going nowhere until you explain your fucking self. Are you fucking that nigga?"

The more upset he got the louder the argument became. Morgan turned away from him so that he wouldn't see her tear-filled eyes. She needed him to leave ... she couldn't handle a confrontation. She didn't want it to get out of hand. It wasn't until this very moment that she realized how risky her affair with Ahmeek was. She should have been fearful of Bash discovering Meek but in her twisted heart she feared Ahmeek waking up to find Bash inside her apartment, inside their bubble.

He was in front of her now, finger in her face, hand

wrapped around her neck as he pushed her hard into the door. Morgan's eyes widened in shock. He was walking a fine line as his fingers tightened around her throat.

"You don't want to do this, Bash," she said. She stared him in the eyes, brow lifted. "I said we can talk. Later. When I'm ready. And you might want to loosen your grip before you do something stupid. At that point it'll no longer be in my hands." Bash slammed a hard hand to the door. It was so close to her head that Morgan jumped.

"You fucked him, didn't you? You got me out here waiting until you're ready but you're sleeping with him?"

"Wasn't no sleeping, homie. Wasn't no waiting neither and those hands around her neck like that . . . it's a bad fucking idea."

Morgan's body froze. Her stomach fell out of her. She was sure it was on the floor. The tears she had been holding in fell as she turned to face Ahmeek. He came out of the room in sweat-pants, his Ralph Lauren boxers showing as they hung slightly off his waist. He was shirtless revealing ink and abs, abs she had traced with her tongue just hours before. His forehead wrinkled as his brow bent. Morgan was ashamed that her clit pulsed. He was so damned fine with his pretty boy looks, mean boy vibes, and his fuck boy dick print. He wasn't one, but damn if he didn't have the type of dick to ruin a bitch's life. He was in fact, ruining her life . . . tearing up a relationship that had been perfectly fine before he had shown her how good it could feel to be loved on by a real nigga. He didn't lie, didn't conceal, didn't control. Morgan's heart ached so good that she couldn't stop the smile that played at the corners of her mouth. He leaned against the wall, chewing on the inside of his jaw, something he did when he was holding back anger. A bad habit. The taste of blood filled his mouth and he rubbed one hand down his waves. He pulled on his beard before locking one hand around the opposite wrist. He was so calm, but Morgan knew that was a bad thing. She knew there were no civil thoughts going through Ahmeek's head.

Bash couldn't do anything but react. He was so enraged he pushed Morgan hard against the door, banging her head against the wood before crossing the room toward Ahmeek. "What the fuck did you just say to . . ." Before Bash could even finish his sentence Ahmeek came off the wall. Morgan watched in horror. They were like two freight trains on the same track headed for one another. Ahmeek scooped Bash, sending him back first into her glass coffee table. Ahmeek didn't care that it was shards of glass everywhere, he let them cut into the bottoms of his feet as he straddled Bash, delivering vicious blows to his jaw.

He clicked out. All logic went out the window. The sickening crack of bones breaking made Morgan place hands over her mouth. She hadn't wanted this. She knew she was to blame. This brutal beating was a result of her dishonesty and Bash was undeserving.

Ahmeek's fist crashed across Bash's face again and Morgan recoiled. It was like she could feel the blow. Meek put a knee to Bash's neck and with one hand pressed his face hard into the glass.

"Arghh!" Bash cried out.

"Ahmeek!" Morgan said. "Stop! He's had enough!"

Meek bit down into his bottom lip because he didn't leave food on his plate. Any man he had ever put hands on he had put dirt on too. Morgan didn't want that however.

"Meek! I said stop! I could have handled it. You should have just stayed out of it!"

He lifted squinted eyes to her and then looked down at Bash who was barely conscious. Bash rolled onto his side groaning. Ahmeek scoffed. He lifted, flexing his injured fist, open and close, to make sure it wasn't broken. He gritted his teeth, temple throbbing.

He flicked his nose in irritation and then ran his tongue across his top row of teeth before he nodded. "Your nigga, your business Mo," he said as he retreated to the bedroom. Morgan's lip quivered as she bent down.

"I'm sorry," she said, frowning. She shook her head as she helped him up to the couch. Ahmeek emerged fully dressed, keys in hand.

"Meek," she called after him. Morgan's lip trembled as she sprang from the couch and rushed after him. He made it all the way to the hallway before she caught him, grabbing his hand. He jerked away from her and Morgan stopped.

"So you're just gonna leave?" she asked. "I didn't say I wanted you to leave but that wasn't necessary! You niggas and your fucking anger issues!"

Ahmeek advanced on her, pinning her against the wall and pointing a stern finger in her face. "Ain't no *you* niggas. Ain't no issues in my head or my heart, Morgan. I ain't Messiah. I ain't Isa. I don't fucking pop off unless it's necessary. Niggas don't run up on me and live to tell about it. The nigga had his hand wrapped around your throat but I'm the bad guy? Fuck out of here."

"Just calm down, please," she whispered.

Meek raised both hands in surrender and back pedaled.

"I'm calm. I'm out of it, Mo," he said. He took the air in her lungs with him as he left. Morgan walked back into her apartment and Bash burned a hole in her with his stare. He sat on the couch, leaned onto his elbows, head drooping as he licked blood from his lip. Morgan went to the kitchen retrieving a wet towel before returning to Bash.

She tried to place it to his bloody face, but Bash snatched it from her hands, opting to do it himself.

Morgan's soul left her body as she exhaled. "I really didn't want you to find out this way. I've been unhappy for a long time, Bash," she said, her voice low.

"Since when? We were good Morgan. We were building together."

"You were building, Bash. I was just following orders. Your mother, she planned out my entire life. She has me lying about who my kids belong to, has me dressing to her standards, speaking, walking, eating to her standards, Bash. All for what? To uphold your family's name. I can't breathe when I'm with you and it's not even your fault."

"How long you been fucking him?" Bash asked.

Morgan was silent as she sat beside him. Her eyes were on the glass pieces on the floor. Those pieces reminded her of herself . . . of her heart . . . she was shattered and although she seemed okay, no amount of glue would be able to piece her together again. Ahmeek was trying and Morgan wished she could let him, but no one knew how hard it was to trust again. The things she felt for Ahmeek were terrifying. They made her vulnerable, they made her ache inside, and she couldn't depend on that feeling to stay. She didn't want to get used to it because her past had taught her that it wouldn't last. Ahmeek would feel good until one day he didn't, and Morgan couldn't put all her eggs in his basket. That basket would grow weak and when it broke she didn't want her soul cracked. Like last time. So she kept Bash around. Bash didn't make her weak. He wasn't capable of it. He provided friendship without requiring her vulnerability. She loved him on the surface but she hadn't explored his depths. She had no desire to. She was satisfied with a shallow connection. A shallow hole could be filled. If she let another man dig deep and then he left, she would never be the same. Bash was safe. Her silence was all the answer he needed, and she knew it hurt him, but she couldn't defend wrong. She was wrong. The way she had carried him was wrong, but she would rather give hurt than receive it. She had been taught that somebody in a relationship always felt pain and she had vowed to never be the one to feel that way again.

He scoffed. "I'm wasting my time with you. I've raised your kids as my own and put the whole world at your feet and you out here hoeing for that nigga!"

He had never raised his voice at her before. His tone shocked her.

"I'm not screaming. I'm not fighting. I just want to talk about where we go from here," Morgan stated.

"You're a fucking piece of work," he stated. "You're worthless. You weren't shit when I met you. A little girl with a drug dealing daddy from the ghetto. I should have left your ass there."

Morgan's eyes widened. "Wow," she scoffed. She went to stand, and Bash pulled her arm, jerking her so hard her knees hit the ground, sinking into the glass.

"Don't walk away when I'm talking to you! You're my fiancée . . ."

"Well maybe I shouldn't be!" Morgan screamed as she pushed him off her. He stood, towering over her. "Yes! I'm fucking him. He knows me! He knows Morgan Atkins. The daughter of a drug dealer from Flint and instead of judging me for it he loves that shit. He fucking cherishes me for who I am right now, today, not who he can turn me into!" Morgan pulled the ring off her finger. "I'm not your fiancée. You're not engaged to Morgan Atkins. I don't even know the girl who said yes to you."

Bash pulled the corner of his bloody lip into his mouth and touched it with his thumb, frowning as he shook his head.

"You don't want to be with me, Mo? You gon' take those kids from me? After everything I've done for you?"

"It just doesn't feel like this is where I'm supposed to be," Morgan said.

"But you're supposed to be with him? They're all the same Mo! He's not sticking around! He gon' leave you just like the nigga before. Wasn't that man Messiah's friend? You would rather crawl around in the gutter as a pass around than marry somebody who can elevate you."

The words jolted her.

"Have some self-respect, Mo!" Bash stated. "I asked you to be my wife. What have any of them ever done besides fuck you?"

Morgan had never felt so low. She placed the back of one hand to her forehead and one hand on her stomach as she tried to stop his words from ripping through her. She was choking on cries, refusing to let them spill. He had hurt her feelings so badly. He had pointed out the obvious and the thought that she was nothing more than a conquest to Ahmeek brought her to tears. Bash sat on the couch, leaning over onto his knees and shaking his head as he stared at the floor.

"Tell me what he is giving you, that I don't?" he whispered, calming, forcing his anger down to give way to what he was really feeling. Loss.

"I don't know," Morgan whispered as a tear fell down her cheek. "He just understands me . . ."

"Help me understand you, Mo. Do you not love me? Because I love the hell out of you," Bash admitted. "From the first time I saw you."

Morgan broke. Even after discovering her in bed with another man, even with the smell of Ahmeek still on her skin, even after taking a brutal beating Bash still wanted her. Was still professing his love. It reminded her of Messiah. It reminded her of how Messiah had taken advantage of her love for him. She was doing that in this moment. Hurting Bash. Taking advantage of him because she knew he loved her more . . . Messiah had turned her heartless. Messiah had turned her into a fucked-up person. Someone who went around selfishly stealing hearts just to break them simply because she could.

"I do care about you, Bash. It's just not . . ." She paused. How could she word this? How could she say how she felt without hurting him more? "You're my friend. I care about you like that. Like I look at you and I see my best friend. We joke, we have a good time. The twins adore you. You're kind, but I'm not in love with you. I can't be because there is shit in my heart that stops me from falling too hard. After Messiah, I can't fall that hard," she said. "I need to remain in control of my heart . . . of my life . . . and your family takes control of me. I have no freedom. Your mom . . ."

"Is a bitch, Mo. Everyone knows she's a bitch. I don't want her to be the reason I lose you. Okay, you don't love me. You can grow to love me though, Morgan. Love grows. I'm not dangerous or gangster or from the streets but I'll love you right, Mo."

"I don't know if that's enough," she answered. "I don't know if I can be who you want."

"Don't throw the past two years away for him," Bash answered. "Just give me a chance to keep my hat in the ring. Wear my ring, Mo. I know I fucked up in Vegas. I was angry and I was dead ass wrong, Morgan. If this is payback for that, let it be done. I fucked up. You fucked up. Now let's get it right."

"You left my kids backstage by themselves," Morgan said, shaking her head.

"Don't do that, Mo. They're mine too. You know I'm here for them like they belong to me," Bash said.

"But they don't. It's clear that you don't really feel that way because you would never have left them if they were yours. If they shared your blood and had your last name."

"And he loves them better? You think he'll love you better?" Bash asked.

"I don't know!" Morgan shouted. "He's just . . ." Morgan sighed as anxiety built in her chest. "I don't know."

"Just give me a chance to make it right." Bash pulled her into his arms. The feeling of his hands around her waist didn't repulse her but the embrace didn't warm her like it should. There was no safety in his touch, no power, no aggression . . . just desperation. He was desperate not to lose her. Morgan was full of regrets. She should have never allowed him to sneak out of the friend zone. He had helped her through some of the hardest days of her life and she felt obligated to give him something in return . . . she was repaying a debt to him by giving him partnership, promising him marriage. She had never even said yes. Not to the proposal, not to the relationship, not to any of it. She had gone along with things because nothing was worth caring about. She had been caught in the grips of depression and grief while Bash made plans for the rest of her life. He had taken her silence as permission. Bash had coerced a space in her life when she was in the worst of states and now, she felt trapped. Morgan never expected to find someone who made her want to love again. She had been okay with settling before. Now she wanted greatness. Now she wanted someone else and guilt was eating her alive because Bash had done his part, he had been a support to her and it still wasn't enough. She wondered if it were true . . . if she could learn to love him. If she could be happy one day with Bash the way she was when she was with Ahmeek. She still couldn't believe that she felt that way about a man she should have no feelings for at all, but it was so potent, and it made her not want to accept anything that came with dilution.

"Okay," she said, giving in. He deserved the chance. That

was the least she could do. "But this is a lot. It's too much fighting and yelling. I need some space to think. Just a day or two. Please."

"Whatever you need, Mo. Do I need to worry about you? With him?" he asked.

Morgan looked him in the eyes and shook her head. "No. It's done. I'll end it."

3

"So, it's nothing fancy. Four walls, one bedroom, one bath. Rent is eight hundred dollars per month. I'll need first and last, plus deposit."

Messiah looked around the small space and pulled in a deep breath. This was a far cry from what he had once possessed. He had fallen so far from the throne he didn't even remember what it felt like to be on top. He had given every dime he had to Morgan. He didn't regret it. She deserved it. He hoped it had done some good. A consolation for breaking her heart. He was down but Messiah had no worries. He could get to the money in his sleep. He wouldn't be down long.

"I'll take it," he said.

He peeled off $2500 from the small knot he had in his pocket. It was half of what he had to his name. He had clothes, his car, his bike, a handful of guns, and $2500 left. A legit man would sell the toys for cash, but Messiah was an outlaw. The all-white BMW represented a status he once held in the streets. A king. The king. He would rather grind up than get rid of them.

The woman placed a key on the countertop and pulled a lease agreement from the folder she clutched to her chest.

"I'll just need your signature on a few pages and you'll be all set," she said.

Messiah took the pen and signed his name.

The leasing agent walked out, and Messiah hopped up onto the countertop, looking around the empty space. It reminded him of Mo's place ... of the day he had moved her into her apartment all those years ago. He was so close to her. In the same zip code, but he couldn't reach out, not yet. Ethic had been clear. Messiah needed to wait until the right time to approach Morgan because she had been through a lot. He wondered what a lot meant. How had she coped after he had disappeared? It tore him apart thinking of the ways she had hurt after he left. He knew she would have a hard time, but he had been in a situation where life and death trumped emotions. Leaving her felt less cruel than making her watch him die. If he could go back he would do things a bit different, because when things became unbearable he would have given anything to hear her voice. He had made a mistake by abandoning her. He just wanted to make it right. He would be unsettled until he saw her face. Seeing Ethic, gaining his forgiveness so easily gave him hope that Mo would accept him back into her life. She would be mad, but he would take that. He would take whatever energy she was giving as long as she let him come home. Messiah grabbed the key and flipped up the hood of his sweatshirt before walking out. He couldn't sit around, waiting. If he was going to come back for Mo, he wasn't coming empty handed. He had to have more to offer than just himself because he knew he wasn't worth shit in her book. He couldn't let anyone else know he was back before telling Mo. Even Isa and Ahmeek had to wait. He would just have to keep a low profile until Ethic gave him the green light. Until then he would put in work to get back on his feet.

4

The money machine was the soundtrack for the evening as Ahmeek and Isa sat around the living room table counting up. Isa balanced a short blunt between his lips as his hands flipped through the bills in front of him. A knock at the door lifted Isa from his seat as he reached for the chrome pistol that laid on the money covered table.

"That's Beans?" Ahmeek inquired, as his chocolate fingers ran through the money in his hand.

"Dropping off the bag. His block's going crazy," Isa stated. He peeked out the blinds before reaching the door and then pulled it open. A handshake amongst gangsters was the formal greeting before the mountain of a man lowered his head to step inside the house.

"Murder Meek," the man greeted. Meek stood briefly, dapping him up with one hand before reclaiming his seat.

"Beans, baby what's good?" Meek acknowledged.

"Shit, everything," Beans said dropping the duffel at Meek's feet.

"We got to bust this down?" Meek asked unzipping the

bag to reveal that it was stuffed to the tip top with banded rolls of money.

"Nah that's all you. That's your cut. Not a dollar short," he said.

"Square bi'ness," Meek answered. Ahmeek resumed counting, glancing up at the 65-inch screen on the wall. The Lakers game played in front of him, but his hands flipped through the bread while he watched, never losing count. He was accurate at all things money. All things logic. Ahmeek was all G. He could bang with the best of them, but he was well aware that his biggest weapon was his mind.

"Bron letting off tonight," Ahmeek noted.

"I had the shit playing on XM on the way over. He going for the triple double, ain't he?" Beans asked as he pulled up his pants and took a seat on the couch.

"Hmm, hmm. Homie bringing that bag home for a nigga. I got five bands on the first half. Lakers minus two," Isa said.

"You covering that," Ahmeek stated, surely.

Isa held out the blunt and Meek grabbed it, placing it between his lips, pulling hard before passing it back. He held it in for an extra beat before blowing it out.

"What's good bro? You grim than a mu'fucka," Beans noted.

"Nigga spell grim," Ahmeek shot back as he put the weed in rotation, passing it to Beans.

Beans laughed and took the blunt.

"Mo Money got this nigga in his bag. Mo crazy than a mu'fucka, man," Isa said, snickering. "I don't never want no bitch like that. One thang go wrong and a nigga whole world fucked up? Nahhh. I'm good, G."

"Fuck you talking about? We talking about feelings now nigga?" Meek chastised, face bent in frustration. "Count this money, bruh. I ain't speaking on Mo."

"I'm just saying nigggaaaaa. That pussy gotta bang cuz Mo out here casting spells like this shit is bewitched," Isa said, laughing.

Meek shook his head, leaning forward on his elbows but offered no response.

"Shorty got ass for days. I'd be chin deep in that shit, my nigga. I heard that shit sliding down a nigga throat like Rosé. Call that bitch mo-wet."

Ahmeek's entire body went still and he sucked his front teeth, running his tongue along the inside of his jawline as his forehead dipped.

"Yo bruh go get that bottle out the fridge, let's pop one," Ahmeek stated, calmly. It was the type of tranquility that made everything go silent when a storm was approaching.

"Hell yeah, I'm with it. I ain't got nowhere to be," Beans stated, eyes on the game. Isa shook his head.

"Here we go," Isa muttered as he went to retrieve the bottle.

Ahmeek finessed his beard and then rubbed his hands together until Isa returned with the bottle.

"You say that pussy slide down a nigga throat like Moet?" Ahmeek asked looking at Beans, deadpanning on him with so much conviction that his malice wasn't to be missed.

Beans froze. "Nigga you for real, right now? You cappin' over pussy, my nigga. As much pussy as we done tossed up. You hit 'em and pass 'em down homie. Pass that shit the fuck down when you done." Beans chuckled.

Isa groaned. "Say less my nigga, damn."

Meek popped the top on the champagne, sending the cork flying. He tipped it to his mouth and out of nowhere he brought the bottle crashing into the side of Beans's face. He hit him so hard that the bottle broke, sending glass deep into Ahmeek's hand. Meek didn't let up. He gripped Beans's collar as he delivered audible blows to Beans's bloody face.

"Call that bitch what? Mo-wet, nigga? You want to know what it tastes like sliding down your throat?"

Meek drew on him, placing his gun right beneath Beans's chin.

"Yo' Meek! Man! I ain't mean no disrespect! Isa man!" Beans screamed.

Isa sat disinterested with his eyes following the game. "Nah, G, that's all you. You got it. That Mo-wet crack about to getcho ass wet the fuck up. Better start praying."

"I just want to know what you said, G, cuz I know I had to hear that shit wrong? What you say you call her? Mo-wet?"

"Nah man! No! I ain't know you was fucking with it like that! Isa was joking. I was just playing man! I'm sorry!"

"What you call her nigga?" Meek sneered.

"Nothing!" the man cried.

Meek pushed him off with so much aggression that Beans fell across the table, fucking up the count.

"That's right, bitch ass nigga. You don't call her nothing. Matter fact when you see her you better lower your fucking eyes, pussy. Goofy ass nigga. I'll fuck yo' bitch then put one between her fucking eyes for that silly ass shit you just said, nigga." Ahmeek was straddling Beans, barking at him, gripping his collar.

"Yo' bruh, let the nigga breathe man," Isa said, chuckling. "Cuz I ain't recounting this shit. Make his ass do it."

Meek pushed Beans to the floor and backpedaled. He was foaming at the mouth he was so pissed.

"Clean this nigga up, man. Bleeding all over my mother-fucking money," Meek uttered as he stormed out the room.

He retreated to the kitchen, snatching open the refrigerator, pulling out water because Morgan had him thirsty. The ways he needed to be quenched in her moisture, drenched in her wet, was ridiculous. As Ahmeek tilted the bottle to his lips his heart dipped. Yes, he was thirsty as fuck. He wrapped his bloody hand in a towel and then ran both hands down his head. Morgan had him on ice. No communication. It had been a week since he'd seen her and he was going crazy. Being away from her had him out of character. He was acting without thought, punishing niggas because she was punishing him. It shouldn't feel this impossible to move around a woman. He had done it before. To dozens. He wasn't shit if he had made them feel this. Morgan had his mind so fucked up that all he wanted to do was mob. He hadn't slept in days. Life had turned into twenty-four-hour cycles of getting money or getting high. He was blown. He wouldn't press her however. It was like she was his karma for all the hearts he had broken, all the women he had used as playthings over the years. Morgan was playing with him like he was a toy for her enjoyment and Ahmeek couldn't get her off his mind.

Morgan lay in bed, eyes to the ceiling, tears sliding into her ears as her mind tortured her. Messari's feet were directly next to her face. His wild tossing and turning had turned him upside down in her bed. Morgan turned her head, letting a tear fall with gravity as she planted a kiss to his perfect little toes.

"Mommy," Yara signed.

Morgan turned her head the other way, staring into the bright eyes of her baby girl. "Where's Poppa?" she signed.

Morgan's lip quivered, and she trapped it quickly forcing a smile.

Your daddy's dead baby. He left me, and he never came back.

The thought tore up everything in its path. Utter destruction. Morgan couldn't contain the sadness.

"He's back at home in London baby. You know the big house?" Morgan signed.

Yara nodded.

"He's there."

Morgan was relieved that Bash had been called away for work. He wouldn't be back until graduation. It gave her time to think but Morgan's heart and her mind were screaming two different things. They were at war and she couldn't decide which one to trust. She wasn't sure about anything at this point. The seeds of doubt that Bash had put into her head were growing. Doubt about Ahmeek's intentions made her ignore every attempt he made to reach out.

"Where is Meekie, Mommy?" Yara signed.

Morgan had to turn her head away as her lips pulled tight in angst and her chest quaked. Morgan rolled up and laid Yara down. "Lie down Yolly Pop. It's time for bed," she signed. "Good night. Mama loves you."

She turned on the night light and fled the room. She gripped her phone so tightly that it felt like it would break. She pressed the home button and her fingerprint unlocked the screen. She was in her pictures before she could stop herself. When she saw his face she crumbled, sliding down the wall until her butt touched the floor. She tucked her legs beneath her, Indian style, and gazed at the four of them. It had been the most perfect day. The zoo. The smile on all of their faces told a story of love wrapped in exhaustion because they had walked around the exhibits all day.

She couldn't even describe the ways she missed him. Morgan gripped her phone in both hands, bringing them to her forehead, and putting elbows to knees. She just wanted to shut off her feelings. To make everything go dark. She had felt that way before. In that garage. Years ago. She had just wanted it all to go away. Morgan didn't understand why this felt like that. The only difference was Morgan couldn't even fathom hurting herself. Meek had acknowledged the bitch in her, the fighter, he had said. So even though she was dying without him, she couldn't do anything but feel the shit. He had called her strong and although many people had told her that before, he was the first person she had ever believed.

Morgan sent the picture in a text with the caption . . . *A perfect day.* Her heart pulled inside her chest as she awaited his response.

MEEKIE
Are you okay?

MORGAN
Yes

MEEKIE
Can I come?

Morgan paused. Her fingers lingered, hovering over the screen. Oh, how she wanted to say yes. She wanted him to fly up the highway and be at her door within the hour, because she knew he would, but she couldn't. What she had begun with him had been a mistake. They couldn't possibly have a future together. Their past alone made it impossible. Morgan couldn't ruin her entire family. She couldn't count on him to be more than a fling. Bash had been consistent for two years. He had stood by her through the birth of babies that didn't belong to him, claimed them, supported them. The only time he had slipped is when her loyalty began to, granted he hadn't known at the time that she was falling for someone else, but perhaps, subconsciously, Morgan had treated him differently, so he had begun to feel disconnected from her twins. *If I let things go back to normal everything will be fine. He would have never left them backstage if I hadn't started this with Ahmeek. Maybe he felt me pulling away, so he pulled away from them too. I have to let this*

*go. Meek will never stick around. He will never commit to a life
with a woman with two kids that aren't his. Bash is here and willing to stay. He's who they know as their dad.*

With tears running down her face she replied.

MORGAN
No

MEEKIE
Whenever you not okay, you know to hit my line, right?

MORGAN
I know

Morgan picked herself up from the floor and wiped her
eyes. She blew out a weighted breath. Just the words in her phone.
Just the reassurance of his texts chased the thoughts of giving up
out of her head.

MORGAN
Thank you

MEEKIE
Every time, love

He knew exactly what she was thanking him for and Morgan smiled. She hoped he would text more. He didn't. Morgan
clicked out of the screen and she wondered if Ahmeek was that
good of an actor or if he could really be different for her. It was
so hard to trust that he wouldn't hurt her and because of that
she let the silence linger. She let it fester and it was the loudest
thing she had ever heard.

5

Aria stood in the long line of students. Her face was knitted in irritation. There were so many graduates picking up their caps and gowns that the task would take forever. She was grateful for the musical distraction in her headphones. She was already putting the eight count together in her head. Her head was bowed, eyes focused on her phone as she typed in a count, so she would remember the moves for later. Aria didn't have time to waste. There was an audition for background dancers on a big summer tour and she had to be there. There was no doubt she'd get the gig. There was never one that she tried out for that she didn't land. Aria secured her bag effortlessly, spending hours in the studio, dancing her life away. She made sure she was the very best. The crème de la crème. College was just a way to get more technical experience under her belt. She had breezed through the school of dance at Michigan State, perfecting the art of her body, learning more about the rigidity and fluidity of movement. It helped her to compete to be both self-taught and professionally trained. Aria was a beast. Her phone rang, and Isa's name popped up on her screen. She smiled, hating the way that just three letters next to each other . . . I-S-A made her insides liquefy. She had waited all day to hear from him. Every time he spoke the name he had given her, Aria's heart skipped beats, but she played Isa real casually. It didn't matter that they were engaged. He was the type of man you had to keep on his toes. There would be no growing bored on her watch. No matter how pressed she was, she'd never show him. He would never know it, but she was head over heels for him.

ISA
Nigga answer yo' MF phone.

"Nope," Aria said to herself. His name flashed on her phone again and she buttoned him again. She decided when he had access to her and despite what he seemed to believe, it wasn't 24/7. She had a life outside of him, and he would have to learn how to respect that. She was still in the training stage with Isa.

"You must want me to bust yo' ass, Ali," Isa said.

Aria never saw him coming.

"Agh! Boy!" she shouted, taken by surprise as he scooped her, making her drop her phone as he pressed her back to the wall and lifting her dress so far up that her thong showed. "Isa!"

Aria tried to climb out of his arms, but he hoisted her higher, tossing her little ass so high that she straddled his face.

Aria had never been so embarrassed.

"Isa nooooo, Isaaaa stop!" she fussed as he slid her panties to the side and ran his tongue along her lips and gave her clit a sloppy kiss.

The other students in line gawked at them.

"Baby, you got me out here looking crazy," she groaned as he kissed her inner thigh. "Put me down." Aria couldn't help but twirl on his tongue for the one time as she pleaded to be released.

"When I fucking call yo' phone you pick up for me. Every time. You put whatever lame ass nigga that's in your face shooting his shot on hold and you pick the fuck up," he said. He bit her thigh.

"Ow, Isa!" Aria swung, knocking him upside his head so hard he dropped her.

"I'ma fuck yo' little ass up," he said. He grabbed her up, tossing her over his shoulder and planting a smack to her ass so hard that her skin burned.

She hollered in laughter as he spun her in a circle and walked away from the line.

"Wait! Isa! I been in this line for forty minutes! My phone!" she protested. He paused and turned to the group of students then walked to the beginning, still carrying her over his shoulder.

"Fuck yo' phone. You probably got hoe niggas calling that bitch anyway," Isa said as he sank his teeth into the skin of her thigh, biting just enough to pull a yelp out of her.

"Excuse me sir, there's a line," the advisor, who sat behind a desk at the front of the line, said.

Isa went into his pocket and pulled out a knot of hundred-dollar bills. He didn't even care to count it. He tossed the entire thing on the desk. "Aria Taylor," he said. "I need that cap and gown up out you."

The advisor eyed the money and went to retrieve it.

"Now you gon' ride with me for a minute?" he asked.

"I have an audition," she said. "At three."

"I'll get you there," he said. He placed her on her feet when they were at his car. All white, BMW. The car he barely drove because he was an adrenaline junkie and his bike suited him better. He removed his keys from his pocket and tossed them in the air. Aria caught them.

"I'm driving?"

"I can't play in that pussy and drive at the same time, Ali. Nigga this ain't *Driving Miss Daisy*. Hop yo' pretty ass behind the wheel," Isa said.

Aria stopped walking, frowning. "Who you think you talking to?" she asked. "I can just go about my day. You interrupted what I had going on."

Isa blew out a breath of frustration. "Ali, I don't want no smoke. Can you just not give a nigga a hard time and drive?"

She rolled her eyes and pulled open the door, sliding in and starting the car.

"Since you making me drive it, I take it I can have it," she said.

"Fuck out of here with that bullshit," Isa snickered. "Buy yo' ass a fucking Honda. Hoes like Hondas."

"That's why your dusty ass mama drive one," she shot back.

Isa hollered in laughter. "Yo' she got one for real. That's cold."

"Where are we going anyway?" she asked, laughing.

"I want to show you something. Just drive," he said as he entered an address into the GPS.

Isa ran his fingers up her thigh, between her legs. "You miss me?"

"Not really," Aria answered.

"Yeah well that pussy saying something different," Isa said as he traipsed through her wet. He massaged her clit as she merged onto the highway.

"Fast lane," he instructed, bringing his lips to her neck and tasting her skin. "Hmm, you taste so mu'fucking good."

Aria's neck fell to the side as he feasted there.

"Go faster," he ordered. His fingers pressed down hard on her clit and her foot pressed down harder on the gas.

"Isa, you're going to make me crazy," she moaned.

"Yo' little ass already crazy," he moaned in her ear. He took a thumb to her bud and inserted his middle and ring finger inside her. Aria damn near lifted out the seat.

"Yo' I promise I hit the fucking jackpot," Isa mumbled in her ear. His tongue was warm and wet against her neck.

"Isaaaaa," she moaned.

"Go faster." Another order. The speedometer was at ninety miles per hour.

She steered the car while he maneuvered her body. She bit her bottom lip and her eyes closed.

"Open your eyes before you crash this bitch." He kept toying with her middle and kissing her neck.

"Isa I'm . . ."

"Damn right you are," he said. Aria came all over his fingers, her thighs squeezing so tight that she trapped his hand.

"Little nasty ass little girl," he teased. He leaned his seat back as Aria sat smugly, smiling and floating on a high all the way to Flint.

When she placed the car in park, they sat in front of a storage facility.

"Come on," Isa said.

Aria climbed out and followed him up to one of the steel orange doors. Isa removed a set of keys and opened it. He lifted the door, revealing tires stacked to the ceiling.

He pulled the string that hung from the ceiling and light flooded the space.

"What is all this Isa?" she asked, frowning. "You own a tire shop or something?"

"Pull that door down," he instructed. Aria reached up and slid the metal door to the ground.

Isa pulled a switch blade from his back pocket and stabbed through one of the tires. He pulled out a gallon-sized ziplock bag. It was filled with money rolls. He tossed it to Aria.

"Shop with it or something," he said.

Aria frowned, catching the bag. She eyed the bag.

"You don't believe in banks?" she asked.

"The money go to the bank after it's clean," he said.

"Why are you showing me this, Isa?"

"In case something happens. You come here and clear this bitch out. If I get knocked, if I get murked out here, you need to know where the stash is," Isa said, leaning against the walls and crossing his arms.

Aria's heart stalled. "Is there something I should know? Something I should be worried about?"

Isa shook his head. "Never that. You ain't never got to worry. I'm just telling you. I want you to be able to take care of yourself if something happens."

"I take care of myself without you Isa," Aria said.

"Nigga when the last time you paid your own rent? I been paying that shit for two years," Isa shot back.

"Just because you pay it don't mean I can't. While you're paying my rent, my money's sitting pretty in the bank," she said.

"Yeah well keep your little paper," Isa stated. He removed a key from his key ring and handed it to her. "You got access to everything that matters now. My name and my paper. That's all I got."

The notion made Aria a little sad because Isa was worth so much more than he gave himself credit for.

"That's not all you got," she said as she closed the space between them. She leaned into him, looking up at him as he peered down into her eyes. "You got me, Isa. I'm never going to need this key. If you bussin' baby I'm bussin', when they put dirt on you, they gon' have to cover me too. You've got me."

Isa wrapped a hand around her waist. "Real shit?" he asked.

Aria nodded. "Real shit." She kissed him, softly. Her touch held such finesse that it hypnotized him as she placed fingertips to his face.

"I get real rough with you Ali," he stated as he reached for her wrists. They were bruised.

"I like it Isa," she said. "I'm a big girl."

"I don't ever wanna be rough on your heart kid," he stated. "I'ma fuck up. Always been a fuck up, but I don't want to fumble you because from the moment I saw your little ass I knew I wanted you. I ain't trying to fuck shit up. I'ma get it right with you and that's on my kids."

Aria pulled her neck back in confusion. "Kids? Isa, what kids?"

"Our kids, baby. Every single one I'ma put in you one day," he stated. "Like ten of them bitches. All boys cuz a nigga don't want no girls."

Aria's tension melted. "Ten boys! Boy fuck you I'm not having ten nothing. You'll be lucky if you get one out of me."

Isa scooped her and turned her toward the wall. "Nah, you gon' give me ten cuz you a good girl. You know how I get when you don't listen," he whispered as he attacked her neck. "A nigga get real savage."

"Which is why I never listen," she moaned. He pulled back staring at her. Challenge lived in Aria and a man like Isa loved to conquer shit.

"I swear to fucking God, you're the best. You got my head so fucking wrapped up in you," he admitted. "For real, Ali. Every minute I ain't with you I'm equating shit back to you.

Thinking of some shit you said or did or gon' say when I get back to you. Shit is fucked up."

"Good," she whispered. "Control the mind and the body will follow." Aria was raised to be thorough. She handled men like men handled women and Isa was hooked.

Isa smirked. "You think you in charge," he stated, kissing her, pulling her bottom lip in so hard it ached.

"I am," she whispered.

Aria's body was trained for him, in tune with him and it was screaming in need. Her nipples against the fabric of her denim dress, the feel of him hardening against her. She reached down, undoing his buckle then freed him. He was inside her in seconds and Aria's mouth fell open.

"I want babies with you, Ali," he groaned. "Can I put a baby in you?"

"Isa, nooooo," she whispered, face bent in pleasure as he fucked her up the wall.

"Yes, baby," he insisted.

Aria grabbed his face tightly and forced him to stare in her eyes. "I say when. I'm not ready for that, Isa and I for damn sure will have a ring on my finger. A ring that's been in place for so long that the skin under it is lighter than the rest of my hand. You got me?" she asked.

He moved his head out of her grasp and then tensed into her slowly. "I got you, baby. You the boss."

Aria couldn't believe how deep she was with Isa. She could have never predicted that the little skinned gangster wrapped in Gucci and ink that she'd met on a whim would be the one to give her butterflies. He wasn't her type at all, but she had a feeling it was the reason why they worked. He made her so damn wild. So unpredictable. She had envisioned her entire life before him and now she couldn't tell what tomorrow would bring. Their love was a spontaneous one. It was unique. It was aggressive and bold. He was hers and as long as he remained loyal, she would be his. She hoped he didn't underestimate her however, because if he ever hurt her, she would bite back. The exchange of pain would be unbearable. She just prayed he knew.

6

Back to the Bricks was a Flint Town tradition. It was a celebration of the city's impact on the automotive industry and it brought people to town from all over just to show off their fancy old school vehicles. The original brick streets of the city's downtown were lined with fully restored, American made, Flint made, cars. Morgan loved the pomp and circumstance of the annual festival. She attended every year and ever since she was sixteen years old Ethic had allowed her to push one of his refurbished cars to show off. Today's choice was a 1985 Cutlass Convertible. This year was no different only this time Bella rode shotgun and Aria was seated in the back seat.

"I've never seen this many people in Flint. This is a big deal," Aria exclaimed.

"The entire city comes out for this," Bella said, leaning forward to turn up the custom radio.

"Whole hood too," Mo added.

Keep showing up and I'ma keep showing love.

The car might have been old school, but Ethic had equipped it with the latest technology inside.

"Who shooting they shot with you B?" Aria asked. "I know you got a little boyfriend or something. You're fifteen. That's usually when it starts."

"I'm not worried about these boys out here," Bella answered, but Morgan didn't miss the blush.

"Mmm, hmm. Let me find out," Morgan teased. "You ain't slick. You ain't spending all that time at Nannie's because you like playing bid whist. What's up with you and that little boy Hendrix?"

"Nosey much, Mo?" Bella asked.

Aria laughed as Morgan let the top down and Aria lifted onto the back as Morgan drove slowly down the block. Aria curled her fingers like triggers as Morgan turned up the music and Aria grooved. The attention the trio drew was inevitable. It was just the way of the world; pretty girls deserved the spotlight and it didn't get prettier than them. It was time for the stunt. Bella might have only been fifteen, but she was beautiful, and next to Morgan and Aria she shined. They were stars . . . hood stars but stars all the same. Morgan knew the program. Women were coming through half naked to flex, Morgan and her crew opted for Lakers jerseys and baggy Lakers shorts and designer sneakers. Her tribal braids were so long that she sat on them as she drove and the beads she had decorated them with had her feeling like a goddess and her face was made up to perfection. She pulled the car into a space, backing in, before turning off the engine and reversing the key so the music continued to play.

Keep it up, I said keep it up.
See I ain't got no time for the fake shit
Been seeing too much of it lately.

Morgan and Bella climbed into the back seat with Aria and the party began.

"Baby girl got a big girl toy. You sure you can handle that?"

Morgan turned her scowl on the guy parked beside her. Old school Bronco, clean, on big tires and all black rims.

"I'm sure I can manage," she said, smirking.

"I'm Reco," the dude said.

"Good for you," Mo shot back.

"Baby girl, most people exchange introductions. I give you my name, you give me yours. That's how it works," he said.

"For one you talking to me from inside the car, from the passenger side. You're already moving all wrong," she said.

Aria laughed and even Bella snickered. The guy climbed from the car. His friends hung out around, smoking, infiltrating the air with the smell of good weed as their subwoofers knocked. They stood sneaking sips of drink from brown paper bags. It was a good day. A hood day and the mood was jovial. Flint didn't get a lot of days like this, but it felt good to be on the scene with her people. She was sure bullets would fly before the day was over but for the moment all was right and it put Morgan in good spirits. It reminded her to be less bitchy. Morgan knew from his lowered eyes that the man was high. She surveyed him in seconds, a habit Ethic had taught her. Size the opposition up from a distance to determine if you're going to allow access.

"Everyone shouldn't be able to run up on you," he had said. The guy wasn't flashy. Normal hood nigga attired, fitted white T-shirt, designer jeans, and thousand-dollar shoes. She knew he had a little bit of paper because his timepiece was expensive, and his teeth were veneers. Not a gap or chip in sight. She was sure that expensive smile had disarmed plenty bitches and the thought made her shake her head. Men as handsome as he was were trouble. He was put together well, and his mouth was charming enough. She wouldn't fall victim to it, but she knew how to give props when they were due.

"You're not from around here are you?" she asked, throwing her legs over the side of the car, so she was facing him. He leaned against the car beside her.

"Nah, me and my people came up from the Chi," he said.

Morgan's eyes landed on the music note tattooed on his neck amongst a mural of ink.

"And you're a rapper?" she asked.

"Not a rapper baby," his friend spoke up as he clapped two rubber banded stacks of hundred-dollar bills together. "The rapper. The next nigga up." He leaned down to turn up the stereo system inside the Bronco and Morgan noticed a familiar anthem that had been shaking shit up lately. She had warmed up to this very song before.

"What are you? His hype man?" Aria asked, frowning.

"I'm his A&R," the man said snickering. "Why y'all so mean? Where the hospitality at beautiful?"

Aria rolled her eyes. "Don't let the pretty face fool you. You get the sour first. The sweet is earned."

The guy was heavy, with a belly, and a full beard. He was handsome with smooth peanut butter skin and a fresh fade. "I ain't mad at that. I can do that," he stated, confident, overconfident in fact.

"What about you pretty girl? You mean too?" A&R asked.

"Nope but my daddy is," Bella shot back. Aria put up those fake triggers and pulled one in A&R's direction as she grooved to the music. He bellowed. Aria's confidence and attitude stayed on a million and men loved it, including A&R.

"Your little sister I take it?" Reco asked.

Morgan smiled and nodded. "And my best friend. My hittas as you can see."

"Baby girl got hittas," he said, licking his lips. "I better be easy then."

"It would be wise," she answered with a small smirk.

Morgan heard the sound of engines revving and the guttural voice of Jeezy. She looked up as Isa and Ahmeek pulled up, different cars, pushing old schools dripping in candy paint on big boy rims, subwoofers knocking. Six motorcycles flanked the two cars. Three shooters in the front, three shooters in the back. All on Kawasakis. Fucking motorcade of the hood. Protection. Always protected. Ahmeek and Isa didn't slip.

"Better tighten up," Aria said. "Murder Meek coming through."

Morgan watched as they backed in to the spaces directly across from where she parked, and the fanfare started instantly. Ahmeek and Isa couldn't even climb out of the car good before men came up showing love and women flocked to them.

Morgan couldn't even focus on the man in front of her. Her heart stalled in her chest. It had been too long since she'd seen Ahmeek. Two weeks and three days in fact. It had been that long since she'd seen Bash too. She was preparing for graduation and the tug of war of her heart filled her with turmoil. She just wanted to enjoy this moment in her life . . . celebrate her upcoming accomplishment. She didn't want to look back on this time in her life and remember feeling torn. She just wanted to be proud, so she had put them both on ice. She had fallen off the face of the earth on Ahmeek without a warning. They had gotten heavy, they had done things that only meant one thing, he had kissed places that made her quiver, explored depths that made her call on God. Then she pulled back. She had abruptly cut him off. They had made plans to go skating. A formal date. Their first formal date. Something that took place outside the seclusion of a bedroom. A place where they could see if their chemistry was more than physical. The fight between Meek and Bash had caused Morgan to pull back. She wouldn't even answer his calls. He had called for a while, but after days of unreturned effort he had stopped altogether. She knew she was sending mixed messages but what was she supposed to do when her heart and head were all mixed up. Her stomach tightened when she saw him break through the fanfare and swagger across the street with Isa at his side. He was like a local celebrity as people, both men and women fought for a bit of his time . . . time that Morgan didn't have to fight for at all. He pulled up his pants then rubbed the back of his neck before finessing his beard. Stressed . . . she knew he was. She could feel his disdain as his fine ass made his way over to her. A&R acknowledged them first.

"Yo! Nigga what up?" A&R greeted, slapping hands with Meek then Isa. "Flint's muthafucking finest in this bitch!"

Morgan rolled her eyes. Too much. The man was doing entirely too much dick riding for Mo's tastes, but it was just how the crew was received. It was warm welcomes, or they would air shit out to bring niggas temperatures down.

Isa slapped hands with the rapper next then nestled himself right between the guy and Morgan, running interference. Isa was always a good man to have on the battlefield. Morgan smirked because he made no effort to play off his intentions. He was breaking up whatever party Morgan's pursuer thought was occurring. "All this pussy out here and you mu'fuckas choose the two that'll get niggas sent to early graves out this bitch."

"Oh, shit bruh, no disrespect G. I ain't know they were spoken for."

The rapper lifted from the car, retreating. If Morgan had been interested, it would have waned right then. The authority Ahmeek and Isa carried over grown men, made grown men seem like boys.

"Shit we should have known. You niggas keep the baddest out the fucking bunch," the rapper said. Isa snickered and Ahmeek trained an indifferent gaze on Morgan.

"Nah, Mo ain't got no chains. She free to choose," Ahmeek stated. He ran a hand over his wavy head and then slapped hands with A&R. "Get with me tonight. I got a bottle for you G. You performing?"

"Yeah we got a joint in the D tonight. Info is on my IG and shit. Come fuck with me," the rapper invited.

"Yeah we'll see," Ahmeek answered. He was speaking to the rapper, but his eyes were on Morgan. She rolled her eyes away from him, smiling because it never failed, he just made her smile whenever he was around. She was sure he was pissed at her and still here she was giddy at just the sight of him.

Isa held up a fist to Bella and she connected hers to his. "Keep these mu'fuckas in line, B. You in charge boss baby," he said. He tapped her nose and Bella blushed as Isa bent down and placed a kiss to the front of Aria's shorts, marking her. His bitch. His pussy. He kissed it whenever he wanted to, wherever he wanted to. "Act right out here Ali before I chop some shit up."

Aria smirked and pulled his face to hers as he came up. "You're going to make me go soft boy," she whispered.

"Nah, you all G, Ali. That's why you mine. I like 'em tough," he stated with a wink. He pecked her lips then pulled back. "Yo' boss baby," he said focusing on Bella. She lifted a curious brow. "Little Henny huh?"

Morgan turned to Isa. "Little Henny what?"

"Ethic's girls are always a problem," Isa snickered.

"Yo' bruh we up," Ahmeek stated. He turned to cross the street.

"You can't speak?" Morgan asked.

He gritted his teeth and turned toward her.

"Nah love, that's you with the silent treatment. I'm playing by the rules you set," he said.

Morgan's heart cracked in two as Ahmeek walked across the street. It felt like someone set it on fire as a group of women surrounded him.

"Bitch, what did you do?" Aria asked.

"Are you dating Meek?" Bella asked.

"No, we're just friends," Morgan said as her eyes prickled.

"Then why is your voice shaking?" Bella asked.

"Cuz that nigga fucking her real good but she playing games. Whack ass Bash got that ass on lock," Aria answered.

"Ahmeek is so fine," Bella gushed.

"B!" Morgan shouted.

"What? He is!" Bella replied. Fifteen-year-old Bella knew the makings of a boss when she saw one and Ahmeek wore the crown well.

Morgan's mouth fell open and Aria shrugged. "I mean well he is, shit!" Aria agreed.

Morgan laughed and shook her head as she looked across the street. "He really is," she admitted, swooning as she blew out a breath of angst.

"Well sis, I love you, but I'm taking my ass across the street," Aria said. "You better come to your senses and bring yo' ass." Aria hopped down, and Bella followed.

"B!" Morgan shouted.

"I mean Hendrix is over there," Bella answered, shrugging.

Morgan sat in the car alone. She was so conflicted because her heart was screaming for her to give in, but her head, her head was telling her that she would lose everything if she left Bash. The fear of Ahmeek doing her the same way Messiah had done kept her behind the wheel of the car, gripping the steering wheel in distress. She knew what heartbreak felt like and she didn't want to be the one to put that on Bash. He had more time invested than Ahmeek. It was only fair that she give him a chance. Plus, the entire city was present. Businessmen and hood politicians alike were lining the city streets. Morgan couldn't just cross the block to stand at Ahmeek's side. The speculation it would cause, the way the grapevine would talk, Morgan just couldn't. Messiah's old girl with his best friend? It was a scandal that she wasn't ready to acknowledge, despite the fact that she was a willing participant. Jealousy seared her as she watched the crew parlay without her. Her gut turned at the amount of attention Ahmeek received. He stayed greeting niggas from around the way. Showing love, giving dap, extending hugs, half smirks gracing his chocolate face as women vied for his attention. Morgan was sick because she couldn't be at his side. She couldn't make her position known. No flex because while they had been seen together in Detroit plenty of times, this was Flint and Flint was small . . . a town where everyone knew everyone . . . they had surely marked her as the little deaf girl Messiah Williams used to fuck with. Morgan felt her phone vibrate and she was grateful for the distraction. She opened the message.

MEEKIE
I'm losing patience, love.

She looked up and saw him coming across the street. She didn't miss his frustration . . . the breath he blew out as he swaggered her way. The dipped brow because he was annoyed as fuck with her. Morgan's eyes appreciated all of him. Bow-legged Ahmeek with the J's, Nike shorts, and white T-shirt that he had freed one arm of because it was smoldering outside. Tattoos everywhere, black skin everywhere, beard full, dick heavy, because the shorts were made of sweatpants material and Morgan was pissed about that. He was flexing, and she wasn't the only one watching. She didn't know why she felt the urge to run, but she started walking in the opposite direction. She maneuvered through the thick crowd, trying to put distance between her and Meek because if he got too close . . . if he touched her, Morgan was going to lose it. She was going to do something that would show the world what they had been up to. She shouldn't. She couldn't. Their business was their business, especially within Flint city limits. The tug of her hand made her spin into him and before she could protest his lips were on hers, her ass was in his hands as he lifted her from her feet.

"Hmm," she moaned as she wrapped her arms around his neck and got lost in the rhythm of his lips. He took heavy steps, carrying her across the street, stopping traffic because neither were paying attention, as they kissed the entire way. Morgan's heart ran rampant inside her chest. An infestation of love mixed with relief filled her anxious soul.

He didn't pull away until she was sitting on the hood of his car.

"Everybody's watching, Ahmeek," she whispered.

He placed his hands to the metal around her and leaned down to take her lips again. "I don't give a fuck, love," he answered. One peck, then two. Each time he pulled back he looked her in the eyes. Their kisses always seemed to last forever.

"I can't breathe," she gasped.

"Me either love, when you're on your bullshit, I can't fucking breathe," Ahmeek said. "What the fuck you doing to me Morgan Atkins?"

"I don't know," she admitted.

"I should be done with you, Mo. I should take my L and let it be," he said as he stood in front of her, holding her close to his body as he spoke the words in her ear.

"Don't do that, Meekie. Don't say that to me," she whispered back.

"You're fucking difficult, Morgan," he said, kissing the nook of her neck. It was like they were alone. The festivities around them were loud and boisterous. Isa with Aria, Bella was sitting on a motorcycle and Morgan knew she should intervene, but she couldn't. She was trapped in a world with Ahmeek. Only the two of them existed even though she knew the nosy passersby were taking note of the new couple on the scene. He was marking her. His. Morgan Atkins. His. His bitch. His girl. Off limits. It was something Messiah had never done. They had lived within the four walls of her old apartment, only venturing out in the college town when she had a performance, or to come up for air and food. They survived in the shadows. They thrived there, because she had been too afraid to tell Ethic about their relationship. Ahmeek was claiming her, publicly, loving on her openly . . . knowing full well it was forbidden, uncaring that Ethic didn't like it, unconcerned that she had an entire fiancé. He didn't care how wrong they were, he was proud to show her off and she loved it. God why did she love this so much? Why couldn't she feel this with Bash?

"I know," she answered.

"You been with that nigga?" Ahmeek asked, taking her chin in his grasp and pinching slightly, pursing her lips, commanding her stare.

She shook her head. "He's been calling. Same as you. I haven't seen him. I haven't chosen him either, Ahmeek. I just don't really know what to do. I just needed some time to disconnect."

He didn't answer. Instead he turned, finally letting the world back in and sat beside her on the hood of his car. Morgan stood, and he pulled her between his legs, resting his head over her shoulder as his arms wrapped around her body. Lovey dovey shit from a man who didn't do lovey dovey at all. Morgan swooned. Her heart ached so good that her legs felt unsteady. His embrace, his touch, was electrifying.

"We done beefing and shit? We all on the same team again?" Aria asked as she leaned inside Isa's car and turned up the volume of his system.

Sssipping on some ssssyzzzurrp. . . . sssssssipping on some sip . . .

"Come fuck it up, Bella!" Aria shouted as she rolled her hips seductively. "You said you're auditioning for majorettes . . . let's see it."

Bella shook her head shyly.

"Come on, Mo, let's make up her count," Aria said. Ahmeek tapped her on the behind, urging her to show off. It was another difference. A clear difference between him and Bash, hell even him and Messiah. Her dancing had been a problem with Messiah. He hadn't stopped her from doing it like Bash, but he hadn't liked it either. Morgan had felt tension every time she graced a stage in Messiah's presence and it always made her dial it back a bit . . . always made her tone it down. She turned eyes of uncertainty to Ahmeek. He kissed the tip of her nose.

"Do your thing, love," he said. Morgan lifted off the car. Aria was already halfway into an eight count. Morgan joined in effortlessly.

"These mu'fuckas love showing out," Isa snickered as he sat next to Ahmeek who leaned back on the hood, arms folded across his chest.

"Eerrtime bruh," Meek answered, smirking.

The crowd circled around the duo as they got lost like the street was their stage.

"Come on, B!" Morgan called, smiling.

"Nooo," Bella groaned. "I can't dance to this. Who is this anyway? It sounds so old!"

"Old!" Aria snapped. "This is classic!"

"It's ghetttoo!" Bella protested.

Aria stopped dancing, but Mo kept snapping her pretty fingers and swinging her braids from side to side. She was in a zone until Aria cut the music.

"Little spoiled little girl think Three-Six is ghetto so let's give her something bougie," Aria stated. The dainty beat oozed out of the car but Isa's subwoofers quickly added kick to it. Aria clapped her hands. "What you gon' do now B? Ariana fucking Grande! She real prissy with it, just like you, little girl, now fuck it up."

Yeah breakfast at Tiffany's and bottles of bubbly.

"Come on B!!" Mo instigated. She walked over to Bella and grabbed her hand, pulling her front and center.

My wrist, stop watching
My neck is flossy
Make big deposits, my gloss is poppin'

Aria was out of there as Morgan stood nodding her head to the beat, her eyes scanning Aria's body, taking mental note of every little tick Aria did with her body. Morgan processed music like a computer, storing files, saving notes, CTRL+ALT+DELETE, on a bitch. She picked up the steps with little effort and interpreted them beautifully, putting her touch on dances that made them unique.

"Okay, B. Just eight counts," Mo said, slowing down

the dance for Bella. "Watch my feet first. It's 1, 2, 3, and 4, 5, 6, 7, 8." Morgan went through the steps. They were holding class right in the middle of the festival and the crowd was tuned in.

"Like this?" Bella asked, following the steps.

"Yesssss, B!" Aria shouted. "How the fuck didn't I know, Bella was fire? Fuck majorettes, we need her on gang shit. Yo' run that shit the fuck back!"

"Don't run shit back bitches, oh no little baby what is thisssss?"

White Boy Nick's voice broke through the crowd as he made his way to the front. "I knew you two would be wherever these money bags are! Got me looking all over the bricks for y'all asses. What we doing, giving out free smoke?"

"This mu'fucka," Isa snickered.

"Hey, Zaddy! With your fine ass. Out here blessing the common folk. I don't even like light skins but whew chile," Nick said, fanning himself. He blew Isa a kiss. Isa extended his hand as if he could see the damn kiss floating through mid-air. Then he tossed it up and took a pretend bat to that bitch. "Get that bullshit outta here."

Ahmeek chuckled as Aria hollered. The circle of onlookers roared in laughter as Nick feigned fake offense, clutching pearls he wasn't wearing.

"I like it when you're aggressive, boy," Nick joked. "Run it back."

Hendrix leaned inside Isa's car and started the song over. He stood and met eyes with Bella who blushed. "Pretty girl who hate attention, figure that," he snickered.

As soon as the song played the foursome started, and Morgan laughed with Bella who picked up the count with ease. When the count was over Morgan, Aria, and Bella stopped dancing, high fiving one another, but Nick took off.

I see it, I like it
I want it, I got it

Morgan joined him and Nick stepped back as the song changed. A new artist. Enchanting. With Bella out of the way she could do her thing. The beat slowed and Morgan matched its pace, eyes on Meek as she approached him.

"Oh, she about to cut the fuck up," Aria said snickering as she shook her head while smiling. Morgan ran her tongue across her lips and then biting her lower lip she walked on tip toes toward Ahmeek. You would have thought she wore stilettos instead of the bulky sneakers. She had turned her seduction on and no matter that she was dressed down, her appeal was turned up.

Promise you won't take nobody
Touching on my body
And make sure you take your time cuz I'm not just anybody

Morgan freaked him. Fearless. Erotic. A fucking beast when it came to expressing herself with her body. She wrapped one hand around his neck, like he was a strip pole and she was about to throw her set down for dollars. She rolled her middle, leaving no room between them. Morgan's mouth fell open and then she bit her bottom lip before turning and bending at the waist.

Can I come over
Don't wanna beee soober
Can I come over
Ride your love rollercoaster
Don't ask me I want it
Boy you know I need itttt

Morgan bounced her ass on Ahmeek, slowly, deliberately, like she had a mission, like the more aggressively she worked him the more control she took from him. She lifted and pressed into him. Her back to his chest.

She reached behind her and wrapped both hands around his neck.

She closed her eyes and rode the beat using her body to heighten the temperature, to raise the stakes. The power she had over him, the way he reacted to her, made her feel like a woman.

"Bitcccchhhh, everybody lost! You better work that nigga Mo Money!" Aria shouted as she snapped her fingers and hit a light groove to the sensual beat.

Ahmeek smirked as he looked down at Morgan who was making a whole show of him. If there was any doubt of anyone watching it was now erased. A woman didn't do what Mo was doing for any man that wasn't hers. The music faded, and he shook his head, running both hands over the top of his head, brows lifted, as he bit his bottom lip. She went to move, and he pulled her by her waist.

"Nah, love. You causing problems out here. You stay right here," he whispered, kissing her on the back of her neck. He left chills in the place his lips graced. She felt him beneath her and Morgan's clit pulsed.

"Big problems. I'm causing real big problems."

He bit her shoulder and she laughed before turning to him. He took his time with her lips, pinching her chin and tilting it slightly before pulling her bottom lip into his mouth. Brazen. Unapologetic. If there was any doubt of whom she was with before today, after today there would be none.

"Bitch, running through the whole damn crew."

Morgan's entire body turned to steel. It was what she had feared. The judgement. The assumptions. The random groupie who had voiced it had only expressed the thoughts of those present. Morgan's eyes closed, snapping shut as she tried to absorb the verbal jab without letting it get the best of her. If she was going to do this . . . be with Ahmeek, publicly, she had to be prepared for moments like this.

The hush that settled over the crowd embarrassed her more. The criticism shrank her . . . it reminded her that this was wrong. Ahmeek arose from the hood of the car, placing hands to Morgan's waist to move her out the way.

"Yo, you know me?" he asked. He ran his tongue across his bottom lip and his temple pulsed. Morgan could see the anger radiating off him.

"Everybody knows you," the girl said. "I'm just saying you ain't got to recycle the same ol' pussy. It's a lot of new new out here."

"Is that right?" he asked. "Com'ere. Let me see something."

The girl sashayed by Morgan, smirking with arrogance until she was in front of Ahmeek.

Ahmeek placed his hand on her neck, rubbing her neckline, one finger tracing the dip in her cleavage that was overexposed before he wrapped one hand around her neck and jerked her into him. She leaned into him smiling because everyone knew that the crew was aggressive. Girls lined up to experience some of that aggression. That smile faded as he whispered in her ear.

"I'ma need you to clear something up for me. You trying to be funny toward her or toward me? Cuz seem like you were trying to play her, but I'm feeling real disrespected right now."

"I would never—"

"I'm not done talking sweetheart," he stated. The girl's face lost color. "I don't take the slick shit too well you feel me? That's me on any given Sunday and if you ever disrespect her again it's gon' be a problem."

The girl's eyes prickled, and she nodded. "Sorry Meek. I ain't know it was like that." Her voice was barely audible. Fear gripped her, and her voice shook.

"Nah, the disrespect was loud, make that apology loud too," he said. He stood, stoic, impatient. The calm he expressed was so out of place for the tense situation that it made the hair on the back of Morgan's neck stand tall.

"You wanted my attention. You got it. My eyes on you, now put on a show," Meek stated.

Morgan shifted in her stance. "Ahmeek . . ."

The girl looked at Morgan with glossy eyes.

"Sorry Morgan. I don't want no problems," she said.

"You sure? Cuz we got 'em if you want 'em? Buy one, get one free hoe," Aria stated.

The girl retreated, walking away in embarrassment.

"Goofy ass," Aria muttered, mushing the back of the girl's head as she walked by. "I want one of you hoes to jump bad out here today."

Neither the girl or her comrades did anything in reaction.

The vibe was tense, and Morgan felt his anger, but she felt her embarrassment more. The mood had been spoiled all because two lovers who weren't supposed to be lovers had been called out.

Morgan turned to Ahmeek and placed a hand to his cheek, controlling his focus, shifting it from the girl to her. She could feel the tension in him. He was pissed.

"Let it go," she said softly. "We knew what people would think. I don't care. They don't know about us. They have no idea how right wrong is." She teared, and he cleared the lone drop that fell down her face. Morgan grabbed the hand that cupped her face and leaned into it, then kissed his tear-covered thumb. "I don't care what they say."

He looked down at her and she tucked herself right beneath him. Fuck everybody. Fuck anybody. She held no remorse for being here . . . doing this . . . in front of everyone . . . even with the fiancé she had waiting for her at home. She was so afraid of what she felt but no matter how much she tried to pull away, whenever he was around, she was pulled closer. It was that strong . . . his draw on her was that magnetic. His arm wrapped around her back and her head rested on his chest as the crowd dispersed.

"We making a lot of noise today little Morgan. I don't even know what any of it means. Where you at with it? Every time I press go, you press stop. You and your games, love. I don't enjoy 'em much."

"I can't promise I'll leave him. I don't know yet. I can't promise him I'll leave you either. I don't know about anything, Ahmeek. I'm so uncertain. All I know is I breathe for this," she said.

It wasn't what he wanted to hear. His jaw locked, and he looked past her, out into the street, like she was invisible. She pulled his chin, forcing him to look at her.

"Meekie, you have to understand—"

"I get it Mo. Y'all got a family," he said.

"But I do want you. I can't lie and say that I don't. I want this too. Can we just keep doing this? Can this just be ours? I won't disappear anymore. I won't not answer your calls or get scared. I just need you to be patient with me."

"You playing a dangerous game, Mo," he said.

"I know."

"Nah you not hearing me. I'm not talking about you, Morgan. There is no danger for you when you're with me, but you risking that nigga life. I told you before we started how I am over mine. Now if you ain't mine let me know, so I can dial it back, but if you mine, Mo . . . damn love, if a nigga blessed to call you mine . . ." He shook his head as if he couldn't believe the privilege had been granted at all. "Look at me." Morgan trained an emotional stare on Ahmeek. "I'll put a nigga on his back over you, love. Don't make me."

Most women would be intimidated by the threat. Some would find the aggression crazy, but it set Morgan's soul aflame. Every fiber in her body wanted to tell this man three words, but he stole her speech when he bullied her with a kiss. Morgan was defenseless against him. All she could do was moan as her eyes closed. There was no denying what she felt. There was no giving this up. It was Meek and Morgan or nothing at all because Morgan didn't want anything else.

7

"This is seed money. You're a man. You don't ask for no hand-outs," Ethic stated as he walked into the abandoned business. Messiah sauntered in behind him, face bent as he looked around the dilapidated building.

"And you're a businessman so I'll put twenty percent on top of your investment when I run it back to you," Messiah stated. The sound of plaster falling off the wall caused Messiah to turn toward the back of the room. "Not gon' lie though O.G. this look like a lot of work. You sure this the one?"

"It's cheap, it's in the middle of the city, and I can purchase it cash, no banks involved. Murder rate in Flint is at an all-time high. Where you think they gon' bring those bodies?" Ethic asked.

Messiah looked around frowning. "This bitch is damn near condemned though."

"The value is in the location of the land not what's sitting on it. We can get in here, gut all this shit, build it up from the studs, and open in ninety days. Williams Funeral Services."

Messiah steeled.

"Word?"

Ethic nodded. "You've run businesses before. This ain't nothing new. Same flip different industry."

"When I left everything else went under. I liquidated it all," Messiah stated. He thought of how he'd had Bleu sell everything. Every house except the one he left for Morgan in her name and every business he had used to clean his street money. It all had to go so that he could cut Morgan a million-dollar check. A goodbye that was worth something because he knew she wouldn't be able to do shit with words. He had left her with a broken heart and a bag. "When I pictured coming back, I ain't picture this."

"Got to think bigger. You open this one and in a year, you open another one, in three years you own three, in five years you got five. It's about generational wealth, Messiah. That street shit will line your pockets. This will last as long as your name lives on," Ethic schooled.

Messiah felt tension tear through his body. "I gave up legacy when I let them pump me full of drugs to save my life. They say chemo helps you live. I think it just makes death slower. I can't make babies man. This will live and die with me so do it really matter?"

Ethic stopped walking and turned to Messiah. The stare he placed on Messiah made Messiah's chest fill with grief. He was so filled with emotion. After surviving the impossible he couldn't even control it. Couldn't even stop it. Lately he had been feeling everything and he hated it. It disgusted him to be this susceptible. Everything penetrated him. Every stare, every word, every interaction. Affected him.

Ethic was silent, but his eyes spoke volumes.

"You don't know what the future holds for you Messiah," he said. "It matters."

Messiah turned away, eyes betraying him, burning.

Ethic walked over to the tools he'd had delivered and picked up a sledgehammer. He held it out to Messiah.

"I know the rage you got in you," Ethic said. He pointed around them. "All this got to come down anyway. Tear it up all you want."

Messiah looked down at the sledgehammer and hesitated before taking it.

A firm hand to his shoulder then a squeeze. A touch. One he allowed because he knew Ethic well. Then solitude filled the room. He heard Ethic push out of the front door, then heard the ignition to his Range Rover as Ethic departed.

Messiah's fist tightened around the long-handled sledge-hammer as it hung at his side. One squeeze. Then two. Then his lip quivered. Eyes burning. Heart racing. Anger coursed through him. He had missed so much time with Morgan. He was so close to her, close to home but still so far away. He couldn't see her. Not until Ethic spoke to her first and until he had his shit together. Messiah had to come with an explanation and an apology. Neither lived on his tongue. The words were stuck in a timid heart that was too afraid to free them. So, he was forced to wait. Wait until he could build up courage to face her . . . wait until his money was right because he wanted to offer her a life. He wanted to take care of her. The anticipation was agonizing. He had been ordered to give her space until the time was right and as bad as Messiah wanted to defy Ethic, he knew he had to prove his loyalty all over again. He had to keep his distance from Morgan for now.

"Aghhh!" The roar that erupted from him bounced off the walls as he brought the hammer up and then forward, taking plaster off the wall. He swung that hammer again. Causing destruction. It was exactly what was going on inside him.

Demolition. Seeing Morgan with someone else was tearing him apart. Condemning him to misery and filling him with an emptiness so vast his stomach was free falling.

Messiah tore down an entire wall before exhaustion forced him to stop.

"Now you got to rebuild it."

He turned in surprise. He hadn't even heard her come in.

Bleu stood in front of him, leaning against the door frame.

"You tore it all down, Messiah. Are you done now? Tearing things down?" she asked.

Messiah heaved as he stared at her.

"Aren't you tired of fucking shit up?" she asked. "Tear yourself down all you want, you're still the dopest person I know."

The hammer fell from his hands and he turned away from Bleu, leaning over onto the countertop.

"When you gon' be ready to do something different, Messiah? You tore it down. Tore your life down. Now you got to rebuild it. I'd love to see that."

Bleu's voice was closer and when he faced her she was right in front of him.

"I can't," he said, looking over her head because he couldn't bring himself to meet her eyes.

"I'm not up there," she challenged.

He looked off to the side.

"I'm not over there either," Bleu said.

Stubbornly he looked down at her and Bleu captured him there, peering so deeply into him that Messiah felt transparent. Could she see all his fears? She had pulled back the curtains and was peeking into his aura without permission. A peeping fucking Tom. Her nosy ass. Messiah picked up her hand and laced her fingers with his then surrendered, placing his forehead against hers.

"Shit's fucked up, B. I'm so close to her but I ain't got shit to offer. I can't go to her empty handed."

"So, give her your heart," Bleu said. "That's enough."

Messiah lifted her hand and admired the ink that melted from his skin to hers. Two tattoos one picture, incomplete without the other half. The greatest friend he'd ever had. Bond tested, turmoil approved.

"What you doing here anyway?" he asked, changing the subject as he hopped up on the countertop.

Bleu dug into her tote bag and removed a prescription bottle. "Your vitamins," she said. "You left them at the house." Messiah took them from her hand and watched as she removed a bottled water and a white paper bag. "You said they hurt your stomach, so I figured you'd need food with them."

"What are you B? My mama?" Messiah snickered.

"Call me whatever you got to call me to take the vitamins," Bleu shot back, smirking as he followed her instructions.

"I would be a much better man, B. If I came up with a mama like you," he said. "God didn't put good shit like that in my life."

Bleu stared at him.

"You know you can talk to me, right?" she asked. "About whatever, Messiah. It doesn't all have to live in your head."

"Some shit you just don't say, B," Messiah said.

"With other people I get it. With me, you can say everything. There's nothing you can ever do or say that will make me switch up on you," she assured.

"I ain't do shit. What's on my soul is something different. Shit is black."

Bleu pulled in air but forgot to release it. The gloom that hung in the air around Messiah. The spark of shame that ignited in his eyes. His deep baritone that normally barked everything with such aggression, was subdued, it was barely a whisper.

"Black like eating dog food off a dirty basement floor? Or black like not knowing who your son's father is because you were so gone on crack binges that you let a man fuck you so that you could smoke for free? Darker than that?"

Bleu had never admitted that second part to anyone.

"Word?" Messiah's brow lifted. "You was hoeing, B?"

"Hoeing, bruh," she confirmed.

Messiah snickered, and Bleu released a small smile that was filled with shame. She looked down as her eyes misted.

"Don't do that," he said.

"What?" she asked.

"Be ashamed of any of the fuck shit you fought through to get here," Messiah stated.

"I'll stop if you stop," she countered.

He nodded and then crossed strong arms across his chest.

"It's hard, B," he said. He pulled his bottom lip into his mouth and bit down.

"I know," she whispered.

"I wake up at night in cold sweats, cuz I don't really like the sleep thing. Late night is when he would come to my room. I can still smell his sweat. Feel the weight of him. He was so heavy I couldn't breathe—"

Messiah searched for disgust in Bleu. He waited for her reaction.

"What the fuck are you looking at ugly?" she asked.

"A change. Now that you know I'm looking for a change in you," Messiah admitted.

"Knowing that doesn't change how I feel about you. I'm sorry that it happened to you. Fucked up shit happens. People are disgusting. Whoever did that to you . . ."

"My father," Messiah admitted. He couldn't even believe he was telling her this.

"Well your father is disgusting. He's filth, Messiah. I hope he dies a long, miserable, painful death for what he did to you. But the man you are. The man in front of me. You're so far removed from the little boy who went through that Messiah. You survived. You don't have to prove anything to anybody and people knowing your past doesn't change who we see right here today. You're a fucking beast, Messiah. A whole king out here. Stop getting in your own way because you're ashamed of shit you couldn't control. You're looking for me to feel sorry for you? Or to judge you? I don't feel none of that. I respect you more. Love you more. Never less. I'll never love you less. If you tell her, she'll understand. She'll take you back, but you got to tell it all. Stop giving her half of you."

Messiah shook his head. "Nah, that ain't for Mo. Shorty ain't built for that. That's just for you, B. For you to know so you can know me. I don't want to hide shit from you. You the realest on my team. I want you to know everything. Keep that safe for me."

Bleu nodded. "Always. I know you can't see Mo yet, but what about Isa? What about Meek?"

"Nah," Messiah said. "She's first. Nobody's seeing my face before her. Except you."

8

"Messari!" Morgan yelled from the kitchen.

"Get Yolly and come here baby boy." She heard the sounds of "Baby Shark" and Morgan groaned as she let her neck fall back, eyes hitting the ceiling. She was so damned tired of hearing that damn tune she didn't know what to do. Morgan cut the strawberries into small pieces and a smirk crossed her face before her eyes went void. Her heart stalled, and her eyes prickled. The smallest things would put her in time machine and warp her back to Messiah. All it took was the sight of a strawberry or someone calling her Shorty to send her back in time. *God please let him be at peace.* The knock at the door snapped her back to the present and Morgan cleared her throat and sucked in a deep breath before carrying two plates to the kitchen table.

"One minute!" she called out.

"Babbbby shark, doo, doo, doo, doo, doo, doo . . ."

Morgan rolled her eyes and chuckled as she watched Messari dance along to the program. Both he and Yara had their hands steepled on top of their heads. Yara couldn't hear but she followed her brother without question.

"Mommy, wook at me!" Messari yelled.

"I see you big boy!"

Yara's bright eyes turned to Morgan and Morgan smiled. "You're doing so good, Yolly Pop. Get it boo!" she signed. His legacies. Messiah's babies made her happier than anything ever could. She often wondered if they were the purpose for all the pain. Maybe she and Messiah were only meant to create these beautiful souls and nothing more. They were beautiful and if she had to survive the turmoil all over again just to have them, she would. She hated when she got like this. When one small thing triggered a bout of depression so strong she felt like giving up. She pulled open the door without looking and without warning every single negative emotion that had tried to pull her into the darkness dissipated. Light flooded into the darkest parts of her heart, into the unhealthiest parts of her mind as soon as she saw his face.

Morgan's heart thundered in her chest and she fingered her wild hair, trying to tame it. She hadn't even wiped the damn crust from her eye yet.

"You got a little something living in your nose too, love. Get that while you're at it," he said, amusement playing in his eyes.

"You're lying!" she shouted, embarrassed.

Morgan turned to the mirror mortified as she inspected her disheveled appearance. Seeing that there was nothing, she turned back to him.

"You're real funny," she chastised. He cornered her against the door and kissed her.

"I see your ass ain't brushed your teeth yet either," he said. Morgan turned her head to the side, and he turned it back, kissing her deeper. Morgan melted and wrapped her hands around his neck, massaging the back of his head.

"What are you doing here?" she asked, breathless as she stared in his eyes. She got lost there. Drowned there.

"This thing is becoming a problem. Wake up, think about you. Go to sleep, thinking 'bout you."

"That doesn't sound like a problem." Morgan beamed, smiling so brightly that her cheeks hurt a little.

"When your mind is supposed to be elsewhere it is," he said. His lips touched hers. Gently. Lightly. A small peck then he stared again, eyes scanning her face. Another peck. The seduction he had mastered was the best part. He took his time with her. Every time.

He pulled back when he felt a tug on his pants leg. He looked down to find Yara reaching up for him.

"You're canceled love, my favorite girl pulling rank," he said. Morgan smiled as he bent to pick Yara up.

"She stay hating," Morgan answered. She closed the door, locked it, and then headed to the kitchen. "Are you hungry?" she asked.

"I can eat," he said.

"Messari, come eat!" she called.

" 'Baby Shark,' Mommy!" he shouted back.

Morgan turned and walked back to the living room. "What you doing boy? If you gon' dance to it you got to swag it," she said, giving him duck lips as she started dancing in the middle of the living room, bending down so she was eye level with her son. She picked him up and blew raspberries against his neck. He laughed, uncontrollably, wiggling in her arms, and squealing. "You want Mommy to dance to this boop?"

Messari nodded. She propped him on her hip.

"Alexa, play 'Baby Shark Remix,'" she said.

Ahmeek stood with Yara, forehead dipped in curiosity. "You can remix a lot of stuff Mo, but I don't know about the baby shark song," Meek said, smirking.

"Boy what?" she frowned. "See I was just joking, but now I'm about to teach you to put some respect on my name mmkay." She placed Messari on his feet. "Go sit next to Meekie, Ssari. Watch ya' mama burn it down." Meek placed a hand on the top of Messari's head and guided him to the couch. Messari climbed up and tried to take a seat in Meek's lap but Yara pushed him off. She was territorial, much like Morgan.

"Yollyyy!" Morgan chastised. "Don't push," she signed.

Messari scrambled onto the back of the couch and climbed onto Meek's neck, while Yara occupied his arms. They were hanging all over him and he didn't seem to mind. His patience with her twins warmed Morgan from the inside out.

"Can I get an introduction or something?" she asked.

"Mommy! You're Mommy Shark!" Messari shouted giggling his heart out.

"Coming to the stage, the girl who's about to mess up a perfectly innocent kid's bop! Mo' Money!"

"Noooo! Her Mommy Shark Meek!" Messari shouted, beating flat hands against Meek's head. Meek winced, closing one eye and Morgan hollered.

"You right homie, let me run it back again, get it right this time," Meek said. "Introducing Mommy Shark!"

"Yayyy!" Messari yelled, clapping his hands. Meek grabbed Yara's hands and the threesome gave her a round of applause as the beat dropped.

The trap remix was much different than the normal song.

Shark, shark, shark, shark, shark, shark, shh-shh-shark, shark, shark

Morgan stuck out her tongue and started dancing. Meek's brow lifted in stunned amazement.

"Yo' love, the level of talent you got is crazy," he said, shaking his head as she turned up to the song. Morgan wrecked the song like she was dancing to a popular hip-hop beat. Stank breath and wild hair, she made up the count as she went along. It was effortless for Morgan. She dragged beats, any beat, without even thinking.

Messari and Yara scrambled down and joined her and Morgan laughed as she picked up her baby girl and danced with her in her arms. Messari did his best, imitating moves he had seen her do. Meek just sat back watching, shaking his head, and biting his lip until the song ended.

"That mommy shit you got going. It fucking wrecks me yo," Ahmeek said as the music faded.

"Language, Mr. Harris," she reminded, with a smile. She pulled his hand, forcing him to stand. "Come on Ssari, let's go eat."

Meek scooped Messari and followed her into the dining room.

"I didn't know you were coming by," Mo said. "I have a ton to do today. I've got to get Messari's hair cut, go to the grocery store . . ."

"Don't play with me," Meek said as he sat Messari in his high chair where Morgan had already placed a plate.

"Excuse me?" she asked.

"Why didn't you just tell me?" he asked. "I could have brought my clippers."

"I ummm," Morgan paused, a bit stunned. "I mean, it's not your responsibility. Bash usually does it, but considering that he's not speaking to me right now . . ."

Meek frowned. "So because he's on bad terms with you he ain't taking care of his kids?"

Morgan couldn't tell him that Messari wasn't Bash's child. She couldn't explain his position, so she opted for nothing more than a shrug.

"I'll take him," Ahmeek stated. Morgan stared at him in amazement. "My set is at the loft, but we can go to Flint and run by the shop. One of my barbers will get him together, put a line on him. Corny ass nigga got homie out here with no line. We got to fix that. Ain't that right?"

"Wight!" Messari shouted, agreeing, and giving Ahmeek a pound with one tiny fist as he stuffed his mouth with the other.

"I wasn't playing about the breath love," he said, one side of his mouth lifting in a smile. "Go take some time for yourself. Get dressed. I can feed them and get this shit together. When you're ready we'll head out."

Morgan felt like she was dreaming. Things with Ahmeek were so easy. She kept anticipating a pitfall, kept bracing herself for some type of interference to detour the rabbit hole she was falling down but it never happened.

Morgan lifted out her seat.

"This one likes to stuff her mouth and just let it sit there, so don't let her put too much in at once," Morgan advised. "I'll be quick. I promise."

"Take your time," he said, not even looking at her as he reached across the table to cut Yara's food up smaller.

Morgan kept one ear peeled waiting for him to call her for help or to hear her twins crying in protest, but it never happened. Even with Bash she'd have to eventually cut her showers short to assist because her babies were a handful. Morgan dressed casually, or as casual as Morgan Atkins could be. White leggings, tan thigh high boots, and sheer short sleeve, high neck, body suit. She went light on her makeup and straightened her hair, pulling half up and leaving the rest down to cascade down her back. When she walked out into the living room an hour and a half later, she found the three of them asleep on the couch. Meek's arms were thrown across the back of the couch and the twins had found a spot tucked beneath him. Fear filled her. She would have to be careful with this. Her babies knew Bash to be their father. They liked Ahmeek and she was afraid of them getting too close to him. They weren't together. They probably would never be together on that level. It wasn't a forever type of thing despite what it felt like. In the deepest chamber of her heart she knew she couldn't be that for him. Forever. His. She wanted to. She wished she could, but they had so many things that prevented that from coming true. A closet full of skeletons that they were both ignoring just to feel what they were feeling when they were in each other's presence.

She walked over to him and lifted Yara out of the uncomfortable position she was resting in. Ahmeek stirred.

"You ready to mob?" he asked.

She leaned down and kissed him softly. "No more stink breath," she teased playfully. She pulled back and he grabbed her, pulling her into his lap roughly. Morgan laughed as she and Yara fell all over him. Yara quickly scrambled out of Mo's arms and went back to Ahmeek.

"Ugh, this little bond y'all have is starting to turn my stomach," Morgan said. "Come on Mommy's Ssari. Yolly don't show Mama no love."

They departed with the twins and as Ahmeek turned out of the parking lot she glanced over at him. She settled into the seat.

"You know what you're doing to me, right?" she asked.

He took her hand and brought it to his lips, kissing it, without answering.

The barbershop was the first stop. This time Mo wrangled Yara and Ahmeek carried Messari. They entered the barbershop and the jovial atmosphere immediately intensified.

"What up boss man?" an older man with a salt and pepper beard and bald head greeted. Ahmeek dapped him up with his free hand as he made his way through the shop.

"Damn bruh that's you?" another barber asked. Morgan felt all eyes in the shop on her and she blushed slightly as she played Ahmeek close.

"Keep it respectful my nigga," Ahmeek stated, showing love once again. A gangster's hug.

"Always, G," the barber replied.

"Everybody this is Mo," he introduced.

"Nigga don't be parading Mo ass through this bitch like she the new boss. Next thing you know she'll be dropping off plants and shit, putting curtains up, adding nail techs and shit, trying to make this shit hers," Isa stated.

"Shit, bruh. If that's what a nigga got to do to pull something like that? Flower pot me my nigga," another barber cracked.

The men in the shop erupted in laughter and Morgan's entire face turned red.

Ahmeek turned to her and kissed her lips. A quick peck.

"That's your little man, Meek?" the older barber asked.

"Nah, this Mo's baby boy. He my partner though. Ain't that right?" Meek asked Messari.

"Wight!" Messari shouted. He was always an octave too loud and Meek smiled at his energy.

"That's a real good look on you, young," the barber stated. "It's time for you to get you one of them. A couple more boys. Put a football team around them queens over there."

He glanced back at Mo and she looked to the floor, smiling. "You'll get him together for me? Not too low. Clean him up. Give him that big boy cut?"

"I got you," he said. The barber tapped the man he was cutting. "Yo, let me get my man squared away and I'll come back to you as soon as I'm done with little homie."

The man didn't protest. He knew better. "What up, Meek?" he greeted. Ahmeek nodded but didn't answer with words, then placed Messari in the barber's chair.

Meek retreated to Morgan's side. There was one chair left and Meek sat, then pulled her into his lap. She held Yara tightly in her arms. Morgan had never felt so pretty, so loved, so taken care of. It wasn't even a huge gesture. Just a quick trip to the barbershop, but he had introduced her. He had made it clear that she was his. Only she wasn't. She hadn't agreed to that. Or were they past that? Were they beyond the point of needing to talk about what they were to one another? They couldn't be much because she was still something to someone else. The world of gray they existed in was full of confusion, but Morgan didn't care because it felt phenomenal.

"You could totally put a plant or two in here. Spruce the place up a little," Mo said, loud enough for the entire shop to hear.

"Aghhh!" the men groaned.

Morgan smiled, laughing as Ahmeek shook his head.

"See! I told you! Fuck I tell you, bruh?!" Isa said, shaking his head and laughing. "Don't let the pretty face fool y'all. That mu'fucka there put niggas in a trance and shit. Watch she have this nigga wearing matching shirts and Air Force Ones before we know it."

Morgan laughed.

"My nigga, 2003 me!" the same barber shouted, pausing to point his clippers at Mo. "What you say beautiful? We can go to the mall and get matching airbrushed shirts right now! I got the Grand Am out front. It's gassed up and ready to go!"

Morgan smiled, turning to Meek who sat comfortably, leaned back as he shook his head.

"You ain't never coming in here ever again, love," he stated.

"I'm saying though. He has a Grand Am. How can I say no to that?" Mo joked.

Everybody in the shop erupted. Meek would get slaughtered every time he walked inside for weeks. He swept a hand down his face and snickered.

Meek sat up and pinched her chin, manipulating her face to his and he kissed her.

"Awwww this nigga got to mark his territory now!" the barber cracked.

"That's right young, put your name on that," the older man stated while pointing at Ahmeek.

Yara placed her little hand to Morgan's face and pushed it away from Ahmeek's.

"Yolly!" Morgan complained.

"Looks like baby girl is the real one in charge," the old man said.

"She got some act right," Meek stated with a wink, pulling Yara from Mo's arms and then patting Mo on the butt. Morgan lifted and Ahmeek stood, lifting Yara high in the air, arms overhead as Mo sat back down.

"Ain't that right Yolly Pop?" he asked. "Ya mama giving up her seat in the whip. It's all yours now."

Yara laughed uncontrollably. Morgan's heart tightened in angst until Ahmeek caught her effortlessly.

"Meek, be careful," she said.

"Over here, bruh!" Isa shouted, clapping his hands together like they were in the middle of a ball game. Meek tossed Yolly.

Morgan's heart clenched again. Yara was so tickled as Isa snatched her out of mid-air. "Uncle Isa a gangster Yolly Pop. Your scary ass mama think a nigga ain't got hands. Like we ain't used to run niggas on the field."

"Those were the good ol' days!" the older barber chimed in. "You young little niggas on the field were like the fucking three amigos. Ahmeek could toss a football a hunnid yards. Isa would snatch that ball out of midair."

"Hell yeah. Just like this," Isa said, tossing Yara again. Morgan stood.

"Meek, you're terrifying me right now," Morgan said, her heart bleeding a little every time Yara left the safety of his hands.

The toddler was laughing uncontrollably, eyes wide and full of joy from the adrenaline of the fun.

"I got her, Mo. I'd never drop her, love," he said.

"Nah, he ain't dropping nothing. He was the best in the state. Y'all remember the game where Messiah bust up and ran them eighty yards in for a touchdown?"

Morgan's body went rigid. Like somebody had snapped their fingers and put her under a trance she was pulled right back in time. His name. All it took was his name to deflate her. Both Isa and Meek knew. They saw the impact as the words crashed into her. Morgan grabbed Yolly from Isa before rushing out the shop. She just needed some air. A little air would clear her mind and she sucked it in, gulping desperately because she could feel her anxiety building. Yara put her hands on the side of Mo's face and planted a kiss on the tip of her nose and Morgan laughed to stop herself from crying. She felt his hand on the small of her back.

"You okay?"

She turned to him and nodded. "Yeah. I'm fine."

"Five minutes. Let me go get Messari and we can go, a'ight?"

Morgan nodded and lowered her head into his chest. He wrapped one arm around her waist and kissed the top of her head before going back inside.

He emerged with Messari.

"Aww Mommy's Ssari you look so handsommeeeee," Morgan sang. Her mood was instantly turned around. "You look so good big boy." Meek wrapped one arm around Morgan and she leaned her head against his shoulder as they walked to the car. When they were safely inside he turned to her.

"Grocery store?" he asked.

"I think I just want to grab something quick and go home," she whispered.

He started the car and pulled off without a word.

Morgan felt warmth all over her body as his fingers laced hers. He always held her hand when he drove. Every time. It never failed. He secured her. He reassured her. He knew she had her ghosts and he understood them. He never judged her. The level of consideration he always took with her was breathtaking. She was damaged. Scarred from the heartbreaks of her past, and she felt them all the time except when she was with Ahmeek. She was silent as he drove back to her place. When they arrived, they took the twins upstairs.

"I'ma break out, love," he said.

She turned to him in surprise.

"Why?" she asked. She wanted him to stay. She could tell by his body language that he wasn't going to.

"I've got business, love. I just wanted to see you before. It's why I popped up in the first place. I just needed to look at you," he said.

"What kind of business, Ahmeek?" she asked.

Ahmeek leaned against the front door, posting up, as he lifted one hand to the back of his head, rubbing, eyebrows lifting.

"Nothing for you to worry about, Mo," he said.

"So why come by? Why come see me? If you're going to see my face again why did you need to see it so badly today, before you handle your business?" Morgan pushed, voice heightened in worry.

"I just wanted to see you Mo, that's all. I'll call you when I'm back, a'ight?" he said.

Morgan had almost forgotten what Ahmeek was into. She had forgotten that he was only gentle with her. The rest of the world received a totally different man.

"And if I say I don't want you to go?" she asked.

"I'd go anyway," he answered truthfully.

She nodded. She remembered this feeling. She had been

here before. Restless nights. Worrying. Being sick to her stomach because someone she loved was out chasing the bag. He was
the king. He held court in the streets. She'd always known but
his reserve made it easy to forget. He was such a gentleman that
she often forgot the gangster that was well hidden beneath.

She knew she cared about Ahmeek. She knew that she enjoyed his presence but the hole in her heart in this moment told
her that her emotions were growing by the minute.

"And if something happens to you?" she asked.

"Shit happens every day, love," he said.

She nodded again, scoffing. She snapped her eyes closed.
This was why she'd chosen Bash. This was why she had stayed
ducked away in his world for so long. There were no hood niggas in London. There was no passion-filled love affairs that had
the potential to tear her apart.

"You don't have to worry . . ."

"But I will worry, Ahmeek. I'll go crazy here . . . worrying . . .
about you!" she yelled.

"Mommy stop yelling at Meek!" Messari fussed.

Morgan sighed.

Ahmeek smirked and lowered himself to Messari's level.
"Come here, homie," he said. Just like a little traitor Messari
ran into Ahmeek's arms. "You gon' take care of your mommy
and Yolly for me homie?" Messari nodded and Morgan pushed
out a breath of frustration as she pulled out her ponytail holder
and ran her hand through her hair.

For the first time ever, she was angry at him. "Don't do
that," she said. "Don't put grown man responsibility on my son
because your ass ain't gon' be here."

Ahmeek stood, brows lifted. "Watch your mouth love," he
said.

"Don't tell me to watch my mouth, Ahmeek. You're being
stupid right now. I'm telling you I have a problem with this."

"You're not in a position to have a problem with anything I do," Ahmeek stated.

Morgan felt like she had been slapped. Like he had balled a fist and delivered a blow so mighty that she stumbled backwards.

"I don't want you to go. It's not worth it. I don't like this feeling. I don't want to relive this feeling Ahmeek!" She shouted. "You should understand that!"

"You not reliving shit with me, I ain't gave out nothing but love with you," Ahmeek stated. He was so passive aggressive. So calm that it made her livid. His self-control made her lose it. He was speaking to her like her wants and needs didn't matter to him . . . like she had no say so.

"If you walk out this door, I promise I'm done. I can't be in this position again . . ."

"You got a bad habit of comparing me to niggas, Mo."

"Mo?" she asked as her neck jerked back.

"Yeah, Mo!" he stated. It came out forceful and Morgan's eyes widened in stun. "What you want from me, Morgan? I'm doing this shit at your pace. You the coach. I'm just running your plays, but I have commitments."

"Robbing semis is more important than being here with me?" she asked.

"Stop talking about shit you don't know, Mo."

"Stop calling me fucking Mo!" she shouted.

"Mommy stop yelling at Meek!" Messari said running back into the living room. Morgan's emotions were getting the best of her. She had to stop because she didn't do this. She didn't fight with anyone in front of her kids. She couldn't. She knew what it would do to them. She picked up her son, kissing the side of his head.

"Answer the question Ahmeek. Whatever is out there, is more important than me?"

"Look at your left hand Mo," he said. Morgan looked down and saw her engagement ring.

"I ain't the one with other priorities," he said. "I'll call you when I'm back."

"I'm asking you to stay," Morgan stated as he turned to the door. Plain and simple.

"I can't, Mo. Isa's waiting," Meek stated.

Morgan had to place Messari on his feet, so he wouldn't be able to see the tears that fell. She retreated. She left him standing at the front door as she went to the kitchen to cry. Morgan gripped the edge of the countertop, leaning forward as she folded in half. She was so sick to her stomach that she couldn't stand up straight. The amount of grief she felt by the possibility of what could happen to him on this run was crippling. He came up behind her.

"Stop, crying love," he sighed. "This is for nothing. I'm coming back. It's a simple run."

Morgan faced him.

"I don't know what we're doing Ahmeek. I mean, I don't know if this even leads to anything. I have a situation and it's not an easy one to leave but even if we never get more than what we have now I want you to know it means something to me. It means everything to me. I don't take a moment of it for granted. I don't take you for granted."

He pulled her into his chest and she wrapped her arms around his waist. "I'll call you. That's my word." She knew a promise from him was worth more than gold. He had never let her down.

She nodded, sniffing and he gripped the sides of her head, tilting it backward before kissing her.

"God why did I let you in?" she whispered as his lips covered hers. "I'm getting attached Ahmeek." He paused and stared her in the eyes. No words. Just a bunch of thoughts telling him to end this now. A bunch of warnings blaring in his mind telling him that Morgan would be the death of him. Then his disregard for them all.

"I been attached, love," he answered.

Another kiss that stole her soul and he was gone, leaving Morgan's head spinning. This was no longer for fun. It was no longer something Morgan could see herself letting go and she had no idea what she was going to do about it.

9

Ahmeek gripped the throttle of his bike, pushing it faster as he rode on the driver's side of the armored truck.

"Yo, G, this shit is easy money." Isa's voice played through the Bluetooth in his helmet. Meek couldn't see him, but he knew that Isa was keeping pace on the passenger side. They were used to robbing semis, escorting this truck down I-75 felt like babysitting.

"Easy as fuck," Ahmeek responded. "But we need to choose a crew. A nigga could be in something wet right now. This shit feels like an errand."

"True dat," Isa shot back. "I'll pull a couple of the runners off the block. Hand out promotions tomorrow. You know that little nigga Hendrix?" Isa asked.

"I'm familiar."

"He's good with a burner and he know how to ride too. He be racing and shit, taking niggas money, betting big on himself. He's got heart. He stay running through the work too. Pills, coke . . . it don't matter what we give him, he flipping it," Isa stated.

"Let's give him a shot then. Set up the meet. This shit is easy money. All he got to do is take a ride," Ahmeek stated.

"And if shit don't work out I'm casing every aspect of the operation," Isa stated.

Ahmeek snickered. "Preparing for the big lick already, bruh?"

"I'm always ready. Hak better walk light. As long as we on the same team I'm chilling but as soon as he on that opposite side, I'm taking one of these big pretty bitches down," Isa stated, referring to the armored truck. "It's only a matter of time."

"Nah G. We gon' do the job, get this easy money and keep it safe for everybody. I got somebody to get back to every time," Ahmeek stated.

"Shorty doo wop under your skin," Isa remarked.

The old nickname filled Ahmeek with tension and the dead air between the calls told a story of conflict that Isa didn't miss.

"My bad, G."

Meek knew what the apology was for. The name had been given by Messiah. Morgan's first love. His friend. His brother. He hadn't heard the term in years and it put mixed emotions in the bottom of his belly.

She had belonged to Messiah first. That was something he thought of daily, something that gnawed at him. Messiah had asked him to take care of Mo, but still the idea of coming after his man did something to him. It broke every code he's lived by for his entire adult life but damn if he didn't love the girl. Damn if he didn't want her. He was too far in to let his ego and his pride get in the way. What he was feeling for Morgan was unlike anything he had ever felt his entire life.

"Eyes up, bruh," Meek said, tone low, distracted because now his mind was miles away, imagining a pretty yellow bone who he knew was lying in bed watching *Grey's* at this very moment.

Both men went silent, letting the loud exhaust from their motorcycles fill the air.

The sound of a third bike echoed in the distance.

"You hear that?" Isa asked.

"It's four o'clock in the morning. Who else is on this fucking highway this early?" Ahmeek asked.

The bike was nearing fast, accelerating at a pace that was breaking the speed limit.

"Whoever it is they ain't coming to play," Isa said. Ahmeek steered the bike with one hand and reached in his waistline with the other. One slip. One wrong move and the night could end deadly.

A bike came flying by. The helmeted driver was pushing at least one hundred and twenty as he zipped past them.

"It's nothing, bruh. Just some random rider," Isa said.

"That ain't random," Ahmeek answered. The man cut in front of the armored truck so close it caused the truck to spin out of control to avoid hitting the driver. Ahmeek drew his pistol and sat up on the bike, removing both hands from the handle bars. He had to ride the motorcycle with nothing less than stellar balance, gripping the sides of the machine with sturdy thighs as he let loose, pulling his trigger.

When bullets flew back, Ahmeek and Isa knew this was a robbery.

"Fuck this nigga think he is? Who tries to rob an armored truck, dolo?" Isa shouted. He picked up speed and veered right. He came off the hip, shooting as well, as the truck sat in the middle of the highway, absorbing shots from both sides. Bullets ricocheted off the steel truck, sparks flew, and the men inside cowered in fear as Ahmeek and Isa tried their hardest to annihilate this intruder. The sound of sirens rang out as red and blue lights flashed behind them.

"Yo, we got to go!" Ahmeek shouted into his Bluetooth. The lone rider took off again and Isa and Ahmeek gave chase.

"What about the truck?!" Isa asked.

"The money's still inside. We're good. We need to find out who the fuck is on this bike," Ahmeek said, gritting his teeth as he squeezed the throttle faster.

BANG! BANG!

Meek dipped left then right, a moving target as the man on the bike in front of them turned halfway to keep firing. Ahmeek lifted his pistol and curled his finger around the trigger but when the rider lifted onto his front wheel, a backwards wheelie, Ahmeek's finger froze.

"Yo, who the fuck?!" Isa shouted. Ahmeek released his throttle and veered off the highway, letting the rider go as Isa followed him.

They stopped at a gas station a mile up the road and Ahmeek snatched his helmet off his head.

"Who the fuck was that?" he asked.

He looked like he'd seen a ghost. He pointed in the direction of the highway. "You saw that shit G. I only know one nigga that can pull off that trick!" The front wheelie was a move only Messiah had perfected. He had fallen off his motorcycle as a kid a hundred times trying to get it right. Goosebumps formed on Meek's arms despite the leather jacket he wore.

"Yeah we know it ain't him though so somebody's fucking with us and when I find out who it is he's a fucking dead man," Isa stated.

Their phones chimed simultaneously and Ahmeek retrieved his, opening the screen. A call quickly followed.

UNKNOWN

He answered but didn't speak first.

"Whatever happened on the highway just now, is your liability. It's bad press for my business and there is an insurance hike for attempted robberies, gentlemen. An insurance hike that I will not be paying. Care to guess how much it is?"

"Whatever it is, we'll cover it. It's nothing," Isa stated.

But Ahmeek knew it was something. It was everything.

"It's two million dollars," Hak informed. "That's $166,666.66 per month gentlemen. Your new debt. The runs are off until I'm convinced it's not fucking amateur hour."

Click.

Ahmeek bit into his bottom lip and squeezed his fist around his phone. "Fuck!" he shouted. "Find that nigga man. Whoever the motherfucker is he's up outta here."

"What the fuck we gon' do about that payment? Pockets heavy bro, but I ain't got two milli."

"We got to grind up," Ahmeek said. "Put niggas on minimums. If they ain't moving through product they getting put off the block. If niggas want to eat it's time to work overtime. It's time to hit a lick too. A big one. Start scouting, G."

"Say less," Isa replied.

10

Christiana's voice was like elevator music. Background noise. Morgan heard her but paid her no attention as she sat at the dinner table with Bash and his mother.

"I really wish you had brought the twins. I've hardly seen them," Christiana said.

Morgan's fingertip lingered over her phone screen as she stared at Meek's name. Her gut was twisted in agony. In absolute worry. He had promised. He never broke promises. Her phone was dry, and it could only mean one thing. Something was wrong. Her heart was locked so tightly inside her chest that her neck tensed in fear. She didn't understand how this had happened. How had Ahmeek infiltrated her so deeply that she was this invested in his safety? She sat there, hearing but not listening. Present but mind gone.

"Mo!"

Her eyes lifted to Bash who sat frowning at her. "You didn't hear my mother talking to you?" he asked.

Morgan shook her head in confusion and then focused on Christiana.

"I'm sorry, what?" she asked, a bit of annoyance resting in her tone.

Christina peered up over her wineglass and those condescending eyes burned into Morgan. The way Mo's attitude was set up she met her stare, unflinching. Michigan Morgan was quite different than the girl Christiana had control over in London. Tension and challenge rested between them.

"Your children? I haven't seen them. I'm family, Morgan. I should see my grandchildren more often. Since you've been back in the States I hardly recognize you. Your temperament is so unpleasant sometimes. Even the way you dress and wear your hair is different. Michigan is unbecoming of you. Perhaps London is a better place to raise your family, Sebastian."

"Bash doesn't decide where I raise *my* kids," Morgan snapped.

She didn't even mean to let the words come out. He looked at her, stunned.

"Your kids, huh?" Bash asked.

"I didn't mean it like that," she surrendered. "We have family here is all. I don't want them halfway across the world. Away from Ethic. I need to be near *my* family. I stayed away for so long. They're playing catch up with the twins. I want to stay here. I can choose a med school here."

"You sure that's all you're staying for?" Bash challenged.

Morgan's phone vibrated against the table and she pushed back in her chair abruptly.

"We're eating dinner, Morgan," Christiana reminded.

"It's Ethic. I have to take this." She was so desperate to hear the voice of this caller. When he called her line she answered, no exceptions. Morgan rushed out onto the patio that extended from the formal dining room and closed the door before she answered.

"Ahmeek?" she whispered. "God I've been staring at my phone for hours." Relief flooded Morgan and her eyes prickled.

"My bad, love. I got tied up. We about to get to it. I just wanted to keep my word. I'ma hit you when it's over," he said. Morgan heard the background noise. Isa yelling something, the sounds of engines revving.

"Don't call. Just come. As soon as you can get to me. I don't care how late it is. Just come."

"I'ma be there. Let me get to this business and then it's right back to you Ms. Atkins. Always back to you," he stated.

"Okay," she breathed.

She hung up and then turned to see Bash rising from the table. His face was tinted auburn because his temper was rising, and his deep brow hollowed her stomach. She felt the anger coming from him as she walked back inside.

"For real, Mo, you're being rude," he said beneath his breath, grabbing her elbow to stop her from bypassing him.

"Ethic was just checking in, Bash. I had to take the call," she said.

He looked at her skeptically. She was playing him and they both knew it. She was insulting his intelligence and the fire in his eyes and the stern hold told her she was pushing him.

He fingered his chin and bit into his bottom lip in frustration as the sound of Christiana cutting through filet mignon clattered in the background. Silverware to china. Knife to plate. It was so quiet you could hear a pin drop. She knew his mother had keen ears and was tuned in to every word they spoke. It was what she hated most. The overbearing ways of Christiana made her feel trapped. This wasn't a conversation that she wanted to have in front of his mother. In fact, she didn't want to have it at all. She wanted to speed through this dinner so that she could go home and wait for Ahmeek. All she wanted to do every day for forever was be with Ahmeek Harris.

"Can we not do this? I'm here, Bash. With you. I'm not out with anyone else. It was a phone call. From Ethic. Now can we eat?"

Morgan tried to walk around Bash but a hand to her stomach stopped her.

"You told me that other thing was done," he said through gritted teeth.

"Sit down Sebastian," Christiana said. "I'm sure Morgan is smart enough to know what's at stake."

"Ma, chill," Bash interrupted. His interference surprised Morgan. He had finally spoken up. He pulled Morgan toward the kitchen, practically dragging her out of the room.

"Give me your phone," Bash stated.

"What?" Morgan's face turned up in utter disgust. "Absolutely not."

"You're full of shit, Mo," he snapped. The finger he pointed in her face set her soul on fire. Morgan slapped it away.

"What's with the finger?" Mo asked, frowning. "You've been doing the most lately. I promise you I'm not that girl, Bash. I saw my sister get her ass beat every day when I was little. That'll never happen to me. I'll call my people and air all this shit out. I've been silent for two years with you, just going with the flow, so you think shit is sweet."

"I forgot your daddy's a gangster," Bash said sarcastically.

"Daddy's a whole killer nigga and I ain't talking about Ethic."

Morgan knew she had gone too far. She wanted to chase down the words but before she could even take them back his hand was around her neck.

Morgan placed two hands around the stern hold he had on her as he advanced on her. Her back crashed into the corner of the ceramic countertops so hard that it took her breath away. His grip was too tight to even scream. She saw her sister in her head. It was like she was six years old all over again. She had pushed Bash too far. The lying, the cheating, the disrespecting had compounded like interest on a bad loan and he was ready to collect the debt she had incurred. This was the straw that had broken the camel's back. He was killing her. She could feel him squeezing the life out of her.

"Don't be disrespectful. I'm a man, Morgan. You can't bait me and think I won't react. Stop. Antagonizing. Me." He shook her violently with every word as his grip tightened. She couldn't breathe. Morgan went back to her childhood. Her mind floating from the lack of oxygen all the way back to when she would pick dandelions out of her backyard and pop off the tops. Her head felt like that.

"Sebastian!" Christiana stood in the kitchen doorway and for the first time Mo was grateful for her presence. Bash released her instantly.

Morgan gulped in air, stumbling away from Bash, using the countertop as her crutch as she hurried out of his reach.

"Mo—"

Morgan backed away further. Her legs could barely hold her up. She was trembling, and her eyes filled with tears.

"Sebastian give Mo some time. The staff will turn down a room for you. We all just need to calm down," Christiana negotiated, her arms extended as she tried to restore order in her home. "Let Morgan rest, son, and you take a walk."

"You're out your mind if you think I'm staying here tonight," Morgan snapped, heaving as she tried to catch her breath while tears fell down her cheeks. She stormed out of the kitchen.

"Mo!" Bash called as he followed her back to the table. Morgan snatched up her handbag.

"I'm getting the fuck out of here." She tore through the massive home with Bash on her trail.

"I'm sorry, Mo. I lost my temper. I wasn't going to hurt you. Please baby, listen. Just give me a second," he pleaded. He grabbed her arm and Morgan pushed him. She went into her Chanel bag so fast he never saw the .22-millimeter pistol coming.

BANG!

Morgan fired, cracking the mirror behind his head.

He steeled.

"My God!" Christian yelled.

"The next one is going through your head," Morgan stated. No shake on the end of her gun this time. She had perfected her aim, steadied her heart. She was the one in control. Ethic had taught her the one with the gun didn't need to shake.

"Mo this is me," Bash whispered. His hands were out, beseeching, submitting. "I just lost my temper baby. You're breaking me down with this thing with you and this guy, Mo . . . I didn't mean to, I just reacted. I'd never mean to hurt you. You know that. You know me, Mo. I've been here."

"Bash, let her leave," Christiana said, her voice unsteady. Tension had become a dinner guest.

"No Ma! Stay out of it! I'm sorry, Mo. I just love you so much. You gave me a family and now you're taking that away. You're not even giving me a chance, Mo. This is me. I've been here every step of the way. College, the birth of those babies. I picked you up when you were low. I'm low right now Mo. You're walking all over me, Mo and I'm asking you to stay. It's always going to be other options. You think I don't have them? Women who are established, who come with entire bloodlines of legacy. Beautiful women Mo but all I see is you. All I've ever seen was you. You don't even know how clear I see our life together. What it could be," he pleaded.

Morgan closed her eyes because she couldn't even see

through her tears. She didn't even know how it had come to this. "Mo. This is me? Your friend, Mo. I been here. Stop pushing me out. I'm here. I'm right here. Every day of those twins' life I've been here. You, Yolly, and Ssari are my family and you trying to give it away." The sincerity she heard in Bash twisted her gut and prickled her eyes. He had lost control, but Morgan had carried him wrong. She was hurting feelings and expecting rational reactions when she knew more than anyone that heartbreak made you lose control.

"I'm provoking you," she whispered. A part of her wondered if it mattered. Should what she did really control his actions? Was there an excuse for what had happened? Did he get a pass because she had been disrespectful?

"You are, Mo. You're breaking me down," Bash admitted. His face was flush in emotion, forehead wrinkled in anxiety and Mo felt her tears brewing in her. An emotional storm was boiling in her gut and she couldn't stop the tears.

Morgan lowered the gun and her face collapsed as he wrapped her in strong arms.

She dropped the gun as he consoled her. Morgan was so confused. At war with herself because she had chosen this life, but it wasn't the one she wanted to live.

She was caught in a love triangle and every time she tried to settle her heart it only got entangled more. Morgan owed Bash everything. To leave him. To abandon him made her feel low, but she didn't love him. Not the way he wanted her to. Not the way she wanted to give love. Her heart was so uninvolved when it came to him. It was just there. Just an organ. Just beating to keep her alive when in his presence. When she was with Ahmeek however, it raced to a beat so fast that it made her breathless. It was passionate and exhilarating. Ahmeek made her feel like she was free falling. Free falling into him but there was no risk because he caught her every time. She couldn't let him go but she owed Bash. She had a debt to pay and he wanted it paid in the form of time. She was doing a bid with Bash. A lifetime sentence. His wife to be. She was betrothed to him and she couldn't figure out how to escape.

11

Nerves filled Aria as she sat in the restaurant. She twiddled her thumbs in her lap. Her eyes hawked the door and every time it opened her anxiety soared. She checked the Rolex on her wrist and blew out a deep breath.

"You know I'm not walking through the front door."

Aria jumped, startled as she turned in her seat.

She screamed as she hopped up, throwing her arms around the man's neck.

"This hug feels so good," he said as he picked her up. He swung her, left to right, holding on tight and then kissed her cheek. "I'm mad as fuck that I ain't seen you in six months."

"I've been busy," she said, smiling as he placed her on her feet.

He pulled out her chair and she sat. Her eyes followed him as he rounded the table to sit across from her. He was a sight and every woman in the restaurant eyed him. He reeked of money and power. Designer everything but no logos, just expensive looking shit on an expensive looking man. Aria knew he big flexed without effort. He was in a league of his own and her eyes sparkled as she looked at him.

"I missed you," she said.

"Can't be true. I ain't heard a word from you," he answered.

Her phone vibrated against the table.

Isa.

She sent him to voicemail.

"One of your little jump offs?" the man asked.

Aria smirked. "Mind your business," she said, laughing.

"You get that bag I sent?" he asked.

"I got it. Thank you for the money," she said. "You spoil me."

"Always."

Aria's heart stalled when she saw Isa and Ahmeek walk into the restaurant.

He did a quick scan until his eyes landed on her. Ahmeek posted by the door, flipping the sign to closed and flipping the lock as Isa made his way across the room.

"Umm, I have to tell you something." Aria rushed her words, leaning into the table as her heart ran rampant.

Before she could even speak Isa was pulling up a chair.

"You must want me to air this bitch out Ali?" Isa said as he turned toward Aria, legs wide, leaning over onto his knees as he grabbed the seat of her chair and pulled her forward. "What I tell you about not answering my calls?"

"Little dawg. Better remove some of that bass out your voice before I whisper something to you," the man said.

"Nope, no!" Aria said. "This is not how this is going to go."

"That's exactly how it's going to go," Isa said, pulling his gun and sitting in on the table, discreetly covering it with a menu.

"Difference between me and you, is you think of your next move. I think of your next move and then my reaction," the man said. "You pull that trigger and you and your man at the door hitting dirt homie cuz you're outnumbered. Not to mention outwitted."

Isa glanced around the room and saw a shooter at every corner table in the restaurant.

"I own this restaurant," the man said.

"Yeah well you might as well press go on that cuz I'm willing to die over mine," Isa said.

"Isa—"

"Nah, Aria, this nigga want to fly. Let me lift him up out them thousand dollar sneaks. Give him his wings," the man threatened.

Isa didn't back down. Instead he lifted the menu and chambered a round, putting the pistol's aim on the man's face.

Every shooter in the restaurant came off the hip, including Ahmeek, who aimed directly at the man at the table.

"Isa! He's my brother!" Aria shouted. Isa popped the round out of the chamber sending a bullet flying into the air before pushing back from the table. He leaned down and gripped Aria's face, pulling her to him. She moaned as he kissed her, an involuntary response because she was livid. She pushed him off.

"Next time answer ya' fucking phone," he said.

"Isa this is Nahvid. Nah this is my EX boyfriend as of like five minutes ago," Aria said, rolling her eyes.

Everyone in the restaurant relaxed when Nahvid nodded to the manager. Nahvid dead panned on Aria. "You supposed to be out here learning something, not dating drug dealers," Nahvid stated, his temple pulsing. "Now I see why your grades are slipping. That ain't the move. I taught you better. Keep your eye on the play and right now your play is your education. I ain't paying for you to cut up out here."

"Your money ain't required," Isa stated.

"Nigga what?" Nahvid asked, standing.

"Isa leave," Aria urged.

"Leave? I move when I want to move and right now, I feel like staying stagnant as fuck," Isa baited.

"This the shit you into out here?" Nahvid asked.

"Exact shit she's into," Isa answered for her.

"Isa!" Aria shouted. "This is my family. Leave."

Nahvid had never been more comfortable. He sat there, coolly, unbothered. Not one feather was ruffled. Not one jewel in his crown out of place as he rubbed his hands together.

"Niggas got thirty seconds to clear out before I step out of character," Nahvid warned. He was looking at Aria. Aria knew that if Isa didn't leave, he wouldn't be able to soon.

"Ahmeek, get him," Aria said, turning to Meek, eyes pleading.

Meek tucked his pistol.

"Yo bruh. That's family business. She in safe hands. Ain't on no bullshit. We up," Ahmeek stated from across the room. "Shit getting real dramatic for nothing."

Isa turned and walked out of the restaurant without another word.

Aria's eyes followed him, and she went to go after him.

"You don't chase no nigga ever. The day you chase a man is the day I end his life. Remember who you are, queen. You above this. I do this, so you don't have to. I don't like nothing about this."

"You don't know him. He's not a bad guy," Aria defended.

"I don't want to know him. Keep that nigga from around me. He's a loose cannon. I'm going to have to blow that nigga head off over you one day."

"Come on Ssari. Keep up with Mommy, big boy," Morgan called as she carried Yara on one hip while carrying a grocery bag in her free hand.

"Wait for me!" Messari called as his little feet worked double time behind her. Morgan could barely get to the elevator the groceries were so heavy.

"Come press the button, Ssari," Morgan shouted. He hurried to her side and called the elevator.

"Where's Pop Pop, Mommy?" Messari asked. He loved Ethic. Morgan was so grateful for Ethic's connection to her children. It was constant. Consistent. Especially since coming back to Michigan. She knew they needed that because Morgan couldn't guarantee any other male figure in their lives.

"Pop Pop's at home, baby," Morgan replied as she held open the elevator and ushered him inside. Morgan couldn't wait to get inside her apartment. It had been a long day of fake smiling with the Fredricks. Bash's repeated apology for their fight was almost worse than the actual offense. He was overcompensating now, smothering her with affection she didn't ask for and attention she didn't want. Keeping her close and not giving her time to stray too far. Morgan had never felt so trapped. She had been forced to sleep at Bash's parents' estate for three days. He hadn't found time to drive her back to her place, so she had been forced to stay. Too ashamed to call Ethic after what had happened, Morgan allowed Bash to keep her there. The only reason she was able to even leave was because Yara wasn't feeling well and Alani had called to let Morgan know they would be taking her to the hospital. The one time Morgan wished that Bash had chosen to come with her, he couldn't. He had final grades to submit for graduation and a faculty meeting at MSU, so he couldn't accompany her to the hospital. Morgan hoisted Yara higher.

"My poor baby," she whispered to her sleeping daughter. When the elevator freed them, Morgan stepped out. She steeled when she saw Meek at her door. He was leaning forward writing something. He wore dark denim jeans that were distressed just like her heart. A lighter colored denim shirt that was rolled up to the elbows revealing Burberry check print. The brown boots he wore brought a real grown vibe to him. Aged him a bit.

Other niggas would have worn Timberland wheats, Ahmeek wore John Vavartos leather on his feet. A brand the hood wasn't even up on yet, because he didn't give a fuck about labels showing as long as he was buying quality.

"Wook Mommy! Meek!" Messari yelled. Meek turned his head toward her and Messari took off down the hallway.

"Aww, the homie," Meek greeted, bending down so that he was eye level with him. "Give me some, man." He held out his hand and Messari shook it. "Her sick!" Messari said, pointing down the hall to Morgan. Meek scooped Messari and then stood, looking up in her direction. They stood on opposite ends of the hall as nerves ate her alive.

"What are you doing here?" she asked.

He backpedaled, taking two steps until he was in front of her door. "Doing some corny ass shit that I didn't think all the way through. You went ghost on me again, love. I can't really keep cool when I don't hear from you. Results in lame ass shit like this," he said pulling the *Post It* note off the door. Morgan walked to him and took it from his hands.

"Will you be my girlfriend? Circle yes or no," Morgan read.

"That's the best I had at the time. Got all the way here and all the poetic shit I had in my head went out the window," Ahmeek said sarcastically.

Morgan smiled softly. There was something about gangsters that went soft for her that did it for Morgan. She stuck the *Post It* on his forehead. "Come back when you remember the good stuff," she chastised. Ahmeek had no idea that the note alone was the perfect gesture. She swooned over it, not because it was the most original, because she was sure he had gotten it from the show she had forced him to watch. But Morgan swooned because he paid attention to the way her eyes sparkled when Derek Shepard had done the same for Meredith Grey. She rewinded it twice just to experience the feels again. Ahmeek was making her believe that real love could be as good as the fantasy she dreamt of in her head. She turned to the door and he walked up behind her, grabbing her waist with his free hand, pulling her into him. His lips on the back of her neck made her quiver and her eyes closed. She faced him.

"Let me come in and take care of you, love. You're sick. Let me make it feel better," he whispered.

"It's not me. Yolly's not feeling well."

His brow pinched in concern. "That's even worse. What's wrong?" he asked.

"Fever. Doctor said it's viral so there's nothing they can give her. Just Tylenol," she whispered.

Ahmeek reached for Yara. She didn't even stir as he moved her to his shoulder, so he knew it had to be bad. The cold was taking a toll on her. The twins occupied his arms and Morgan unlocked the front door.

Messari scrambled out of Meek's hold as soon as he was inside.

"You can lay her down in my bed," Morgan said.

He disappeared down the hallway as Morgan went into the kitchen to put away the groceries she had purchased. Soup and Pedialyte were the doctor's orders for Yolly Pop so the grocery run on the way home had been a must.

"Ssari!" Morgan called as she headed to the second bedroom next. When she pushed open the door Morgan sighed. "Ssari nooooo," she groaned. Her beautiful son's brow dipped in confusion as his lips puckered into a pout.

"Me drew a picture Mommy, wook!"

The wall in front of him was scribbled in red crayon. Frustration mounted in her, but she couldn't even be angry. Just looking at Messari softened her.

Morgan admired her son. His expression. The sternness that always captured his features was all Messiah.

God, I wish he could have met you. He would have loved you. She hardly ever allowed herself to think of Messiah. She had run from her past and refused to slow down from fear of what might happen if it caught up to her. The tears she would cry, the hole she would sink into. She couldn't. So, she buried it all. Suppressed it because she was no longer the girl who could fall apart without remorse. Her children needed her but the heaviness pressing on her in this moment was so vast that her eyes prickled. Life was never supposed to be lived without him.

"Come on baby, it's bed time," she whispered, shaking the ghosts from her head.

A quick bath and Messari was ready to go down for the night. She carried him to her bedroom where Meek laid on his back, feet touching the floor as Yara laid across his chest. Her fussy baby was content. Morgan's mind drifted again. *Would Messiah be good with her?*

"No fair! Me want to sleep with Meek!" Messari protested. He ran across the room, struggling all the way along his short climb up the mattress.

"Come on lil' homie," Meek said, lifting one arm.

Morgan's eyes betrayed her as tears blinded her. She flicked the light switch and turned to leave.

"Mo—"

Her feet halted.

"Come here, love."

Morgan crossed the room and sat on the edge of the bed. Morgan leaned onto the bed, her face hovering over his as he took her chin in his fingertips.

"I don't want you to do nothing else right now except lay up under me with these babies," he said. "Cuz this shit right here make a nigga think about life in a totally different way, Mo. You got me moving totally different. I'm a different nigga with you."

Morgan exhaled. Ahmeek Harris. Her unpredictable love. She would have never guessed life would lead her to him. Messiah was heavy on her mind and she wondered if he would approve. She closed her eyes, greeting him behind her lids because she knew he would be there.

"He would have killed us," Mo whispered.

"Who?" Ahmeek answered, frowning.

"Messiah."

The name turned Ahmeek to steel and he blew out a sharp breath.

"It's so weird," she offered. "He's just been on my mind today. Like I feel him. I've fought this feeling for years but today it's like he's calling out to me. I can almost hear his voice and I haven't felt him this strongly in such a long time. I'm not trying to disrespect you. I just miss him and being here with you makes me miss him more. You remind me of him. I fight thoughts of him when I look at you." She stopped talking and shook her head because she knew she wasn't explaining herself the right way. "I'm sorry."

"Yo," he said, jarring her attention. "You don't got to hide that you still love him. I know that part already, Mo. I was there. I know what y'all had. I loved that nigga too. I miss him too and you're right, he'd bring war to my door on every day of the week over you. If he were here, we wouldn't be here. We'd never be here, doing this, not with one another. It would have never even been a thought."

"And that makes me sad," she replied, her tone low and heavy. "To think of not knowing you like this. To not be with you like this. You mean so much to me. It's hard to picture us going back to what we were."

"To bring bro back, I would watch you from afar so that nigga could breathe. It still fucks me up, Mo. He wasn't supposed to get sent up out of here like that."

She had never been able to talk about Messiah to anyone before, especially not Bash. Meek's understanding felt like a gift, but she couldn't take much more of this conversation. She still didn't even know how Messiah had died. Every time she thought of it, she broke down. She didn't even know what had become of his body and she didn't want to know. She knew the details would eat her alive. There had been no goodbye, no closure. Just a check. A million-dollar insurance payment. Morgan felt her body filling with emotion.

"I'm so sorry. We can talk about something else. I shouldn't have brought him up."

"You can talk to me, Mo. About whatever. Even the shit you think I don't want to hear."

"You're so good to me," Morgan said. She was still in disbelief at how good Ahmeek could be. Men like him, hood, rough around every edge, normally left scars behind. Instead, he was healing hers. He was cocoa-butter to her scarred heart and slowly but surely the evidence of injury that had been done to her before was fading away.

Morgan leaned down to his lips. Their kiss was moving. Soul-stirring. It aligned the moon and the stars or at least that's what Morgan told herself.

"Now about that date," he said. "A nigga trying to pick you up, take you out, make you smile, do all the basics, flowers, kiss you good night at the end, walk you to your door. I want to slide to third base if you let me get lucky. All that shit."

"All that shit Mommy," Messari repeated.

Morgan laughed. "You're such a bad example."

Meek smirked and looked down at Messari. Messari was tucked so tightly against Ahmeek and it felt right. It felt like this was her family. Like Meek would maybe want to stick around.

"Don't be like me homie. Be like your mama. She's the

good one," he said, smiling. "What you think? After Yolly's better? Maybe Friday, you'll stop playing games and let me do this with you the right way? Make me work real hard to earn these kisses you been giving me for free."

Morgan bit her lip as she sat on the bed, smiling... blushing.

"If Yolly's better, yes I'll go out with you," she said.

"On a real date? In public, love. Fuck who's watching, fuck who's around," he said. "You gon' bet big on a nigga, Mo? I swear to God, I'll never put you in a position to lose if you put your money on the kid."

She nodded. She didn't know how she would get away from Bash. She was sure he would come to her, smothering her again, invading her space, overwhelming her with his presence. She couldn't say no however. She didn't want to say no. All she would ever tell Ahmeek is yes. He left no room for dissatisfaction. All she ever did was smile with him.

"Okay," she agreed. She climbed into bed with him and he adjusted. "We're all over you. You have to be uncomfortable," she laughed. Yara was taking up his chest. Messari under one arm. Mo's big ass under the other.

"I'm good."

He rubbed her shoulder as she moved closer.

She felt the tear slide down her nose and she sniffed. *I love him. Just let me keep this. Just this one time. You always take people from me. Let me keep this one person. Just this one man. Please get rid of everything stopping me from having this with him.*

12

Morgan had never been so nervous in her life. She didn't know where the anxiety came from. Ahmeek wasn't new to her. They had been alone and intimate so going skating should have felt carefree, but it wasn't. Morgan changed clothes three times and switched the twins' outfits twice. Ahmeek had insisted that they join the fun and Morgan had swooned because it meant he didn't think of her as a separate entity. If he was taking one out, he was taking them all out. It was second nature, not forced, and Morgan was appreciative. They sat at the bay window in her apartment looking out like they were waiting on the school bus. A date with Ahmeek Harris. Who would have thought? There was some guilt living in her bones because none of this was ever supposed to be, but how could she not let it be when it felt so glorious? Morgan could hardly sit still. When he pulled up, she jumped up. She waited for Ahmeek at the door only to make him wait a full minute before pulling it open.

"Damn, love, you live to fuck me up," he said at first glance.

Black body suit under an oversized, army fatigue jacket. She smiled. You would have never thought she had cried herself to sleep from the turmoil they were causing by choosing to explore the possibilities ahead. Her face was made up in pretty nude tones and a pair of Bdonnas Apeshit boots were on her feet. Her twins matched her, both dressed in army fatigue joggers and matching jean jackets. Jordans graced their feet.

"So you wasn't gon' let a nigga in on the fatigue memo, huh?" Ahmeek asked. "I want to be down. Why I'm the odd man out?" he asked. She blushed.

"I didn't know you wanted to be down. Can't assume these days. Men say one thing and do another," she answered.

"My actions and words match, love," he said as he tapped her nose. "Always. How is Yolly feeling?"

"Much better," Mo replied.

"You ready?" he asked.

"Yeah I just need to grab their bag and my purse," she answered.

She reached for the bag and Ahmeek relieved her of it then grabbed Messari while she wrangled Yara. They walked to the car together.

"You ready to have some fun homie?" Ahmeek asked Messari. Messari nodded his big head and Ahmeek laughed.

"We can take my car since the car seats are already installed," she said.

"You don't drive me when I'm taking you out, Mo. I'll grab the seats. Unlock your doors," he stated. After ten minutes of preparation the twins were strapped in and Ahmeek climbed into the driver's side. He reached for her, turning her face to him. His eyes swept over her.

"You want to tell me what or who made you cry?" he asked.

Morgan's heart stopped. Her 2 a.m. crying session had lasted for hours. She hardly slept a wink as thoughts of Messiah haunted her. As thoughts of Bash disturbed her. She felt like she was repeating Raven's history with Bash but she felt obligated to stay. Between fearing the future with Bash and stressing over her past with Messiah it was hard to enjoy the present of Ahmeek. She wondered if Messiah would hate her for loving Ahmeek if he were alive to see it. Morgan had so many things blocking her happiness and night time was when the burden weighed on her the most. She had no idea how Ahmeek knew. She held her sorrow in during the sunlight. Like a vampire it lurked in the shadows. She had put on extra concealer, so he wouldn't be able to tell. It wasn't in her features however. The confusion was in her soul.

"It was just a really long night," she replied. "I don't want to talk about that."

"When you do want to talk," he paused and reached for her hand then pulled it to his lips to kiss her fingers. "About that or anything else, I'm always around for you. I'll make listening to you a priority whenever you need me to. I don't ever want you to feel like you got to figure it all out in your head."

She nodded, and he dropped the subject as they pulled away.

He reached for her hand and Morgan laced her fingers through his as her head rested comfortably against the seat. She rolled her neck to the left and a smile spread across her lips. The music pumping through the speakers made her close her eyes.

Don't listen to, what people say
They don't know about
Bout you and me

It spoke to her as she shook her head, side to side, slowly to the beat until she rolled her eyes out the window, enjoying the peace that the inside of this car provided. She had been through so much turmoil the past few weeks when all it took was this to make it go away.

They arrived at Rollhaven, a Flint landmark, and corralled the kids into the building. It was deserted, and Morgan frowned as they made their way to the skate rental booth. Morgan ordered three skates and Meek took the twins to the nearest booth to get them laced up.

"Where is everyone?" she asked, while waiting for her own pair to be retrieved.

"The rink is closed. He rented it out for the day," the worker said.

Morgan lifted eyes of disbelief up to the manager and then rolled them over to Ahmeek who was helping Yara slide her little feet into skates.

"Yo, are these cool for them? What if they fall?" he asked.

The manager nodded. "They'll barely roll, and we have walkers on wheels for them to hold onto," the woman explained.

Meek nodded and finished with Yara before moving onto Messari.

Morgan was stuck. She couldn't move as she watched him with her twins. She couldn't help but smile. He was so patient with them. It wasn't that he was doing what Bash didn't, because he too was amazing with Ssari and Yara, but women expected men like Bash to be fatherly. A nigga like Meek. A hood nigga. A street nigga. Those hands that loaded clips and pulled triggers, weren't supposed to be able to be so gentle. They weren't supposed to undo knots from roller skates and wipe dried snot from beneath the noses of toddlers. When Ahmeek handled her kids Morgan felt like crying, because she had never thought it would be possible to love someone again. She still didn't want to admit it because it was creeping into her life too fast. Overnight her feelings for him had changed. It had gone from friendship to more and she didn't know what to call it, but she could hardly live without it. Times away from him, time spent in the presence of Bash instead, was torture. It was wasteful because Morgan only wanted to be one place . . . near him. She wondered if he would feel the same if he knew the twins belonged to Messiah. He left her kids and rolled over to her.

"You good?" he asked.

Morgan blinked away the emotion that had built in her eyes and nodded, giving a tight-lipped smile because there was a big part of her that was fearful of this . . . this crossing of lines. They had ventured into forbidden territory, but it was too late to turn back. Morgan was in the middle of a landfill and her next steps were important. One wrong move and her life would explode. The detonation would be catastrophic, yet still here she was, risking it all.

"Here you go, sir," the manager said as she brought two guiders from the back. Ahmeek took both and then grabbed Messari. Morgan scooped Yara. They took the twins to the wooden rink and placed them on their feet.

"Hold on like this, Yolly Pop," Morgan signed. "You too," she signed to Messari.

The twins stumbled forward, slowly, as Ahmeek chuckled.

Morgan and Ahmeek skated behind them.

"You're on roller skates Ahmeek," she teased.

He shook his head. "When I thought of impressing Morgan Atkins, I thought of handbags, trips, not this. This is the last thing I'd thought I'd have to do."

Morgan snickered and turned backward as she skated directly in front of him, smoothly, gliding like there weren't wheels on her feet. Morgan had effortless rhythm and it showed, even on skates.

She heard the doors clang open and watched as Isa and Aria walked into the rink.

"A double date?" she asked, her brow lifting in surprise.

"I thought if your girl was here, you'd give a nigga a break and let me kick off these skates," Ahmeek admitted.

"Never that," she answered.

"Yo, nigga I'm clowning you, bruh. Mo got your ass out here on eight wheels my nigga. Next thing you gon' be on a uni-cycle for that pussy," Isa cracked, hollering from the sideline.

"Umm, don't talk too much shit because you're definitely skating," Aria said. She blew a bubble with her gum and Isa stuck his finger in it, popping the stickiness all over her face.

"I'ma kill you!" she screamed as she picked the pieces off her face.

"Shit talking ass," he sneered.

Aria and Isa disappeared for a few minutes as Morgan and Ahmeek skated with the twins.

Isa rolled onto the floor clapping two stacks of money in his hands. "My nigga. You know I'm with the shits. If I'ma do this goofy shit let's make it interesting."

Ahmeek rubbed the back of his neck. "Here yo' ass go, G."

"Nigga I got five thousand on a race. Matter fact. I got fif-teen on it. I'ma smoke you, Ali gon' burn Mo fancy foot ass, and I got Yolly Pop for the last five."

"You betting on babies, boy!" Aria hollered.

Morgan laughed.

"You ain't said nothing but a word. I'm with making a quick fifteen bands." Morgan shrugged.

Meek smirked.

"A'ight nigga. Let me smoke your ass real quick," Ah-meek said, taking the bait. Morgan loved it. It was like they were teenagers without a care in the world. For men who car-ried the entire world on their shoulders, for the first time in years they were having some fun. Mo and Aria brought the adolescents out in them, forced the clock back and required them to partake in things they'd missed coming up. The fellas lined up first.

"On your mark," Ali said.

"Get set!" Morgan stated.

She leaned down to Messari. "Say go baby boy."

Messari looked at Ahmeek and Isa. "Go!" he yelled.

Isa gave Ahmeek a shove, throwing him off balance and Aria cheered. "That's right nigga! We don't fight fair!"

Isa reached the wall first and Ahmeek laughed as he pointed at Isa. "You a cheating mu'fucka."

"Let's gooo!" Isa screamed. "Come on Ali. Show me you worth something baby."

Aria snickered as she stuck up her middle finger. She clapped her hands and danced on her skates as the DJ played a popular song through the speakers.

"Gone with all that dancing. We trying to win, man!" Isa fussed as he picked up Yara and lifted his hand for her to give him a high five. Her small hand met his.

"Go!" Messari yelled out the blue. Morgan stumbled as she took off, but she won by inches, her long legs giving her an advantage over Aria's short stature.

"Baby girl a winner nigga. Get ready to run that bread," Ahmeek bragged, winking at Morgan who was winded as she skated into his arms, laughing.

"Come on, Mo. Tell Yara that it's all on her," Isa said.

Morgan laughed as she signed to Yara. "Do you want to race, Yolly Pop?"

She nodded then shimmied out of Isa's hold. He set her on her feet and Morgan kneeled in front of her kids. "Okay Mommy's babies. Race to the wall okay, as fast as you can. Hold on tight. On your mark," she signed. "Get set." She looked up at her friends who stood smiling. "Go!"

Her twins racing was the cutest thing she had ever seen. They were neck and neck until Yara fell. Morgan went to help her up but paused midway when she saw Messari turn back and notice his sister on the floor. His little face dipped in concern and he wobbled back to get her.

"Aww! Morgan how cute are they?" Aria sang.

Messari picked Yara up and they used the same guider all the way to the wall.

Ahmeek and Morgan skated over to them. They picked them up.

"Good job man," Ahmeek said, holding out his fist to Messari for a fist bump. Messari balled his fist and tapped Meek's.

"It's a tie," Aria said. "Looks like the twins get both pots. Aria went into Isa's pockets and pulled out the knots. "We into building trust funds around here."

She tossed them to Mo.

"Put it in the bank for 'em man," Isa griped. It was nothing for him to cash out fifteen thousand on the twins but losing any type of challenge stung for his competitive spirit.

"We'll make the deposit after we leave," Ahmeek whispered. "We'll make it an even fifty."

"Meek that's not necessary," she said. "Isa you either. The twins are taken care of."

"Nigga if you don't take that bread. We know you do your part, Mo. We gon' do ours too though," Isa said. "They family. Period. Even though they daddy a bitch."

Aria slapped his chest. "Boy!"

Morgan shook her head. "Don't, Isa. Not in front of them. I know I'm here, but I'm kinda still there and . . ."

Ahmeek pulled her hand. "No explanations needed, Mo. He won't be discussed again."

He put a hand to her cheek, his thumb feathering it as four fingers wrapped behind her neck.

"Come on homie. Uncle Isa buying pizza. You like pizza?" he asked, taking Messari from Ahmeek. Aria grabbed Yara and they skated away leaving Meek and Mo in the middle of the floor. The strobe light bounced colorful balls all over them and they just stood there. He was probing her. Testing her. Playing chicken. Seeing if she would abandon the mission first but Morgan had her foot to the floor, speeding, headed straight for him. She didn't fear the collision ahead. She placed one hand to his chest, as he snaked her waist pulling her as close as close could get, then her cheek rested against his shirt. Her eyes closed without commanding them to. It was just instinct ... just a level of comfort that she didn't even know they had developed. His cologne invaded her fortress. He rested his chin on top of her head and she heard a heavy sigh.

"What's wrong?" she asked, eyes still closed.

"This is fucked up. Us. Me and you, but I don't give a fuck Mo and I don't know what that means. From the outside looking in this looks bad. Makes me look disloyal, like I'm snaking my man. I don't know. Niggas can call me what they want to call me. I'm all that cuz I ain't giving this up. I can't move around you, Mo."

Morgan shook her head. She was so overwhelmed. He made her heart race. She was submerged in this moment. "You make my scars feel beautiful," she whispered.

Morgan moved one hand to the back of his neck and turned her face sideways so that it rested on his chest. The steady hum of his heartbeat soothed her, and she closed her eyes as he wrapped his arms around her, tighter, securing her every insecurity.

"Ahmeek?"

"What up, love?" he whispered.

Morgan stalled. She had an overwhelming urge to say those three words, but she didn't. She wouldn't because it wasn't logical to love someone so fast. The intensity of what she felt had to ease up. She told herself she felt so invested because it was new and exciting but in the folds of her heart she knew exactly what it was. She just couldn't speak it. Not yet. Maybe not ever. The last time she had said those words she had given a man the power to destroy her. He noticed her hesitation and he pulled back to pinch her chin, arresting her stare.

"I know," he said.

And she knew that he did. He knew because he felt it too. He kissed her, and Morgan didn't care that Isa and Aria were witnesses. It could have been a room full of people and Morgan would have done exactly this.

Morgan lowered her head to his chest and he kissed the top of her head. "Come on. Let's go eat.

He grabbed Morgan's hand and she pulled back. "Wait," she said, holding up a finger before she skated over to the DJ booth and whispered to the man standing behind it. Monica's soulful voice crooned through the speakers moments later.

> *I looked at you a thousand times*
> *So when I looked at you there was something new*
> *How could I be so blinddddd*

Morgan approached him, smiling.

"I want to skate first. While they have the kids. You got to hold my hand and skate with me."

Ahmeek hated doing anything corny but still he took her hand, coquettish, a bit embarrassed, but he did it. He held her hand, using his thumb to make circles against her skin as he rolled around the rink with Morgan for an entire song. Morgan had a way of making a hood nigga feel normal. Of lowering the stakes. Of making them ponder regularity. Her smile was disarming and Ahmeek surrendered every time.

They made their way off the floor and Aria smiled at Mo.

"What?" Morgan asked.

"Bathroom break," Aria said. She stood and grabbed Messari. Morgan grabbed Yara. "We'll be back."

"You can leave them," Ahmeek stated.

"Potty training. They probably have to pee," Morgan stated.

"Where homie going? You can't show him how to do that," Ahmeek stated. "I've got him."

Morgan paused, shocked.

"My nigga YOU BETTA!" Aria shouted. "Murder Meek!"

Meek shook his head, snickering, as he switched back into his shoes. He stood and took Messari from Aria's arms.

"You wild as fuck, Aria," he said, smirking.

He stopped next to Morgan and leaned into her ear. "Relax Mo. I've been shooting straight for a while now. It ain't rocket science. I can take him to the bathroom for you."

She nodded, and she turned to watch him head to the bathroom.

"Bitch, bathroom now. I'm not even patient enough to pretend like we not about to talk about this shit," Aria said.

Morgan followed Aria into the women's restroom.

"Morgan Jacqueline Atkins!" Aria exclaimed when they were behind closed doors.

"I knowwww," Morgan whined. "You don't even have to tell me because I already know."

Morgan took Yara into a stall and lined the toilet with tissue before placing her down. "Pee pee like a big girl, Yolly Pop," Morgan signed.

"He makes you really happy, Mo. Like I've never seen you

like this. Ever. Even before," Aria said through the stall door. Morgan heard the drops of urine from her daughter and waved her fingers wildly, signing her cheers for Yara before wiping her and emerging from the stall. Aria was right there. "And Ahmeek! The smiling, the closing of roller rinks, the dates in the middle of the day. You know he had a run today? He's supposed to be out of town on a money mission, cuz Isa was complaining about missing it. Do you see his face, Mo? That man is fucking done. He's cooked. He's literally high off you. You got that gangster ass nigga roller skating, Morgan. Roller skating, bitch! He is crazy about you. Are you sure this just started? Y'all weren't creeping back in the day."

"Don't even say that. I don't even want that to be a notion because when it was me and Messiah it was just us, nobody else mattered. I didn't even see *you*. All I saw was Messiah. He was my whole world. Ahmeek didn't matter because he didn't exist. The world didn't exist. We lived on another planet. There was nothing between Meek and I back then. No flirting, no nothing. We were just friends and God I wish it could have stayed that way. It should have never gone further than that, but now . . ." Morgan paused as she helped her daughter wash her hands. Normally she would be scrambling with two sets of hands but Ahmeek wasn't just a body, he wasn't just around. He assisted. He took initiative. He made it easier and she appreciated him despite how small the gesture of taking Messari to the restroom seemed. She turned to Aria. "Now he's . . ." Morgan paused. "I think I'm in love with him Aria."

"Oh Mo," Aria whispered, enthralled in a love story that didn't even belong to her.

"And I feel so guilty, the shit is eating me up. I'm still engaged to Bash because I know I can't do this with Ahmeek. It's not right, but I can't let this go. I can't help it," Morgan whispered, her words breaking as tears came to her eyes. She was still so haunted by Messiah's ghost. His memory would always be fresh, and it would always burn. "But God I love him. How do I love him already?"

"Because he's a good ass man," Aria said. "And your man is waiting on you." Aria used her thumbs to wipe away Mo's tears. "So, stop crying and go to your man. Fuck guilt just love him."

Morgan nodded and hugged Aria before emerging from the restroom. Ahmeek stood with Messari on his shoulders as Morgan approached with Yara.

"You ready?" he asked.

She nodded.

"I'ma get with you bro," Ahmeek said as he and Isa acknowledged one another, saying goodbye, fists locking then joining for a quick hug. An embrace for Aria and then Ahmeek headed to the door with Morgan at his side. The two of them looked like a couple in love. The twins rounded out the picture making them look like a family in love. How complete the picture could be if it were true. It wasn't until Morgan tucked her twins in the backseat and her phone went off did she remember they weren't.

BASH

My mother was at State today. The commencement cap and gowns came in early. I told her to grab yours. She's going to drop it off. She said she'll be there by 9.

Morgan's heart hurt a little as she read the text. How dare he text her without addressing what he had done. Where was her apology? Where was his remorse? Her chest tightened with anxiety and she knew that she had led them here. Things had never been this bad between them when they were in London. He had never ever spoken to her in an elevated tone. Flint was a curse to their relationship. Ahmeek was a curse to the relationship.

"What's wrong?" Meek asked as he slid into the driver's seat.

"Nothing," Mo said. "I'm just tired of living a life designed by everyone else," she admitted.

"I don't know what to say to that Mo," he admitted. "I would say come home with me, but I know you won't. I'm not sure what you want, love. So, you tell me what I can do. Whatever you want me to do, I'ma do."

She shook her head. "I don't know. I'm so confused Ahmeek. Just torn between what I should be doing and what I want to do. Who I should be with and who I want to be with. It's just..." she flipped her hair out of her face, clearing her bangs, as she leaned her head against the head rest, "complicated. Life is just suddenly so complicated."

Morgan picked up her phone and sent a reply to Bash.

MORGAN
I'm not home. Tell her she can bring it by in the morning.

BASH
Where the hell are you?

And there it was. The control. The rules. The invasion of privacy and the overbearing need to know her every move, her every thought, his need to weigh in on her decisions, down to what she wore. It was well intended, but it bugged the hell out of Morgan. Morgan knew if she did what she was about to do she would be setting herself up for an argument when she finally went home. She knew it would make Bash livid. She didn't care.

She powered off the phone and then took a deep breath to calm her nerves.

"Take me to your house Ahmeek," she whispered.

He didn't even respond. He slid the car into drive and pulled off. The lull of the road and exhaustion of the day's events put the twins to sleep instantly.

Morgan was silent the entire ride and he allowed her to be. They both knew that between the two of them she had the most to lose. When he pulled up to his home Morgan felt his eyes on her. He threw the gear in park and left the car running as she stared out the windshield at the house in front of her. It was modest but beautiful. A white Victorian with black shutters, two levels, and a fenced yard. Someone slipping would think it wasn't up to par for his lifestyle. Someone flashy would want him to have a bigger place, a more luxurious pad, but they would be underestimating Ahmeek. He owned his home and each one beside it and the one behind it. His name was on every deed, so he didn't need to floss on just one. He had many.

"You know I would never leave you bold out here, Morgan. You know that, right? If the shit blows up. Whether this shit between us lasts a week or a lifetime, I'ma look out for you regardless. So, you don't have to be nowhere you don't want to be. I just wanted to let you know."

Morgan didn't respond with words. She simply climbed across the seat and straddled him. The discomfort of the car didn't bother either of them as she kissed him. A fist to her hair and a hand around her waist kept her in place as their kiss deepened. Morgan teased him, pulling back, retracting her tongue and placing soft touches of her lips to his as she stared at him through lowered lids. One kiss, then two, then tongue, then a bite to his lower lip. Ahmeek groaned. She felt all of him beneath her and Morgan pulled back to stare at him. Her soft hands caressed the back of his neck.

"I'm in trouble Ahmeek," she said. Her heart was beating so hard it sounded off in her ears. She couldn't stop this runaway love affair. She had no desire to.

He kissed her again. Just once. "Yeah?"

"Yeah," she confirmed with a head nod.

"Let's get them inside," he said.

She climbed out of his lap and out the car. They took the twins upstairs to a spare bedroom, but as soon as Yara felt Ahmeek put her down she woke, crying. Ahmeek scooped her up and carried her out the room so that she wouldn't wake Messari. Morgan planted a kiss on her son's forehead, pulled the cover up to his chin and then joined Meek in the hallway. He walked Yara back and forth down the narrow space, bouncing slightly as she laid her head on his shoulder. This man could have his pick of the litter and here he was putting up with her and not one, but two babies. Morgan was enamored.

"I love you, Ahmeek," Morgan blurted.

His feet paused, and he stared at her so hard that Morgan began to shake. He walked up to her, forcing her against the wall, trapping her, before stirring her soul with another kiss.

"This ain't love Mo. The shit that got a nigga rocking babies that don't belong to me and putting on skates to impress a pretty girl. Love ain't enough to pull that type of effort out of me. This is addiction, Mo. Three niggas lost their lives because too much time went by without me seeing you. All because I was in a mood. All because I pictured you doing the shit you do to me on the nigga you got at home. You make me reckless Morgan. Shit I'm feeling ain't normal."

Only a man who had never been in love would describe it like a vice. Morgan was a weakness, a distraction, and Ahmeek had never made room for those things before . . . until now.

"You can't take that out on other people, Ahmeek. You can't fly off the handle when you don't see me. You know my situation. I thought we were on the same page. When I'm with you I'm yours," she whispered. "And when I'm not . . ."

"You're his? On God I'm gonna end up killing that nigga, love."

"I'm yours, Meekie. Just yours. I'm not having sex with him. You don't have to wonder about that. I belong to you, Ahmeek. Just you. He'll never touch me after you. I couldn't even bear it. All I want is this."

He pressed his forehead to hers. She placed her hand on Yara's back who was now dead weight in his arms.

"Put her down and let me save a life," Morgan whispered. "Can't have you walking out into the world tomorrow in your feelings."

Ahmeek scoffed, then kissed her lips, before slipping into the room to lay Yara on the bed.

Morgan heard Yara fuss and Ahmeek was patient, rubbing her back until she settled. By the time he emerged back into the hall Morgan was naked.

"That's how you carrying it?" he asked.

She nodded, biting that bottom lip. He pulled his shirt over his head.

"Drop them drawers too," she said, arrogantly, confidently. She wasn't this girl all the time . . . the one giving out commands, the one exerting her power.

Ahmeek followed orders. His eyes never left hers as he unbuttoned the jeans he wore and stepped out of them.

"Everything," she instructed. His underwear came next and what he revealed was so thick and heavy that Morgan sucked in air. "Boy . . ." She shook her head, smiling, blushing. Just the sight of that blessing made her shy. Morgan wasn't super experienced but the men that she had chosen to give herself to were sexual beasts. Both skilled at pleasing her, yet completely different in their approaches. She had never thought anyone could bring her pleasure like Messiah, but Ahmeek's touch held such finesse that she climaxed instantly when he entered her. There was no build up. It was just pleasure. No waiting, no earning it, no working for it. No taking dick she couldn't handle to earn her orgasm. He approached her, hand on his strength as he lifted one thigh into the crook of his arm. Morgan gasped as he slid past the silkiness of her longing, easing in so slow then pulling out to rub the head of his dick against her clit three times, like he was typing in the passcode to her desire before diving back in.

"Meek," Morgan moaned. "Ahhhmeeeeekkkk." Again, he pulled out, and massaged her clit, driving it, rotating it like it was the steering wheel to her body and he needed her to turn right.

"Fuck," he groaned. "So fucking wet, love."

He took her leg that was propped in his arm and straightened it slowly, grabbing her calf and lifting higher and higher until Morgan's leg was in a full split. Thank God she was a dancer. Thank God her legs could even comply. Her sex was wide open, and he was so deep inside her that he could feel her pulsating.

"Meek!" Mo whined. Her face so twisted in an ugly grimace and she clenched her teeth.

He fucked her there making Morgan cry out in pleasure. His stroke was so precise, so deliberate. He didn't just throw shots hoping to do a good job. He had her g-spot in his crosshairs and was tagging it again and again. Morgan couldn't keep quiet if she wanted to. She was so loud he had to feed her his tongue, drowning her moans in kisses, in love, so she wouldn't wake the twins. He released her leg and it draped over his shoulder then he scooped her and lifted the other leg to his other shoulder. He moved her to the hutch that sat against the wall in the hallway. Everything that was on it was sent crashing to the floor. Her pelvis hung halfway off as he gripped her

hips, fucking her so good Morgan couldn't even match his intensity. She just laid there, receiving, unable to give back to the
charity of Ahmeek, because she was selfish in this moment and
she just wanted to nut. Dick so long and so wide she felt every
inch. Morgan was delirious. "Aghhhhhh, mmmmmm, ohhhh
myyyy, yessss," she moaned as he reached down to play with her
clit while he hit it. "Ahmeeek!"

"I know, love. Damn," he groaned.

Morgan came so hard that she shuddered. Violent waves
of pleasure caused her stomach to cave in and Morgan pulled
at her hair from the intensity of it all. "Oh my God!" she
whimpered. "Ahmeek, Ahhhmeek . . ." she said his name over
and over until only pants came out. Her chest heaved, and she
wasn't even the one putting in the work.

Meek pulled out in the nick of time, because if he didn't
he knew they were making a baby tonight and as beautiful as
a mother Morgan Atkins was, he wasn't ready to be a father.
Once he started dropping seeds inside Morgan she wouldn't be
going home to another man.

He lifted her, and she wrapped her legs around his waist.
They were drunk, off each other, high off this passion, unable
to stop kissing one another as he took labored steps toward his
bedroom. His strong thighs held up all her weight as he carried
her to his bed. He hovered over her and paused.

"What are you staring at?" she whispered.

"The one who's going to fuck shit up for every woman after
this moment. You're never going to be mine love, but I'ma always be yours. Whenever you need a nigga, you come find me. I
don't give a fuck about what happens between us. Good, bad. If
you stay near, far. If we talk every day or if we haven't talked for
years. If you ever need to hit my line, don't think twice, don't
talk yourself out of it. You call me and I'm pulling up dumping
over you. Every time."

Morgan was overwhelmed and before she could even think of a response his head disappeared as he went south. Her eyes rolled to the back of her head as he brought her to orgasm, all over again.

This was more than just an affair. She was in big trouble and Morgan didn't care because it turned out she was good at being the bad guy.

13

Bleu opened the memory box that she kept beneath her bed and her heart clenched. Even laying eyes on it made her body fill with anxiety. She flipped the lid and her lip trembled as she reached inside. She closed her eyes and memories slid down her cheek in the form of tears.

I've been so sick. I can't hold anything down, Bleu said. My best friend died not too long ago and it's just been really hard to pull it together. This pit in my stomach never goes away.

Bleu looked at her doctor with angst filled eyes.

"Well, Bleu the reason why you've been sick is because you're pregnant. That mixed with the loss of a loved one explains your loss of appetite, the dropping weight. It's not depression. There's a baby in there."

Bleu sobbed as she thought of those days after losing Messiah. Her best friend's seed had grown inside her for months and she had been clueless. He had left her with parts of him. Those parts had destroyed her relationship with Iman, but Bleu had refused to get rid of her baby. She had needed it. She had looked forward to loving it. A boy. Messiah Honor Williams II.

Bleu hadn't even known that she was pregnant until she passed out on the hospital floor the day Messiah died. She was four months along and she had been so sick with worry over Messiah that she didn't even realize she was expecting their child. Bleu picked up the hospital band that had been on her son's wrist.

The amniocentesis results show that your baby will be born with Down syndrome, Bleu. You can choose to terminate or . . .

"I'll never terminate this baby. He's important and he matters, and I'll love him, no matter what."

Bleu couldn't get that day out of her head and she bawled on the floor in her bedroom as her thoughts haunted her. Days had only gotten harder after that. She carried her son until birth and from the day he took his first breath she knew that he wouldn't grace her life for very long. He existed for 380 days before complications returned him to God. Bleu was destroyed.

She didn't even hear Messiah enter the room.

"B? Who the fuck I got to fucking see about these tears?" Messiah asked. She could hear his chain yanking against the invisible fence that contained his aggression. Her crying would always rile him up. Bleu quickly put the things back into the box and put the top on, standing to her feet and wiping her eyes.

"I'm fine," she said, sniffing away tears. "You can't knock? You don't know how to call before just showing up?" She was agitated, and Messiah frowned.

"Fuck nah, I can't call. I don't need permission to come see about you. Fuck is going on, B?" he pressed.

"Nothing, Messiah, I just had a hard day," she said, sniffing. She moved the box beneath the bed with her foot and Messiah eyed it.

"What's in the box?" he asked. His tone was chilling, and his brow dipped as his nostrils flared. "I swear to God, B if it's what I think it is, I'ma hurt you in this bitch. Saviour is right down the hall!" he barked.

"It's not!" she protested, grabbing his arm as he went to grab it. "Messiah mind your business."

Messiah pulled away from her and flipped the top off the box. Bleu's stomach went missing. He bent down, placing a bawled fist against her floor as he picked up the photo. He looked back at her. Bleu was keeled over onto her knees, face buried in her hands.

"B? What is all this?" His voice softened, relieved at the fact that there were no drugs in the box.

"Messiah just mind your business. Put it back," she demanded. He stood with the picture in his hand and walked up to her, standing directly in front of her. The top of her head pressed into his stomach as she kept crying.

Messiah's eyes fell to the box. He pulled out the hospital bracelet with Bleu's name on it and his eyes went wet. He knew. He knew before he even looked at the smaller bracelet, but he picked it up for confirmation.

He read the name and his chin trembled.

"B—"

His voice was barely audible. He turned away from her, box in one hand, hand sweeping over the top of his head with the other.

"You had my son? My son was sick?" Messiah asked. He didn't even sound like himself. "My son was sick, and I left him? I left you? B, look at me."

Bleu lifted her mess of a face and he kneeled in front of her, getting on both knees to wrap his arms around her. He pulled her from the bed and into his arms as he rocked her on the floor. "I'm sorry. I didn't know," he said, sorrow filling him, making him feel like he was choking. "Is that why Iman ain't here with you?"

She nodded and wiped her tears away. "He gets Saviour, but he and I are done."

She looked down in shame. "He was beautiful Messiah. The doctors said he was defective. Born with so many illnesses, but he was ours you know and to me he was incredible."

"You're beautiful, B. You're fucking—" Messiah scoffed, shaking his head in disbelief. He didn't even know how to describe what he felt for Bleu in this moment. "I love you, Bleu. I ain't know that for a long time, but the moment I realized it, I've fucked with you hard every day since. I wasn't here for you. I'll never not be here for you again. I give you my word. I'll give you my life Bleu. Damn, you gave me a son and I didn't even get to meet him. We made a son."

"We did," she whispered. "Two fuck ups made something amazing."

"Two negatives equal a positive, B," Messiah said, half smiling as he flicked her chin with his finger.

"Your bad ass paid attention to something in school, huh?" Bleu cracked. He was grateful for her lightheartedness and she sighed. She was so strong. Her resilience was his favorite part of her. They stayed right there on her bedroom floor. Her back to his chest, hands intertwined as Messiah rested his chin on top of her head.

"Tell me about my son. Don't leave nothing out," he said.

They stayed up all night until her words turned into whispers and whispers turned to heavy breathing. He picked her up from the floor and put her in her bed. She groaned when her head touched the pillow but didn't awaken and Messiah turned to leave. He made it to the bedroom door before he stopped. He looked back at her and his eyes prickled. He pinched the bridge of his nose before sniffing away his emotion and forcing himself to leave. His heart tore in half because he wanted to stay but his mind ran in circles because if he wanted to be here how could he be there with Mo? Wherever she was. He felt his alliance being tested. He hoped the day never came where he had to choose between them. He would never be able to. He would end up losing them both before he ever allowed himself to put one above the other. Bleu was simply a friendship that he couldn't let go of. She was an intricate part of him now and Messiah prayed that the bond with Morgan wouldn't suffer because of it.

14

The sound of cartoons blaring pulled Morgan out of her sex-coma. She groaned as she pushed up from the bed. She felt like she had just closed her eyes. They were so heavy she just wanted to surrender to the plush mattress for a little longer, but her kids were loud. She heard laughter and if they were awake, she didn't have a choice but to say goodbye to dreamland. Morgan slipped into the sweat pants that Ahmeek had shed the day before. They drowned her, but she wore them anyway and slipped into his T-shirt, closing her eyes as the scent of his cologne hugged her. She took bare feet to hardwood floors as she followed the sound to the kitchen. She paused in the hallway when she saw Ahmeek sitting at the table with the twins. Morgan folded her arms across her chest and leaned against the wall. A fly on the wall as she watched him fix them cereal.

"Me no want milk Meek!" Messari yelled.

"No milk? All right, homie, no milk. Dry cereal it is," Meek replied. "What does Yolly Pop like?"

"Her like milk," Messari answered for his sister.

Yara sat quietly, picking up Froot Loops and putting them

into her mouth before holding one up for Ahmeek. He bent down and opened his mouth and Yara pet the top of his head, like Ahmeek was her obedient dog.

Morgan's entire body hummed. She felt safe with this man, in this house, watching him in this way. If she could wake up to this every day, she would.

"Good morning," she said softly.

Ahmeek lifted eyes in her direction.

"Good morning love."

His attention went right back to the twins. "So, a nigga can't really cook all that good, but I figured what kid don't like cereal right?" he asked without looking at her as he let Yara put another colorful loop in his mouth.

"Thank you for feeding them," she said. "You're really great Ahmeek." She said it with a bit of something in her tone. Sadness. Dread.

"Come here," he said. Morgan walked over to him and he pulled her into his lap.

"That thing you said last night?" His hand massaged the back of her neck as she looked down at him. "That's how you feel? That's real?"

She nodded.

"Words, love. Use words," he ordered.

"That's how I feel Ahmeek," she said. "I love you, but I'm terrified. When it was just sex . . ."

"It was never just sex, Mo," he interrupted. She felt the invisible bulldozer he was taking to the wall she had built around herself.

She scoffed.

"Fear and love aren't even supposed to be spoken in the same sentence but for me it's . . ." She paused, shaking her head as her stare went blank. She traveled back in time, playing back the picture of her first love in her head. "I don't know Meekie.

This just feels like a dream. Like I need to get my head out of the clouds and snap out of it."

"Yo," he said, pinching her chin and arresting her focus.

"If you're not afraid of the dreams they're not big enough, love. A nigga dream about you. Scary as shit thinking about loving all that pain away I see in your eyes, Mo. I don't know how to make that go away, but in my head, I see us years later. In a pretty ass house, the twins are older and it's one on the way. There's a ring on your finger and ain't no gun on my hip. Ain't no weekly licks to hit, no runs to make. It's just me and you doing a whole lot of fucking and a whole lot of loving and that look in your eye . . . that shit that makes you doubt me is gone. Big dreams, love. That's the only way I know how to do it. You gon' dream with me, Mo?"

Morgan nodded. This mental high he gave her made it feel like maybe . . . one day . . . that dream could come true. "How did we get here, Ahmeek? I don't know the way back. I'm lost in this." She wrapped her arms around his neck and rested her head over his shoulder.

"Do you really want to find your way back?" he asked.

"No," she answered. She felt him slide a hand between them, reaching inside his hoodie and he pulled out an envelope.

She leaned back. "What's this?" she asked, smiling.

"An early birthday gift. I know you got the twins, so it was real hard to plan around them, so I included them. If you can make the time that is," he said.

"Uh-ohhh!" Messari shouted. Meek and Morgan looked to find the whole gallon of milk was spilling all over the table.

"Sawwry Mommy!" Messari said.

"I got it," Meek stated.

Morgan stood, and Meek attended to the mess as she opened the envelope. Her mouth fell open in stun.

She turned to him, eyes wide in disbelief. "Ahmeek," she

gasped. "A trip? You want to take me to Disney World?" She held up the four tickets and the brochure to the Ritz Carlton and shook her head in amazement. She had been before. Ethic had taken her when she was a kid, but to have a man want to take her and her kids felt glorious. Ahmeek made her feel special. He was never afraid to step outside of his rigid boxes to make her happy.

"I want to take you to the altar, love, but you're young. You need time. This will do for now," he said, licking his lips and smirking as he soaked up the mess with paper towels. Morgan's entire face turned red.

"And you bought four tickets? I could have gotten a sitter. I'm sure Disney World isn't your idea of a good time."

"They go where you go. A good time is wherever you are, love. So Disney World it is. If you'll come," he said.

"Of course, I'll come. I'll go anywhere with you," she said. She rushed him. Rushed him like her emotions were rushing her. Bash was wrong about Ahmeek. He had to be. He wasn't like Messiah. He wasn't just here to indulge in sex. He wasn't going to leave her without warning. She felt it. It was like a pulse that kept her alive. Ahmeek and Mo stood in the middle of the kitchen, lost in each other, lips dancing, hearts racing, his hand on her ass, her arms around his neck, massaging the back of his head. Morgan almost forgot that her children were in the room until she felt a little body squeeze between them. She looked down and Yara was holding up both arms for Ahmeek. Morgan smiled. She was scooped into his arms instantly.

"I swear she's so rotten," Morgan chuckled, shaking her head.

"Pot meet kettle," he said, snickering. Messari was next, climbing out of the chair and running over to Morgan. Morgan picked him up. This had all the makings of perfection. All the makings of a man and his family. She never could have predicted that Ahmeek would be the one to put her heart back together.

"I can't really do casual Ahmeek," she whispered. "If I leave him and you pull out on me . . ."

"I wouldn't ask you for your time just to waste it," he said. He pecked her lips. "I'm right here. Be here with me. Be my lady, Mo."

She was stunned to silence and he knew he had put her on the spot, so he gracefully changed the subject. "I've got to get with Isa about something. I'ma be in the streets heavy for a little bit. I've got some loose ends to tie, but coming home to you and these kids at the end of it all would do me well, love. If you're comfortable here, you can stay. If not, I'll take you home."

This man. This whole man. Ahmeek was nothing like anyone assumed him to be. He knew what he wanted and he actively pursued it. He wanted Morgan Atkins and since the day he had decided that, he had made it be known. He was playing for keeps and Morgan was losing a pointless fight trying to resist him. Everything about him felt good. Her insides ached around him. The things he said made her melt, but the things he did were affirmation that it was more than bullshit. It was more than casual. They were so far off the deep end that Morgan could envision her entire future under his tutelage. She never wanted to leave. Never wanted to give up this feeling. If she could she would just leave without notice. Quit Bash like a bitch quit a job she hated, but she couldn't. She owed him more than that. An explanation. Her relationship with Messiah had ended painfully and abruptly without warning or closure. She couldn't keep leaving doors of her heart open. She had to close this thing out with Bash before she could move in with Meek. She needed a clean break.

"I need to go home. Settle this once and for all. Give

me time. While you handle your business and keep your late nights, I'll handle mine and end it with Bash. A week. That's all I need. My birthday is in a week. When you pick me up, I won't be going back. I'll be coming home. To you Ahmeek. I want to be here with you," she promised.

15

Seven days of no Morgan Atkins. Seven days of darkness because she was the light. His light. Ahmeek pushed into the trap house with a duffel in his hands and one hanging from the strap on his shoulder. He hadn't gotten his hands this dirty in years. He normally moved a lot less recklessly, putting middle men between himself and his product, but he and Isa needed all hands on deck. The debt they owed Hak couldn't wait. He had barely slept in a week. He had distributed so much cocaine and bottled so many pills that he'd amassed two months' worth of the insurance premium they'd incurred for Hak. Ahmeek tossed the duffels to the ground like they were worthless, despite the fact they were filled with cash. Exhaustion pulled him to the couch. He groaned as he sat back and lifted his eyes to the ceiling. He was over this part of the game. He had been for a while. A part of him wanted to just pay the two million to Hak but it would liquidate his pockets. It would take every dollar he had and the selling of assets to cover a bill that hefty. He would be left with nothing and there was no guarantee that Hak would re-instate business as usual. Ahmeek had to hustle for the money and keep his money squared away. His investments were fruitful. Business was good. He had enough money to take care of himself. Enough to care for Mo and her kids if it came to that. His money was making money. He couldn't ruin all the years of hard work. He wasn't fresh out the sandbox anymore. He was ready to put away childish things. Mo made him want to give up anything that took time away from her. So instead of giving his last dollar to pay Hak, he hustled. He hustled like nobody else could hustle flipping work like minimum wage workers flipped burgers. He put himself on a shift, put his team on an impossible plan. His infamy grew, his organization quadrupled, every truck coming down I-75 was relieved of its content. It didn't matter what it carried. If it was a produce truck, Meek robbed it and sold the contents back to black-owned grocery stores in the neighborhood. If it was jewelry it was taken to local pawn shops and fencers. Cars were broken down and sold for parts. The drugs sold themselves. He had never gone harder and the type of focus it took meant he hadn't been able to make room for anything else.

His phone vibrated in his pocket and Ahmeek lifted off the couch a bit to retrieve it from his back pocket. Morgan's name popped up on his screen. He couldn't even fight the smile that took over his face.

He saw a link to a poem. "A Poem of Friendship" by Nikki Giovanni.

> *We are not lovers because of the love we make, but the love we have.*

Ahmeek opened his browser and typed in the line to pull up the full poem. The depth of it rocked him. Every word written felt like a tribute to what they shared. He read it three times.

Once to introduce himself to the work. Twice to understand what the poet was trying to say. A third time to feel it from Morgan's perspective. He loved the fuck out of this girl.

Reading the stanzas made Ahmeek's stomach tighten. They were so serious without being serious at all. They had no type of commitment. Ahmeek thought of calling her but Morgan truly was the best type of distraction. If he heard her voice even once, he would lose focus. He would go soft and he needed to be hard for what he was doing. He needed to be cold. He opened their message and his fingers moved across the screen as he typed a response.

> *If you can't find something to live for, you best find*
>   *something to die for.*

Ahmeek pressed send. His phone buzzed almost immediately, showing that Morgan had awaited his reply.

MORGAN

What poem is that?

MEEKIE

No poem, love. Just a little Pac. Lol. He got it wrong though. For you I'll do both. Live and die, for you, Morgan Atkins.

He waited. Ahmeek shook his head as he sat up, leaning forward onto his knees. He had never felt like such a sucker. Morgan Atkins had him caking in the middle of the night.
Sending love notes and shit.

Ahmeek was on some soft ass shit and he fucking couldn't get enough of it. Mo brought out the boy in him. He had gone straight from a kid to a gangster. He had missed nights of staying up all night on the phone with girls he liked. He was busy pulling triggers and working corners at the age. Morgan made him feel like a sixteen-year-old kid.

Another message came through.

MORGAN
Finish handling your business. I'll finish handling mine. Then it's all about us. I love you Meekie. Be careful.

He clicked out of the screen and tucked every emotion she had just exposed. He grabbed the duffels and began to remove the money that was stuffed inside. He began the count. He hated that he was being pulled right back to the bowels of the game. He wanted to elevate. He had his exit all planned out in his head but with this looming debt over his head he knew that he was now deeper than he had ever been before. He only hoped that he would be able to play both roles and be a man who could be consistent for Morgan and be the ruthless gangster that the streets required.

16

One Week Later

"You look beautiful, Mo," Bash complimented as he sat on the edge of her bed, leaned over to slip his size 13 feet into expensive Tom Ford shoes.

"Where are we going anyway?" Morgan asked. "I told you, I don't really feel that well. I could have just stayed in this year."

"No, there's no staying in. Twenty-one is a big one, Mo. I want to celebrate with my girl. Is that too much to ask?" He lifted and swaggered over to her. He was especially handsome in the grey tailored suit. He shined like money, beard full, cut freshly tapered, and penetrating stare. He really was so handsome and so kind, but Morgan could barely stomach Bash. It was Christiana's pushiness, her forcefulness that made Morgan's disdain for her fiancé grow. She felt like she was being held captive by the Fredricks family. It wasn't Bash whom she disliked. It was the world he was attached to. The pomp and circumstance of London society. The rules. The overbearing mother-in-law. It was all too much for Morgan. Bash had been consistent. The slip-up in Vegas, him leaving her twins, had exposed a side of him she hadn't known existed however. It showed he wasn't all the way invested in her children the way he claimed, and Morgan hadn't been in the mood for him since.

"Can you please just cooperate today?" Bash asked. "I promise by the end of the night you'll be happy."

"I doubt it," Morgan mumbled.

Morgan was becoming horrible at hiding her melancholy. If she was going to celebrate she wanted to do so with Ahmeek. She wanted to smile and laugh with him, blow out birthday candles that rested atop a cake that he got for her; make love all night and sleep it off in the morning. Bash was nowhere in her mental plans.

Her phone buzzed, and Morgan reached inside her cross-body handbag, removing it.

AHMEEK

I'm outside.

Morgan's heart dipped in anxiety. He hadn't told her he was coming, but it was her birthday so of course he would come. He was the type of man who would be ready to shower his lady with affection.

"I need to run to the car real quick," she said.

"We're headed out, Mo. You can just grab whatever it is on the way out," Bash answered.

"No, I need to finish my makeup and what I need is in the car. I'll be another half an hour before I'm ready to go anyway. Just keep an eye on the twins. I can go grab it . . ."

"I'll grab it for you," Bash said, standing.

"No!" she shouted, louder than she meant to. "My car is filthy. You won't even be able to find it. Relax. I've got it."

Morgan walked out of her apartment. The sundress she wore flowed effortlessly, playing an illusion with her hips as she approached Ahmeek's car. Morgan wanted to run to him but instead she kept her cool. He got out of the car just to open her door and then pulled off without a care in the world.

"What are you doing here?" she asked, smiling. "I thought you said you had business to take care of today?"

"It's your birthday, I can't pull up?" he asked. There was something different in his tone. Intolerance, a bit of frustration.

"I just didn't know you were coming. I can't stay. He planned something," Morgan whispered.

"Yo, when we giving this nigga his walking papers, love?" Ahmeek asked.

Morgan heard the impatience in his tone and she felt it in her gut. Ahmeek was tired of sharing her, tired of filling half her world with happiness only to send her home to someone else.

"It's not that simple," Morgan whispered.

"It ain't that hard either," Ahmeek answered. "I know you know that I will take care of you, Mo. Hell, you can take care of yourself, so I'm not understanding the issue. The nigga is either walking away or he can get carried away. I'm sure he got a good six men somewhere."

Pall bearers. Ahmeek was in the mood to send Bash away permanently. Morgan was in the mood to let him.

"Ahmeek . . ."

She reached for his face and he maneuvered out of her grasp.

"Nah, love, no finesse. You get away with the shit I let you get away with. I don't want to be pacified. I want you to go in there and tell that nigga to get fucking lost," Ahmeek said. "So I can put my head between them pretty ass thighs and give you birthday licks. Twenty-one. A nigga owes you twenty-one licks. I'm ready to lock you down, love. Don't stop, don't pass go."

"Meekie," she whispered. "Just give me some time. I promise I will."

"Just not today," he scoffed and nodded his head as he turned the wheel, driving in one big rectangle, spinning the block, just to sneak and have this conversation with her. Ahmeek didn't sneak anywhere and the fact that he had to jump through these hoops just to keep time with Mo was beginning to wear on him. He pulled back up to her apartment and put the car in park. He leaned over and reached into the glove box and handed her a box.

Morgan opened it. A set of keys lay inside.

Morgan lifted eyes to Ahmeek.

"To the loft," he stated. "It'll be empty until you fill it."

"You want me to move in with you?" she asked, shocked.

He didn't answer. He just looked out his window, forehead wrinkled in irritation as he played with the hair on his chin.

"Can I call you, later?" she asked. "I just need some time, Ahmeek. I promise I'll call you."

He reached into the center console and removed another box. Morgan opened it and a Jeep key rested inside.

"It's in the back of the parking lot. Black Jeep, black tint."

"Like the one I wanted when I was a little girl," she gasped in shock.

"The one you said you got jealous of when your daddy wouldn't buy you a real one to match the ones your Barbie dolls had," Ahmeek stated. "I hope you like it."

"I love it," she whispered. Guilt filled her. If she could spend all day with him, just the two of them, it would be a perfect celebration. It was the only gift she wanted.

"I'm up, Mo," he said as he put his car in reverse.

He was angry at her and Morgan's eyes filled with tears.

"Don't call me Mo. Call me what you normally call me," she whispered. Her lip trembled.

His jaw clenched as he grit his teeth and flicked his nose.

"Your nigga waiting on you, Mo," he answered.

"Meekie," she pleaded, whispering. "I can't get out until you tell me we're okay."

"We're good, Mo," he said.

"No, we're not! Call me love, Ahmeek. It's my birthday and you're calling me Mo. You never call me Mo! I don't want to be Mo to you," she cried. Her eyes burned so badly, and her heart was racing.

"And I don't want to be your side nigga," Ahmeek stated, much calmer than she could be in this moment.

"Meekie you're not," she protested. "I don't think of us like that. Stop saying that."

Ahmeek popped his locks. "I speak facts. Have fun with your man," he said, still refusing to look at her.

Morgan's lip quivered, and she opened the door. As she slid out, he caught her fingertips and pulled her back. He fisted her hair and then his lips covered hers. A full sixty seconds turned her to putty. Everything about Ahmeek made Morgan's body react. Her nipples tightened, she could feel the seat of her panties dampen, and her mind erupted. This orgasm he gave her . . . this mental stimulation . . . the exploding of her heart and such . . . Morgan whimpered she was so affected.

"Happy birthday love," he said before letting her go. Morgan climbed out of the car and stood there heartbroken as she watched him pull away.

"I don't really want to leave my babies today," Morgan said as Bash pulled up to Ethic's estate. "I want them with me on my birthday." She was trying to keep things light. A family outing was better than a romantic date. She had no idea what Bash had planned for her, but she knew that she didn't want it to feel anything close to a date.

"Relax, Mo. Just let me do my thing, okay?"

Morgan sighed.

"Bash we need to talk," she said. She could hardly find her words. Mo knew Christiana would make good on her threats to ruin everything she had worked for, but Morgan didn't care. She couldn't care anymore. Ahmeek was worth the sacrifice. She would lose everything to gain him. The idea terrified her but losing him scared her more.

"We can talk later Mo. Let's have some fun today. Celebrate you. It's all about you," Bash said. He was too excited. Sweet and Morgan was moody. She wished he was more of an asshole. Breaking things off would be easier if he were. They had their moments. Their conflicts. Like any normal couple, but Bash was an accommodator. Inconsistencies between them didn't last long. Conflict was easily resolved. Even after his major fuck up in Las Vegas he had rebounded strong, spoiling her and apologizing until all was back to normal, but Morgan craved something else. She had a new normal that didn't include him. The enthusiasm that lived in his eyes told her that now was not the time to blow things up.

Tonight, I'll tell him tonight.

Morgan climbed from the car and grabbed Yara from the backseat as Bash took Messari. Morgan didn't even knock. No need to. Ethic's home was her home. It would always be the place she ran to when she needed refuge from the world.

"SURPRISE!!!!"

Morgan's foot hadn't even crossed the threshold fully before she heard the chaos.

"Oh my God! You did this?" Morgan asked, beaming from ear to ear as she turned to Bash, coyly, hiding her face as a titter bounced off her lips.

"Happy birthday!" Eazy screamed, wrapping his hands around her waist.

"Thank you Eazy!"

"Happy birthday Mo Money," Bella was next.

Morgan hugged her.

"Hey Mo! Happy birthday baby girl," Alani greeted.

Ethic was last and Morgan walked up to him, cheesing.

"I can't believe you're twenty-one. I still see a snaggle tooth little girl when I look at you, Mo," Ethic said as he pulled her into his arms. He kissed her cheek, burying his face against the side of her head before kissing her cheek again . . . once then twice. "Happy birthday, baby girl. I want you to enjoy your party. You deserve it. You deserve all the happiness in the world, Mo. Before you leave, after things wind down, I want to talk to you."

"Is everything okay?" she asked, pulling back.

"Everything will be fine, but it's important," Ethic said.

"Should we talk now?" she asked.

"No, you should enjoy your party," he stated.

She nodded as Ethic kissed Yara's cheek and took Messari from Bash, before crossing the room, leading Alani to a chair.

"There's a DJ outside, Mo," Bella said as she led the way.

"Okay, lead the way," Morgan said. She carried Yara to the back, Bash followed behind her.

A DJ spun on the deck and as soon as Mo walked through the sliding door she noticed that no expense had been spared. The backyard was set up extravagantly. Rose gold and gold accents everywhere. Expensive linen and an acrylic wall with her name on it had been built in the backyard. Professional linens and tables were set up. A tile dance floor had been set up in the middle of the massive lawn. Her favorite flowers were everywhere.

"This is amazing," she smiled. She turned to Bash, feeling so bad about the way she felt about him. "You're a really good guy Bash. You're such a great friend to me and I hope you know that."

"Bitchhhhhh!" Aria's voice carried through the air and Morgan's eyes found her instantly. Beyoncé dropped through the speakers.

You a bad girl and your friends bad too
We got the swag sauce she dripping swagu

Aria owned any dance floor she ever graced and to Mo's surprise Isa was out there with her. Isa swagged casually beside her, pinching a blunt between two fingers with one hand and holding up a Styrofoam cup in the other as his lanky frame caught the beat in a lazy two step as Aria showed out in front of him.

We like to party!

Morgan made her way to the dance floor and with Yara in her arms she bounced playfully.

"Happy birthday Mo," Aria laughed, pausing long enough to kiss Mo's cheek and then Yara's. Isa passed his cup to Aria and took Yara from Mo's arms. Yara laughed as Isa did a cool bop with her as his dance partner. She beat on his face, hands slapping his cheeks as he took her for a spin. A blunt and a baby were his accessories. It was an old school ghetto kickback in the middle of the opulence Ethic provided. Mo was in heaven. There was only one person missing.

She turned and met eyes with Bash who sat in one of the chairs beneath the huge event tent.

"Be careful sis, don't get that nigga hurt," Isa called after her as she made her way to Bash.

"Boy!" Aria fussed.

"I'm just saying. My nigga ain't here so I'ma hold him down. It's fuck nigga Friday in this bitch," Isa said as he hit the blunt. He turned his head and blew the smoke in the opposite direction of Yara. "Say fuck nigga Friday, Yolly Pop. How you sign that shit?"

"Give me my niece!" Aria shouted. "And stop starting shit with that man! Don't you always tell me to mind my business?"

"And yo' hard head ass never do it, either, now I know the fuck why," Isa snickered.

"Yo, bruh, have some respect. It's kids here. My kids are here. Watch your mouth," Bash stated. He stood as Morgan made it to his side.

Isa stopped dancing. Morgan knew it was a problem when his hand went to his hip. "Nigga what?"

Isa was across the dance floor in seconds, but Morgan and Aria stood in his way.

"I ain't afraid of you, man. It's whatever you want to do," Bash said, rolling up his sleeves.

"I want to murder you, nigga," Isa said. Aria was in front of him pushing his chest as Mo pushed Bash in the opposite direction. "How about that? I ain't just talking nigga. I'll put you where them worms be, pussy!" Aria passed Yara to Morgan, so she could use all her strength to stop Isa. Tired of dodging Aria, Isa put his hands under her armpits and picked her up, carrying her toward Bash.

"Bella go get Ethic now!" Morgan yelled. Eazy took off running toward the house first.

"I'm right here, man. I'm not running!" Bash shouted back.

"Bash, my babies are out here!" Morgan screamed.

Ethic was halfway across the lawn when Morgan heard the voice carry through the speakers.

"Isa, you wild as fuck, G. Let that nigga breathe, man."

Morgan froze. Her blood solidified in her veins and she

lost feeling in her hands as she felt Yara slipping from her grasp. Her legs ached, like she was too heavy, like she could no longer support her own weight. Everything went still. Even the breeze that had given her a slight chill ceased to exist.

"Hey, Shorty Doo Wop."

Messiah stood before her living, breathing. She blinked once, then twice . . . he wasn't real. He couldn't be real. She heard his voice in her head sometimes saying those exact words because she had been his . . . his Shorty Doo Wop . . . and she never wanted to forget what he sounded like, but she had never seen him before. Not while she was awake. Never outside her dreams. Morgan felt like she was in a daze as she turned her head to Ethic. She saw pain in his stare, confirmation, that what she was seeing wasn't a figment of her imagination. Ethic made his way to her side.

She couldn't find her voice as she turned her head back to Messiah. He stood, dark denim, black sweatshirt, wheat Timberlands, and a low-cut Caesar. His locs were gone. His image blurred. Tears. They were blinding her.

My leash . . . why would he break my leash?

His hair had been her favorite part of him and him cutting them felt like a personal insult. It was gone but he was here. How?

Morgan couldn't even hear. It was like she had gone deaf all over again, everything was tuned out or was everyone as speechless as she was?

"Come here, let me see you, Shorty," Messiah signed. It was like he had shot a gun that started a race. Morgan's body reacted. She passed Yara to Ethic before he could utter one word. She barely made sure her child was in his arms before she ran to Messiah. She plowed into him and Messiah fisted her hair, pulling her into his body so tightly that they became one. Her heart raced against his chest and Messiah swore he felt it, beating, pulsing, her heart making his heart stronger. Her pulse, her energy, keeping him alive. She always had been life for him . . . always had been his reason for living. Her feet no longer touched the floor as he hugged her. Morgan sobbed. She bawled, and everyone present was silenced at the intensity of the love before them. Everyone stared but no one moved, except Messiah. He took weighted steps, carrying her into the house, bypassing Alani and the kids, and up the stairs because he didn't want to share this moment. He couldn't because he was going to lose it. His levies were about to break. He could feel the burning in his eyes, and no one could see that but her. He entered Bella's bedroom.

"Shhh," he soothed. Morgan trembled so viciously in his hold that even her teeth chattered. "I'm right here. Shhh. Shorty stop crying."

She wanted to but she couldn't. Her body was in an uproar. Her heart was going haywire. Her lungs wouldn't suck in enough air. Her eyes wouldn't stop leaking. She was dying right there in his arms. Messiah had returned to her and she was about to leave him. She was about to die. He would have to say good bye because Morgan couldn't live through this. It was too much. He placed hands, real hands, tangible fingertips to the side of her face as he pulled her off his shoulder. "Let me see my girl," he whispered.

He cleared the snot from her top lip with the swipe of his thumb.

"Pretty ass," he admired. Morgan's hands were leaves on the limbs of a tree. They shook, shook so hard she thought they would fall off as she placed both hands to his face. Her holding him, him holding her. No sound but her tears as they stared at one another.

"How are you here?" she finally said, scraping up the remnants of her voice. "Messiah. How?"

"I told you I'ma always come back to you, Mo. I'm never leaving you, Shorty."

Morgan's chest felt weighted as it dipped in turmoil. "Where have you been, Messiah?"

Messiah's eyes closed involuntarily. His name on her lips. Those zz's. He had waited a long time to hear her say it. It disturbed him at his core, ripping up all his reserve and he bit down on his bottom lip to stop himself from breaking down. Damn if Morgan was the only person on Earth capable of making a bitch of him. His heart was pounding in anxiety just at the sight of her.

"I've been trying to get back, Shorty. I've been—"

Morgan pushed him. "Where have you been?!" she shouted. Her face folded in excruciation. This was real. This was a dagger, another dagger through her heart. The realization that he had been living and breathing somewhere without her, that he had stayed away for two fucking years without her . . . it destroyed her. "Do you know what I've been through?" she asked. Memories of her inside that car all those years ago flashed through her mind, playing the mini-movie of her life since he'd gone away. Her shock had worn off and was replaced with inexplicable rage. It pulsed through her as she remembered the last time she'd seen him. He had humiliated her. He had told her he didn't care. That she hadn't meant anything to him. He had reached inside her chest, fisted her heart, and ripped it away from every single strand of flesh that kept it lodged inside her body. She had been hollowed out ever since, like a carcass. She was empty.

"I'm so sorry, Shorty . . ."

Morgan pushed him, he barely budged. "You murdered me!" she screamed. She pushed him again, jerking him but not moving him.

"I'm sorry," Messiah said, lifting hands of surrender.

"You're disgusting! I hate you! I fucking hate you! It's been two years! Two!" Morgan pushed him, again and again. Then she slapped him. Her hand landed across his cheek so viciously that the impact turned his head. Morgan's fingers curled into a fist and she swung. "You just left me here! You just left! You destroyed me!" Messiah arrested her hands and Morgan sobbed against him. "How coullllldddddd youuuuuuu?" she cried, melting. His sudden emergence in her life leveled her.

Morgan's cries were so loud that a crowd gathered outside the door. When it opened, she was on her hands and knees, sobbing, as the emotional storm wrecked her.

"Shorty, don't do this to me. Baby, please. Mo, just let me explain. I can explain," he said.

Morgan smelled Ethic before she saw him. "Ethic help meeee, please, help me," she sobbed.

"Morgan . . ." Messiah's voice was injured, pleading. Damn. He hadn't meant for her to feel any of this.

Ethic picked Mo up from the ground, scooping her into his arms. He didn't even acknowledge Messiah as she wrapped arms around his neck and hid her face in his chest.

"Mo, baby . . ."

"Messiah," Alani's voice corralled him. He walked toward her, lip trembling and without ever knowing where his feet were leading him he fell into her arms.

Messiah held onto Alani like she was his mama . . . like she would heal his aching soul . . . like if she told him it would be okay it magically would be just that . . . okay. Messiah was a motherless boy and a womanless man and the way Morgan had reacted to him had obliterated him. The shit hurt so fucking bad that it almost numbed it, so much pain that he could barely feel it.

"Morgan?" The man's voice calling Mo's name caused Messiah to pull away from Alani.

"Messiah! No!" Alani called after him, but he was already out of her grasp.

When he stepped into the hallway, the sight of Morgan, in someone else's arms, not Ethic's, but Bash, it was like a bullet. Cancer couldn't kill him, but this could, it would. Damn why was his heart bleeding? He could feel it. The squeeze inside his chest. Bash met his stare and Messiah took steps toward him until he saw the two children that Morgan was reaching for. She grabbed a baby girl from Bella and a boy from Eazy and Messiah stumbled, backward, like someone had delivered a blow that knocked him off balance. He had seen them before. He knew she'd had them. The Instagram posts had shown him she was a mother now, but to see it up close. To see those innocent eyes, those pretty faces, that matched her face almost exactly, and to see Bash, their father, it was a filet knife to Messiah's soul. Karma was sliding that bitch back and forth, cutting away hope. Any chance he thought he had at getting her back felt miniscule.

"I need to leave," Mo said.

Messiah turned and placed balled fists on top of his head. She was leaving and dragging his heart behind her like the soda cans he used to hook to string on the back of his bike. He wanted to stop her, he wanted to fucking kill the corny nigga beside her, but the destruction he had caused was too great and there were so many eyes watching. He didn't want to make a bigger scene than they already had. He had made a spectacle of her before. Doing that again would cripple her. Perhaps, the first time had already done that . . . her eyes looked different. Staring into them felt . . . different. Morgan's light had been extinguished. He had done that. He had seen it turn off two years ago when he left her. The moment he had shouted, "I don't give a fuck anymore." He had noticed the change in her. It was like he had hit a switch, cloaking her in darkness. She had gotten used to the gloom and now that he was trying to pull her out, now that he wanted to live in the light with her, she was forever changed, forever cloaked in gloom. Fuck.

17

Messiah sat on the floor in Bella's room. He hadn't moved. Couldn't move. The sting that caused his eyes to prickle was moving through his entire body. Morgan's disdain was electrocuting him. His knees were bent, arms wrapped around them, one hand clasping the opposite wrist. His head was bowed. Regret pushed it down. Like a dog being punished his face was pushed into his mistake. Messiah's blood boiled as he pictured Morgan walking down the steps with her kids and her man, only he wasn't her man. He could never be her man because the position wasn't vacant. It would never be vacant because Messiah was never quitting on the job. The image tore through his mind like a tornado, causing his chest to fill with a cloud of hurt so potent that it felt like he couldn't breathe. He clenched his teeth as he rocked back and forth.

"Messiah?"

The voice was so damn soft Messiah felt like there was an angel sitting on his shoulder.

"I'm good," said, his voice gritty.

"Okay," she said. Messiah saw Alani lower into his view as

she sat on the floor in front of him. Her round belly was so big that it sat in her lap as she tried to sit Indian style. "So you will definitely have to help me get up from here," she said, out of breath and smiling.

Messiah scoffed and shook his head but didn't speak. He didn't know Alani well. Didn't know her at all in fact. All he knew was that Ethic loved her and that she had forgiven him after he'd killed her daughter. She had forgiven a tragic mistake. Pardoned the unfathomable and as she sat before him she almost glowed.

"Alani—"

Ethic's voice came from behind Messiah. It was territorial. Protective. Stern.

"Ezra."

Her voice was sterner. More protective. It was so matter of fact that Messiah had to look up because he couldn't ever remember anyone taking that tone with Ethic before.

"We're fine," she said.

He looked up at Ethic who dead panned on him. There was a silent conversation between them.

Walk real fucking light with my wife.

Messiah heard the message without the utterance of words before Ethic left the room.

"Is she happy with that nigga?" Messiah asked.

"Not with him," Alani answered. "No.

"Why did you come today, Messiah? If Ethic asked you to wait until after her birthday. Why did you come anyway?" Alani asked.

"I just wanted to see her. I been back too long and I ain't seen my Shorty," Messiah stated.

"So you ruin her birthday?" Alani asked, frowning in confusion. "You put your needs before hers and decide when and how she should receive the news that you're alive? And you choose a house full of spectators to witness the reunion? You had to know seeing you would unravel her and you wanted people to see her like that?"

Her words hit Messiah. Arrow to the heart.

"I didn't think about that," he said.

"That's your problem, Messiah. You think of you first and her second. You have to always think about her. How she's going to feel. If what you want supports what she needs. Morgan is a sensitive girl. She's a woman. We need to be handled delicately."

"How did you forgive him?" Messiah asked. His chin quivered, and he put his head down. "When you found out what Ethic had done, you loved him anyway. I need her to love me like that. Through everything, you know? So how did you do it?"

Alani paused, closing her eyes as she sucked in a deep breath. He took her in. She really was beautiful. Even with the roundness from her pregnancy filling her face. Alani radiated. She wore the confidence of a woman who was sure of the decisions she had made in life. She was cloaked in peace like she had come to terms with the turmoil that had led her to this home, with this man, in this role. It had taken her awhile to grow into this woman, to wear this heavy crown, but she did it gracefully like she had been on this throne her entire life. When she opened her eyes they glistened with emotion.

"He was my air, Messiah. I didn't have a choice but to forgive him. If I wanted to live, I had to breathe, and he was air," Alani whispered. "You abandoned her when she needed you most. She's been through a lot."

"I've been through a lot!" Messiah blurted. "I was sick when I left, and I fucked Shorty over so bad that I couldn't look her in the eyes and ask her to hold my hand while I died. I snaked Shorty. I pulled the rug from under her feet. I couldn't ask her for shit after that. I'm not even supposed to be here but

I'm here and I want her so damn bad, man. I just want her. I'm sick and I don't know if I got one day or a hundred but they hers if she want 'em. I just want her to want 'em," Messiah's chest rocked, and a rare sob surfaced before he swallowed it down, choking on remorse. He trapped his emotion so tightly inside him that the vein in his forehead bulged.

"Oh, Messiah," Alani said. She reached out and wrapped a soft hand around his forearm. She gave a gentle squeeze and Messiah recoiled, snatching away from her so viciously that she fell forward a bit.

"Messiah—"

His reaction was like she had touched him with fire. An instinct. To pull away. From touch. From the touch of someone he didn't trust. Alani knew that instinct well.

"Who hurt you, Messiah?" she asked. Emotion filled her eyes as she watched him pull himself from the ground. "Somebody hurt you, bad. Touched you the wrong way. Someone who loved you."

"You don't know shit," he snapped.

"That's why you're afraid to love people. Why you walk around hurting people who love ya' ass."

Alani climbed to her feet.

"Stop talking about what you don't know," Messiah said. "Don't bend my name."

"Sexually? Somebody abused you sexually?" Alani pressed. "Couldn't be a woman. You would find that brag worthy. A hood nigga getting pussy early. You would brag on that. A man hurt you."

"No!" Messiah barked it so loud that Ethic entered the room. Alani's eyes widened.

"Get out Ethic," Alani ordered. She didn't even look at him. Her stare was on Messiah's. His burned into her. Eyes glossy, red, tortured. "We're fine. This ain't for you. He's not going to hurt me. I'm a big girl. A little yelling ain't never hurt nobody. I yell at your ass all the time."

"Al—"

"Ezra!" The authority in her voice silenced him instantly. His eyes met hers. "See. I yelled. Nothing happened. We're fine. Right, Messiah?"

She challenged Messiah with her stare again. A long silence filled the room as they faced off. He was like a wild animal . . . cornered . . . trying to decide if he was going to surrender or fight his way out of this corner. His chest heaved as he relented.

"Yeah," he answered.

Ethic's reluctance ate him alive, but he retreated from the room.

Alani knew she had pressed Messiah too hard. He didn't know her. Didn't trust her.

"Where are you staying, Messiah?" Alani asked.

"I'm around," he answered.

"You got food in your refrigerator?" she probed.

"Nah, I got a partner who's a chef," he answered.

"You don't know how to cook for yourself?" she asked.

"Oh, I'm a sous chef when it come to that work. A nigga burn his eggs though, every time," Messiah stated.

Alani's eyes softened. "You sound like somebody else I know," she whispered.

Messiah was grateful that the conversation had eased into the slow lane. When Alani put her foot on the gas pedal it made tension creep up his spine.

"I go grocery shopping every Saturday morning. I go early though at like six o'clock," she said. "Can you take me in the morning? Ezra is busy and Eazy can't carry all the groceries by himself. You can stay for breakfast afterward and get some things for your place too," she said.

She was asking him. Messiah heard the question, but it

didn't seem like he had a choice to decline. It sounded more like a demand and he wondered how she'd made him feel obliged to say yes when he really wanted to say no. He didn't even know if he was allowed to say no. The hand propped on her hip and the raised brow that awaited his answer put a tremor in his chest.

What the fuck? He thought. It was like she just might reach out and pop his ass if he said the wrong thing.

"Yeah, I can do that," he agreed.

Alani nodded. "Good."

Messiah's chin tilted a bit and he stared down the bridge of his nose at her.

"Be her air?" he asked.

Alani nodded. "Give her life. Don't make her feel like she wants to die," Alani answered. "And be patient with her. You can't just show up and expect things to go back to the way they used to be between you two. Morgan is a different girl. She has different needs and a lot has happened since you left. You have to understand that you can't control how people move on from you. If you want any chance of fixing things you have to love without judgment. I'll see you tomorrow morning."

18

The exhaustion that plagued her penetrated her bones as Morgan pushed through her front door, carrying Yara on her shoulder.

"You sure you don't want me to stay?" Bash asked.

She turned to him and placed a finger to her lips. She knew the sound of his baritone would stir Messari. He was a light sleeper and would pop up off Bash's shoulder if they weren't completely silent.

She flicked the light switch and kicked out of her boots before traipsing through the apartment to her nursery. She placed Yara down in her crib as Bash put Messari down to rest. Morgan turned the baby monitor on and then crept out of the room.

"So, you really want me to leave? I could stay," Bash said.

Morgan shook her head. "No, you should go to your place tonight."

"Are we okay, Morgan? Messiah being back. Does that change anything with us?"

It changes everything. Things have been different. You were never the one. You could never be the one.

She didn't have the heart to let the words fall from her lips. Not tonight. A night where her entire world had been flipped upside down she just wanted to be alone. She didn't have the strength to fight. She was stunned, lost, confused . . . so many emotions swirled in Morgan. She didn't know how she felt. Relief. Anger. Love. Hate. It all bombarded her at the same time. She could barely breathe. A knot of apprehension tore through her stomach. Morgan just needed to sleep. Rest. Close her eyes and let the darkness give her momentary solace because she couldn't take this. Reality was merging with her dreams anyway because that's where Messiah lived. How the hell had he walked out of her head and into Ethic's backyard? How had her dreams come true? She could see him. She could hear him and suddenly she wondered if she could touch him. If she could run her fingers through his locs . . . no . . . she couldn't. They were gone.

He cut his hair. His locs. My locs. How could he cut them?

"Morgan?" Bash said, brow dipping in discontent as he awaited her answer.

"Yeah, yeah, we're . . ."

Who the fuck told him to cut his hair?

"We're umm . . . yeah, we're good," she finally managed. "I just need time to think. Just tonight. Please Bash. This is a lot."

He nodded and kissed her forehead. Morgan pulled back. Her body went rigid. There was a time when something as simple as a forehead kiss would have been hazardous to Bash's health. That forehead had been reserved for one person . . . until he had lied . . . until he had died.

How?

Bash stared at her, lingering for a moment before walking out of the apartment. As soon as she heard the door close

Morgan felt her eyes prickle. She had wanted to fold when she'd laid eyes on Messiah but there were so many people watching, waiting for her reaction. He was waiting for her reaction. If she had learned nothing from Christiana over the past two years, the one thing she had learned was how to retain a poker face. Morgan's insides were in turmoil as she made her way to her kitchen. A bottle of tequila. She had never needed it more. She pulled a bottle from her pantry and didn't even bother with a glass. She grabbed the first thing she saw, a red cup, and filled it to the top. Morgan lifted the red cup to her nude lips. One large gulp and her jaw slackened as she let the liquor linger on her tongue before lifting her head to the sky and letting it slide down her throat. She looked at the ceiling, shaking her head, back and forth, forth and back, disbelief. Morgan was in utter disbelief. She took another sip, grabbed the bottle, and melted to the floor. For so long she had wondered why no funeral had been arranged. Why she hadn't been contacted about his body. Why Bleu hadn't known where he was buried. There had been so many unknowns.

Because his ass was alive. All this time. How could he leave me here? I would have gone with him. Wherever he was, I would have gone. I would have run with him. Just like Raven. Just like a moth to a flame. I would have . . .

Morgan's knees met her chest and she finished the cup then poured another. The burning that accompanied withholding tears was unbearable and when she could no longer hold them, they fell.

Her phone rang and Morgan crawled to the couch, snatching the strap and pulling it to her. She retrieved it and answered the call.

"Aria, I'm dreaming. Tell me this isn't real," Morgan cried.

"Open the door Mo. I'm outside," she said.

Morgan sniffed, wiping her runny nose with the back of

her hand before pulling herself from the floor. She didn't even know where she found the strength in her legs to make it to the door, but with a dizzy head she pulled it open. Aria leaned her head against the door frame.

"I brought liquor and Twizzlers," Aria said with a sympathetic smile as she held up a brown paper bag.

Morgan scoffed through the emotion that overwhelmed her and stepped aside so Aria could enter.

"He's back," Morgan whispered, tilting her head back to look at the ceiling. Her tears ran, pooling in her ears.

"He is," Aria said. "Leave it up to Messiah . . ." Aria shook her head. "It has to be a relief Mo. He's alive. That's a good thing, right?"

"It's the best thing," Morgan whispered, sobs wracking her as she lowered her head. She rushed toward Aria crying so hard that she couldn't breathe. "How could he leave me here? It's been so long." Morgan pulled back closing her eyes and shaking her head. "I'm fucking Ahmeek."

"You're doing more than that, Mo," Aria said.

"I told him I would leave Bash. After my birthday I was supposed to move in with him, Aria. He's waiting for me. He gave me a key to his loft. He gave *me* the loft and a car and now Messiah's back. Oh my God, he's back. I don't even know what to feel."

"This is a lot for anybody, Mo. I just want you to take your time with it. Process it. The last thing anyone wants is for you to get overwhelmed. Messiah has a habit of making you feel worthless. Making you feel like you can't keep breathing."

"I can breathe just fine without him Aria. He taught me that I could live without him. That's what scares me most," Morgan admitted. "He left and I died a little on the inside. Walked around not even noticing anything. Nothing was funny. Nothing was beautiful. Everything just irritated me.

Even the sounds of my babies sometimes made me cringe. I almost wanted to be deaf again. I've never said that to anyone. What type of mother thinks that?"

"One who was left devastated. One who lost her peace when their father died," Aria said.

"Ahmeek makes me feel like I'm the best person he's ever known. He makes me feel like I'm doing a good job with the twins. He loves to watch me dance. He's always amazed by it. Not even just at the shows, but when I'm here and putting some bullshit eight count together in the mirror, he just watches. And him and Yara," Mo whispered that last part and closed her eyes. "I could have spent the rest of my life watching him with her. Now I have to give him up."

"You don't have to do anything, Mo. You don't owe Messiah any explanations, but he owes you a long one. You've got to talk to him, and you have to tell him about his kids," Aria said. "That's a card you've been holding, and you should have played it."

"I can't," Morgan said, shaking her head. "I don't even know him. Like who is he? He lied to my face, plotted on my family. I have no idea who he is. I'm so fucking mad at him, Aria, I could kill him. I can't turn my kids over to a man I don't know."

"Morgan. If you do this everything changes. You can't cry victim and do something like this. If you don't tell him, you become wrong. You haven't been so far. You aren't wrong for anything else you've done, but this . . . if you keep that man's kids from him? That's dead ass wrong, Mo and if he finds out and murders every fucking body over his kids, he'll be justified."

"I just have to be sure about him first. He was going to kill Ethic," she snapped. She had never told Aria that. She had never wanted to look foolish enough and admit that she had fallen in love with a man who would do something so cruel. She hadn't

wanted to make it seem like she had been a mark, a way in, a
ploy for Messiah to get to Ethic.

"Morgan. You're playing with me, right?"

"I wish I was," Morgan answered. Morgan had never shared
the depths of Messiah's betrayal with Aria. It was so much more
complex than just heartbreak. Familial warfare was a part of
their history. "He's dangerous Aria. I'm not trusting him with
my kids until I'm one hundred percent sure he's here for the
right reasons." Morgan's gut churned. Turmoil bubbled in her
like lava. All-consuming. Re-introducing her to an aching that
paralyzed her. "How is he here?" She kept asking the same question over and over again. It felt like she was dreaming because
she had dreamt this dream before.

Aria went to the linen closet and retrieved a blanket and a
pillow. "I don't know, Mo. The part of me that knows Messiah
doesn't think he would ever do anything to hurt you. I can't
even see him wanting to hurt yo' fine ass daddy."

Morgan released a small laugh, letting some of the woe on
her heart go, but damn. It was so heavy. Messiah's return was
almost harder than his disappearance. She knew how to mourn
him. She knew how to let go of the past because she hadn't
wanted to hate him from the grave. But to see him again was
crippling. It meant he had chosen to abandon her. It made all
her resentment rush back like a flood. She could hardly keep
her emotional bearings.

"I'll take the couch," Aria said, plopping down next to
Morgan.

"I'm okay. I don't need babysitting. I really just want to be
by myself. I just want to cry. I want to cry without anyone being
here to hear me. He cut his locs, Aria. Why would he cut his
hair? I loved his hair," she whispered, eyes filling to the brim
and then spilling. Crystal tears ran down her cheeks. "I used to
love *him*."

"Do you still?" Aria asked.

Morgan's face crushed, painting a story of hurt. "He took my soul away when he left. He broke my heart and the first thing I felt when I heard his voice was a pulse. I felt him in my veins, Aria. I just wanted to touch him to see if he was real."

A knock at the door made Morgan's heart tense in anticipation. Aria lifted, leaving Mo on the couch, doubled over in complete agony.

"Morgan, it's Ahmeek," Aria said unsurely. "I'm going to go. I know you're okay with him here." Aria looked at Meek. "Call me if she needs anything." Ahmeek didn't look at Aria. His eyes were fixed on Morgan. He nodded though. He heard her. He knew the stakes. Mo's emotions were out of control and she was dangerous to herself when that happened. As soon as Isa called his line with the unbelievable news his stomach hollowed. Gratefulness and uncertainty filled the space where his future once lived because he had no idea what this meant for him and Mo. Aria walked out the door.

Morgan turned, holding onto the back of the couch with one hand. They were silent. Staring at one another like they were soaking each other in, noting every detail, because they weren't sure if they would get the opportunity to again.

Ahmeek stood in front of her, brow furrowed in worry, eyes shining with confusion. The sight of him both stirred and disturbed her soul. Ahmeek, Messiah's left hand, and her lover. What a fucking complicated mess she had made. Her lip quivered.

"Is it true? He's alive?" Meek asked. There was something in his tone. A break. Hope wrapped in disbelief, with a bow of sadness on top because Messiah's return changed so many things.

Morgan couldn't even find her voice. She just nodded.

She rushed into his arms, sobbing. How had they gotten to this place?

"He's back!" she cried. "God, Meek, what have I done?"

He held her tightly and grit his teeth, palming the back of her head, pressing her into his body. They were tormented.

"What have *we* done, Mo? Not just you. What have we done?" he said.

"I'm dying!"

Meek gripped the sides of her face and placed a kiss on her forehead. "Mo, I know what this means. He's back and we can't. We shouldn't have in the first place."

Morgan wilted in his arms. "I'm so sorry!"

"Shh." She needed his consoling. She needed it so badly. "Stop, love."

"I can't, Meek," she sobbed. She was sucking in air. Hyperventilating. Panicking. "Meek, I can't breathe."

"You can," Meek stated. "Because you're the fucking catch, Mo. You can dismiss niggas and keep sitting pretty. I'm not what makes you dope, love. Neither is he. I need you to remember that. Shit about to get rough, love. Real rough. Confusing. Chaotic. It'll probably hurt a little bit, maybe a lot, but you're in control, Mo. The queen is always in control. So you can do anything, Morgan. No matter what happens or who's in your life, you gon' always come out on top."

Morgan pushed out air, grasping his forearms as she lifted pained eyes to his. She sucked in a deep breath.

"I love you," she whispered. "Two hours ago, I could see my whole life with you. I'm in love with you, Ahmeek."

"I know, love," he answered. "You don't have to prove that. I know what it is with us. I know what it is with you and him too. I can't even be mad at it, because my nigga is breathing, Mo. A nigga I thought I lost is breathing." Ahmeek flicked his nose and sniffed back emotion as his eyes glistened. He kissed the top of her head. "He's my brother, Mo. I thought he was dead." Meek released her and turned from her, lifting both hands to his head. She heard him lock his emotion away. The sniff of his nose was the only thing that gave him away. Morgan touched him and he shook his head. "I got to go check on him. I wanted to come here first. I wanted to see you, Mo."

He turned and blew out a sharp breath. She reached up for him, soft hands wrapping around his neck as he pressed his forehead to hers. She sighed. This felt so good. Bliss. It was all she ever felt with Ahmeek. There was no flux of emotions. No fighting. No battling. Just loving. That's all they ever did was love. He didn't waste time fighting or confusing or disappointing or deceiving. Love was just a word with Messiah. He said one thing and then did another. It was a verb with Ahmeek. He put it into action every single day. Even in this moment when everything they wished they could have was in jeopardy, the way he looked at her was full of love.

"I love you. I love you. I love you so much. I love you Meekie. I love this. I love us," she whispered.

"Mo," he interrupted.

"No, just let me say it, Ahmeek. Let me tell you. Let me say it a million times just in case something changes. Just in case—"

She stopped talking. "He's back, Ahmeek. I don't know if I'll ever get to say this to you again so just let me say it now. We are real. This with you is real and I'm in love with you. I felt magical on that dance floor with you in London while Stevie Wonder played in the background. I've felt that same feeling every day since. I left London because I wanted to be near you. I wanted to use Friday night card games as an excuse to see you."

"You came home for me?" he asked, disbelieving.

"I was gone for years, Ahmeek. You gave me a few hours in London, and I wanted more. I wanted you. It's crazy, I know, but I bought a ticket home before you ever stepped foot on the plane to leave. I came home for you," she confirmed.

"I want to kiss you, love but in the back of my mind I'm seeing my nigga. He's back and that shit is fucking me up," he admitted. "I've got to go talk to bro, man. I got to figure this shit out. You okay? Here by yourself?"

"No, but because of you I will be. The queen doesn't fold. I'm your queen, right?" she asked.

"Every day of every week, love," he answered. He kissed her forehead and Morgan placed her fingertips on the sides of his face. They lingered there and then Ahmeek pulled back, opening the door. Morgan felt her body revolt when it closed behind him. She gripped her shirt as a nagging filled her chest. Morgan felt like she was drowning. Her past was colliding with her future, taking away her chance to be with this man and it was unbearable. It was like she had to decide who to love all in an instant. Meek or Messiah? Did she even want to traipse back down the road that led to Messiah? It was bumpy. Rough. Meek was smooth. Meek was effortless and she was letting him walk away. Morgan snatched open the door.

"Ahmeek!" She shouted his name with a desperation he had never heard her possess. He turned from the elevator and she ran to him. His embrace was like a sanctuary and her heart thundered as he picked her up, arms wrapped tight around her back, lips on hers. Her feet never touched the ground as he took wide steps, carrying her back to her door. They stood outside her place, submerged in one another. Her hands on his face then around his neck, finessing the nape of him. She sniffed, crying, as she inhaled this man. Every single second that she had wasted with him before was now a regret. She kissed him so deeply that he stumbled forward, removing one hand to put it against the wall and then pulling her waist into his body. Morgan was a mess. An emotional hurricane.

"What are we going to do?" she asked as she lowered her head into his chest, squeezing her eyes tight. "I can't pretend like this didn't happen. I couldn't choose between you and Messiah, now he's back. I only have one heart Meek. Who am I supposed to give it to?"

"Can't give that bitch to nobody because I ain't never give it back."

Messiah. Fucking Messiah. His voice made Morgan freeze. Her limbs turned to steel. His baritone made the hair on the back of her neck stand up. She gripped Meek's collar as her forehead hit his chest in disgrace, she turned her head to the side away from Messiah as she sobbed. "Meek please, make him leave. I can't." Morgan's heart was on the floor. She couldn't handle this. She couldn't do this right now. Here they were. The three of them. Her transgressions were out in front of them. Clear as day. There was no excusing what Messiah had just interrupted. Three people and only two seats at the table.

"Just go inside," Ahmeek instructed.

"I can't," she cried. "I can't walk. I can't breathe. Ahmeek. God!"

The sight in front of Messiah was devastating. He knew he had himself to blame, but the sight of Morgan leaning on his man for help, clinging to him in her time of need, saying his name so intimately. It tore away pieces of his soul. It was like someone was fileting pieces of him from the bone, slicing flesh clean off, it hurt so bad. In that moment he wished that he had let the cancer take him because witnessing this . . . damn . . . no man was supposed to see this shit. He knew he'd left instructions for Meek to love Mo through her loss, but none of that mattered right now. He saw red.

"Yo, bruh," Messiah started, lifting his hands and clapping them together one time in warning before bringing praying hands against his mouth. He shook those hands, pointing them at Meek as he spoke his next words.

"I swear to fucking God I will end you my nigga," Messiah

threatened, mouth sneered in unbelievable rage. He had never felt anything like the hatred that coursed through his veins in this moment.

Meek released Morgan and came off his hip, pistol in hand because he already knew how Messiah would carry it. M&M&M. At a standoff. Messiah drew on Meek, gripping a .45 in one hand. Meek knew Messiah was seconds off the trigger because Messiah's free hand gave him away. Those fingers were rubbing. Messiah was itching to lay somebody down. They stood there, squared off, both gripping pistols in their palms, trigger fingers in position, but guns resting at their sides.

Messiah shook his head. "I'ma need Shorty back," he said.

"You know me. I don't keep what don't want to be kept," Meek said. Morgan trembled under the safety of one of his arms, squeezing her eyes so tight they hurt. This was a bad dream, the worst nightmare she'd ever had. Her heart thundered, and she just couldn't catch her breath. She loved Messiah, but she was terrified of him, so confused about who he was. Had she ever really known him? Mizan's brother. He had told her she didn't matter. Screamed that she was easy to forget and now he was here. Where the fuck had he been the past two years if not in a grave? Dying was better. Dying meant he was forced away from her. Choosing to stay away . . . leaving her . . . deserting her . . . was unforgiveable. Morgan's legs lost all strength. If Meek pulled away from her Morgan would fall to the floor. She would crumble, so she clung there, because between the two of them, she trusted Meek more. She had loved Messiah first however. She had loved Messiah blindly and she could still feel the pull of his energy drawing her to him. Her body begged her to go to him, but she couldn't oblige. Her mind screamed for her to stay away. She loved them both, but trust was nonexistent between her and Messiah. Meek didn't lie. He didn't deceive.

Messiah had destroyed her, was destroying her in this moment and she couldn't even face him.

Messiah's lip trembled, and his face broke into lines of agony.

"Shorty . . ."

"Meek please! Make him leave . . ."

Meek stepped to Messiah, reaching out to touch him and Messiah smacked his hand down so hard that his own skin felt the sting of the connection.

"Nigga you touch me I'ma put them simple ass thoughts in your head on the floor, pussy!" Messiah was livid. He knew how this had happened. He had thought he would be okay with it . . . the idea was more noble than the reality. His friend and his girl. They were his. They both were his people and they had coped with his disappearance by leaning on one another. Witnessing it was fucking eating Messiah alive. Messiah rushed Meek, throwing a blow so vicious that Messiah felt the bones in his hand break on impact. Meek tossed Messiah, returning with aggression, matching Messiah's energy. They tore up the entire hallway of her apartment building as they attacked one another, blow for blow, neither backing down. Friends turned adversaries over their affection for the same woman.

"No! God! Stop!" Morgan shouted. She pulled Messiah's arm and he turned around so fast that he didn't think first. He was in a blind rage and he didn't snap out of it until he felt his hand across her face.

SLAP!

The blow was so powerful it sent Morgan to the ground.

Meek hemmed Messiah up, one hand to Messiah's collar and a forearm to Messiah's neck. No air. Messiah couldn't breathe, and he didn't want to after the realization of what he had done hit him.

"The FUCK is you doing, nigga?" Meek barked, spitting and jerking Messiah hard against the wall as he spoke. He was livid. Meek wanted to pop Messiah. Pull the trigger and make the nigga disappear. Had he been anyone else he would already be slumped. If Meek had been anyone else the same would apply, but they were brothers, even with two hearts full of disdain and confusion, it was hard for either of them to come to anything other than blows. Fists you could recover from. Once bullets flew there was no coming back from that. Morgan was a good girl with a thing for bad boys. She was addicted to the butterflies and she had two plugs. Two drugs. Fucking addicted to the thrill. M&M ... Meek and Messiah. Two killers, both deadly, equally cunning, at an impasse because not only did they both love the girl on the floor, they loved one another.

Morgan was on all fours, weeping, as she held her face with one hand, trying to stop the ringing in her ears. She opened her mouth, flexing her jaw to see if it still worked. It felt shattered. A bomb had gone off inside her head and the sight in front of her was blindingly white. She could barely see.

"Mmm," she groaned as she reached out for the wall. "Meek ..."

Meek grit his teeth and jerked Messiah hard against the wall in frustration before releasing him to go to Morgan's side. Even killing Messiah came second to Morgan Atkins. She was hurt. She was his priority and Meek went to her side without hesitating because he was able to do what Messiah could not, put his emotions to the side for the woman he loved. Messiah stared down at them in agony. His lip trembled, and he turned to the wall.

"Fuck!" he shouted as he punched it, again and again, again and again, again and again. He balled those bloodied knuckles and brought them to the side of his head then placed them to the wall, resting his head on top of them. His lips flattened, and his nostrils flared as he pulled in air, trying his hardest to calm himself.

You're going to lose her nigga. Straighten the fuck up.

"Morgan . . ." He took one step toward her.

"Stay away from me!" she cried, putting up one hand to keep him at bay as terror played a motion picture in her widened eyes. His hand print was on the entire right side of her face. Ahmeek picked her up from the floor, carrying her in his arms as she bawled on his shoulder while holding her injured face.

"Mo, I'm sorry," Messiah whispered, putting his hands on top of his head in distress. He hadn't meant to hit her . . . would never . . . could never . . . his temper . . . his aggression . . . it had gotten the best of him. He had just reacted. He wanted to hurt Ahmeek, never her, never ever her, she had just been in the way. She had just caught him by surprise. He wanted to touch her, to pull her into his arms and cry, to tell her why he was so fucked up, why his love felt like pain. He wanted to beg her to dismiss Ahmeek, because although Ahmeek was the better man, he would never, could never love her more. No one could. Messiah would pour out every ounce of blood that kept him breathing for Morgan. He would die for her, had damn near died just for the slightest chance to come back to her. He wanted to plead. The image before him enraged him and he wished he could punish them for this love they had built . . . the love that was palpable at first sight, but he knew he had no right. He had told Meek to do exactly this . . . to love Mo back to life . . . to help her . . . to show her love still existed after him, but this wasn't after him. He wasn't gone. He was standing right here and the jealousy he felt from seeing his friend and the love of his life together had made him black out. He had flipped the fucking switch so fast that he hadn't even realized he was seeing red. His temper was uncontrollable because even now, after hurting her, he still wanted to inflict pain, still wanted to curl triggers, like it was a fetish. Perhaps it was, because the thought of laying Meek down made his dick hard. Messiah wanted to murder somebody. He remembered nights like this . . . when he felt like sending niggas to their maker and he would race to Morgan, rushing through her door, just to expel the energy . . . pull up on her just to fuck her good, to murder something . . . sex with her had been like therapy . . . but now he was picturing her with Meek. Her face was on the floor and fear lived in her eyes. Eyes she wouldn't even bless him with looking into. Messiah couldn't breathe. He was fucking choking. Their bond . . . Messiah scoffed . . . the audacity of Morgan and Meek to have a fucking bond . . . it was wrapped around his neck and squeezing tight. Their love was killing him.

"Bro, man," Meek stated. "Another day, G. I'm a man. I stand ten toes behind everything I do. I'll pull up on you. Let me get her settled first."

"Let *you* get her settled," Messiah scoffed in disregard . . . in disbelief. "Let you get my . . ." Messiah pinched the bridge of his nose as he gritted his teeth. "I ain't dead, Mo. I'm right here, Shorty. Right here, baby. I ain't dead, but this shit . . . you with him. That's gon' kill me. It's gon' kill me, Shorty," his voice cracked, and he cleared his throat, swallowing down the lump stopping him from breathing. She wrapped her arms around Meek's neck, body convulsing she was sobbing so hard. She wouldn't . . . couldn't even look at him.

Messiah turned, taking burdened steps away from them, lowering his head as tears fell from his eyes. He quickly sniffed them away and burst through the door that led to the stairwell because if he stood in front of the elevator to wait for it to open, they would witness his undoing. Nobody, not even Mo could see the ways that she was breaking him. Messiah needed privacy to feel the destruction that he had caused.

Meek carried Morgan inside and sat her down on the kitchen island before moving to the freezer. He pulled out a frozen bag of vegetables and put it against her face. She winced in pain.

"Look, Mo," he whispered as he caressed the uninjured side of her face, moving her messy hair from her eyes as his dark stare burned into her. "If you want me to back off, I'll do that. I want to be clear where it's laying with you. I love you. I do. I'll put it all on the line for you, but I know out of us all your position is the hardest and I just want you happy Mo. I want to make you happy but if Messiah changes shit . . ."

Morgan panicked as tears came to her eyes. She saw his lips and she knew what he was saying but she was reading the words, not hearing them. She couldn't hear him. She rolled terrified eyes up to him.

"I can't hear," she said. Her chest heaved. "Meek, I can't hear you! I can't hear! Something's wrong."

19

"There is damage to the inner ear. We'll need to remove the implant then re-install a new cochlear device to see if the nerves are viable for auditory reconnection," the doctor said. Morgan read his lips and dread filled her.

"So two surgeries?" she signed.

"Yes, two surgeries. One to remove the implant and another to re-install."

Morgan's lip quivered as two large tears spilled down her cheeks.

"Do you want to tell me how this happened?" the doctor asked. "If you're unsafe . . ."

Morgan shook her head as her chest rocked. "I fell," she signed. "I'm fine."

"The gentleman in the hallway. Is he hurting you? Your face is bruised," the doctor pushed.

"No, he wouldn't. He didn't do this," Morgan signed.

The doctor sighed because they both knew that she was withholding something. "I'll prepare for surgery in the morning. The nurses will get you settled in."

The doctor opened the door and Meek sat on the floor, leaning against the wall with her twins in front of him. Yara had his car keys and Messari had his cell phone. Morgan gave him a sad smile that melted into tears. He climbed off the floor, wrangling her children into the room.

"You sit here, homie," he said putting Messari in the comfortable chair. "And you sit here." He placed Yara right beside him. He handed them his possessions again and Yara lifted the phone to her mouth.

He pulled it from her hands and held the phone near his face to get her attention. "No, no." Morgan stood and took the phone from him. She gave it to Yara and signed, "No. No. Don't eat it." He was cute. He tried, but he didn't know sign language. He couldn't converse with Yara and Mo didn't like when people tried to make up their own language to communicate with her child . . . like she was a pet they were teaching or something. People had done that to her, her entire life and she hated it. She knew Meek meant well so she held her tongue and gave Yara the phone. She turned to Meek who placed hands on the sides of her face.

"I can't hear, Meek. There's damage. I need surgery," she said. Insecurities filled her because she couldn't hear herself. Her insecurity over the sound of her voice, the projection, the volume, it sprouted instantly. It made her not want to speak at all. She was back to being the poor deaf girl. She could see the pity in Meek's glance. He wouldn't want her like this. No one would want her like this. She was back to being damaged goods. "How could he?" she asked.

Meek wrapped strong arms around her and she withered in his embrace. He pulled back, pinching her chin between two fingers and kissed her lips.

"You're going to be fine. I'ma pull up on Messiah, iron shit out. Let him know how it's laying. Let him know you waited . . .

that we waited before this happened. Everything will be okay," Meek said. Morgan couldn't focus on his eyes to see if he meant the words. She had to focus on his lips. It would be the only way for her to understand what he was saying because Meek couldn't sign. She already felt disconnected from him and it had only been a few hours. She closed her eyes and rested her head on his chest. She wasn't facing the door, so she didn't know it had opened until she felt Meek tap her shoulder. She turned, and her brow lifted in surprise as Bash stared at the two of them then rolled eyes over to the twins, then back to her. Confusion filled the room.

Mo's lip quivered, and she opened her mouth to explain until she felt Meek's hand, gripping her chin, manipulating her gaze until it landed on him.

"You don't owe nobody no explanations, Mo. None. Not one," he said. "You want me to stay or go?"

Morgan turned her head to Bash, Meek turned it back. "Look at me. What do you want?"

Her eyes misted. She couldn't even tell him how she felt. All of a sudden, she had a fear of speaking. It was like it had come back . . . the muteness that came with her deafness . . . like they were a package deal. She felt Bash's eyes on them. She stared at Meek. His handsome face blurred behind the emotion in her vision. She wanted him, but then there was Messiah. He was back and somewhere down inside her, beneath the anger, behind the betrayal, in the depths of her soul underneath the abandonment, even after this slap, she still loved him. She didn't want to hurt him. Even though he had hurt her. Even though she was in this hospital because of him. Even though she had spent the past two years questioning everything he had ever told her. She still loved him. She didn't want him . . . could never have him because things would never be the same, but she didn't want to hurt him. She didn't want to hurt either of them. Messiah the boy who had broken her and Ahmeek, the boy who was fixing her, who had the glue that could mend her heart. Then there was Bash. Morgan looked over at him. He stood flabbergasted and red in the face.

Bash was . . . boring.

"Aye man it's time for you to leave," Bash said. He made the mistake of touching Ahmeek's shoulder and without a thought Meek introduced his burner to Bash's middle, pulling him close so that the twins didn't see what he held in his hands.

"Yo, you put your hands on me again and I'll lay you flat boi," Meek stated.

Meek saw red and his heart raced because he knew Morgan was about to dismiss him. He wasn't even angry at Bash, he was angry at life, at Messiah, at himself for ever falling for Morgan in the first place. Now he might lose her and he suddenly understood the rage Messiah had expressed years ago on Bleu's front lawn when he was put in the very same position. Losing a woman like Mo just made a man murderous. It made him bleed emotion. He felt her indecision and he knew why. Messiah was back and what once seemed like a possibility had become an impossibility in an instant.

"Morgan call off your dog," Bash said, trying not to show his fear.

She pulled his arm, but Meek didn't give. He stood there. Eyes burning into Bash's, intimidation shrinking Bash because he was so fucking angry. It wasn't even about Bash. It was about Morgan Atkins. It was about Messiah. It was about the tug of war that he was in with his best friend's girl . . . a battle he should have never indulged in but now that he had, he couldn't let go, no matter how much the rope burned as he held tight. Morgan put herself between Meek and Bash, pushing Meek back. He tucked his gun in his waist, pulling his jacket down over the handle but his eyes never left Bash. Morgan pulled his face down, using his beard as her leash to get him to look into her eyes.

"Stop," she mouthed.

He nodded and sniffed then ran a hand down his face as she moved her hands up the sides of his face, wrapping them behind his ears and then pulling his forehead to hers.

"Stop." She opened her mouth and spoke the words, using every single ounce of courage she had to speak without being able to hear. She didn't know how she sounded. She hoped she had whispered it, hoped that it sounded the same as before and didn't highlight her disability. A tear fell down her cheek as he kissed her lips, her eyes closed, his eyes open, hawking Bash, daring Bash to do something about it. The emotions filling the moment were too high to continue to be discreet. He wanted to kiss her so he did, she knew it might be the last time so she let him.

"This is bullshit," Bash muttered, before storming out the room.

Morgan pulled back. "You should leave, too."

Meek took in the vision of her, the fucking unbelievable beauty that was Morgan Atkins and he nodded, kissing her forehead before grabbing his belongings from the twins. He finessed the tops of their heads gently, then looked back at her one time before walking out. Morgan blew out a breath, over-whelmed, and gripped her stomach before turning to her babies.

"It's just us," she signed to them. "They all want to be every-thing to me. I just don't know which one belongs here. Maybe none of them. Maybe it's supposed to be just the three of us." Morgan fisted her hair and spun away from them in distress, doubling over as anguish destroyed her face. She gritted her teeth and struggled to fix her face as she stood straight. Her thumb chased away her tears and she sniffed uncontrollably as she tried to stop the flood. Three men loved her. Why couldn't she find it in her to love herself? She knew why . . . she knew that one of them . . . Messiah had made her feel so worthless that she didn't see a point. She didn't feel valuable, worthy. He had destroyed her. Morgan cleared her throat and pursed her lips before blowing out one last breath. She turned to her babies. Her beautiful, sweet angels. They looked at her with unassuming eyes, shining so bright and innocent that Morgan's lip trembled. She got on her knees in front of her babies, in front of Messiah's babies and kissed the tops of their heads. "We'll be okay. I promise," she signed. "I promise you."

Ethic stood on the ladder, pulling the heavy plywood up each step. He put the wood to the broken window of his shop and then pulled the nail gun from his tool belt. He fired four studs through the sturdy wood. He heard the screeching tires of an approaching car and reached for the other gun on his hip. He relaxed when he saw Messiah and he came down off the ladder. Messiah didn't even shut his car door as he hopped out, frantic, worked up, angry.

"She's fucking that nigga!" Messiah said. "She's fucking him! I saw red. I didn't mean to, man." Messiah's lip trembled as he held up his hands in front of his face. They were swollen and bloodied. "I didn't fucking mean to, man. She's fucking my best friend and I lost it. What's wrong with me?" Ethic's temple throbbed because he heard the makings of remorse breaking through Messiah's distress. It could only mean one thing. He could see the regret hanging from Messiah, but it didn't matter. If Messiah had done what Ethic suspected, it was already too late to make amends.

"Grab that board for me and hold it up," Ethic stated, using every inch of discipline he had to remain calm. "Your problem Messiah is that you don't think before you act. You let another man control your emotions and your reactions. You don't take pause," he said as Messiah lifted the board. "That's how you lose your temper. When you don't think. When you don't take a minute to weigh the consequences to your actions."

"I hit her. I fucking hit her. She's everything to me man and I ..."

Ethic grabbed the back of Messiah's neck and slammed it against the wood.

PHEW.

He pulled the trigger.

"Aghh!" A nine-inch nail went through the center of Messiah's hand. "Fuck!"

"That's the hand you hit her with?" Ethic asked as he leaned onto Messiah's injured hand, adding pressure to the nail that impaled it. Messiah grit his teeth, screaming through a clenched jaw. He writhed in pain as Ethic leaned on his bleeding hand.

"I'ma say this to you one time, Messiah," Ethic said. The calm in his tone was terrifying, because it didn't match the anger that Messiah knew was coursing through Ethic's veins. "You ever touch her with anything other than love again and I'll kill you. I taught you to be a man. Men have self-control. You fucking act like I taught you something when you're dealing with anyone who belonged to me first." Ethic eased up a bit, removing some of the pressure on Messiah's injured hand. "I love you like you're my own. I think you know that. I'm glad you're home. I'm glad you're well but I will never allow you or any other nigga to harm her and think there aren't repercussions." He pressed down on that hand again and Messiah grimaced. That pain was so great Messiah thought he might pass out. "You won't intimidate, you won't raise your fucking voice ... you get mad you better whisper my nigga, because she come to me and tell me you abused her in any way. Mentally, physically, emotionally ... I'm coming to kill over mine." Ethic tapped Messiah's chest.

"I'll touch you right there. Lay you down flat with no fucking remorse if you ever touch her again. Do you understand? I want it to be clear because this isn't a conversation to be had twice."

"It's clear," Messiah said, gasping and cringing in excruciation.

Ethic reached for the hammer in his tool belt and used the end of it to grip the nail in Messiah's hand.

"Wait! Man! Damn . . . you couldn't hit a nigga. You had to put a fucking nail through me, O.G.?" Messiah asked, gritting his teeth and breathing heavy as he prepared himself for what he was about to feel.

"You lucky I ain't put a nail in your coffin, G," Ethic answered.

He pulled out the nail swiftly.

"Fuck!" Messiah shouted. Ethic walked inside and grabbed a towel than wrapped Messiah's hand.

"I need help man. I don't want to be bad for her. I want to love her. I do love her. I just want my girl back." The vulnerability leaking from Messiah made Ethic exhale. A long deep breath left his body because he knew that Messiah loved Morgan as best as he knew how. He wasn't fluent in any other emotion besides rage and Ethic knew that Morgan was the test dummy for Messiah's affections. It was a dangerous place to be. "I need you to show me how to love her. Teach me, man. Teach me how to love her the way you love Alani. I'm fucked up. I don't know how to do that. I just want to love her." Messiah sat on the ledge of the boarded-up window, nursing his bloody hand, elbows resting on his knees as his head drooped in despair. "I just gave her up. I told him to take care of her. Told him to love her and now he with her, but I just want to be with her and I want to murder that nigga . . . knock off that corny nigga too . . . I just want to kill everything standing between me and her."

"Listen to me," Ethic said as he sat beside Messiah. "Morgan has had niggas like Bash sniffing behind her since she was twelve years old. She's settling with him. I wasn't aware of Ahmeek. I thought they were friends, but if they're more than friends, it's because he's giving her what she's missing without you. She's searching for you in him. He's familiar. Your worries shouldn't be another nigga being with Mo. It should be making sure you're worthy of Mo. She has some shit to tell you. Same way you've got some shit to tell her. Y'all need to talk. You're connected to her in ways that another man will never be. She'll let you come home when you act like you deserve to. Get your shit together, Messiah. Leave the streets alone. Get your temper in check. It's not just her. You'll have two kids involved. They need a home. They need somewhere safe. They need stability. Be better for her. I've seen her with the nigga Ahmeek. I've also seen him with her. She's searching for the best part of you in every nigga she meets. I told you that before . . . that if you moved incorrectly . . . if you went away, got locked up, died . . . the woman you love would spend her life trying to identify you in other men. You went away and you came back and not one, but two men have ties to your girl. You gave them opportunity. The nigga Bash ain't no problem. You can sweep him up out the way with ease, but Ahmeek, the nigga you ran with, the nigga you got money with . . . she smiles with him Messiah. If you ever want to get her back you got to learn how to ease her pain, not cause it. You got to man the fuck up. There's a competition for her heart and right now you're losing. What you willing to do to get your girl back? What you willing to endure to fix what you broke? Because it's hard work. It's painful and if you ain't gon' see it through to the end don't even get her hopes up. Don't even start if you not gon' finish it. But if you love her, you fight for her and you tear yourself apart to build her back up. It was easy making her love you the first time because you were all she knew. Now she knows better. Now she's had others. Only the best man will win."

Messiah bit back his emotion as Ethic put a firm hand to his shoulder.

"Let's go see about that hand," Ethic stated. "The best man will win indeed. Better make sure it's you."

20

Morgan hadn't realized how much she missed this type of silence. The deafening silence. The ominous silence. The kind that nothing penetrated. Not the drip of leaky sink. Not the call of a bird outside of a window. Not even the hum of the machines around her. She heard nothing. She felt the tears though. Felt her heart beating. Felt her mind spinning. Her gut tensing. She couldn't believe he had smacked her. The side of her face was swollen, lip busted, and the makings of a bruise was forming near her ear.

Alani sat near the bedside holding Messari as Yara colored on the floor. Alani had come prepared. With a bag full of distractions for the twins and Morgan was grateful for her help. She felt the squeeze of her hand and Morgan didn't turn her head to look but she gave a squeeze back. Her life felt like it was in shambles. The man she wanted she couldn't have. The man she hated, she kind of also loved, and the one she was indifferent about she had hurt. Nobody deserved to be hurt. She was dead wrong, and she told herself that when she was out of the hospital she owed Bash an apology. If she had made him feel even a fraction of what Messiah made her feel, she wasn't shit. Still, even with Messiah putting hands on her, she felt him in her soul. She had wondered why she had always lived with him. He lingered in the deepest chambers of her heart. There was just an energy she felt. A whisper to her soul. Like he was somewhere out there calling out to her, "Shorty." Now she knew why. Alani lifted Mo's hand in the palm of one hand. Their eyes met and then Alani swept her hand across the injured side of Morgan's face.

"Ethic's on his way up," Alani said. Morgan read her lips and nodded. "I'm going to head out with the twins. Get them to bed. We'll be back in the morning, okay?"

Morgan nodded and then swung her feet over the edge of the bed to stand. She picked up Messari and kissed his cheek then bent to scoop Yara. She hugged her daughter tight and then handed her off to Alani.

They made their way out and Morgan sat there, feeling shut off from the world. It wasn't as bad as she remembered. When she was younger being deaf had felt like a flaw. Right now. With chaos in the hearing world, she felt lucky to be able to turn it all off. Ethic pushed open the door and Morgan's lip trembled. He always made everything better. He was comfort, but when she saw Messiah step in after him it felt like a bomb had detonated inside her.

"Why is he here?" she shouted. She didn't even care that she didn't know how she sounded. She had to scream. Needed to yell.

"Shorty, can I just talk to you for a minute? I'm sorry, Mo," he pleaded. Morgan's entire body trembled, and she broke down, tears running down her pretty cheeks as he approached her. "Your face. Your ears, I'm so sor—"

Morgan was on top of Messiah before he could even finish his sentence. She swung.

"How could you?!" she shouted. She didn't even care how she sounded. She screamed those words from the pit of her soul. "I hate you!" Her fists flew so viciously, and Messiah folded into her, wrapping his arms around her waist, burying his face into her breasts as she beat him. "How fucking dare you! Fuck you! You left me here to die!" She connected with the back of his head and Messiah allowed her to get her blows off. He could feel her soul cry and in his twisted heart, he absorbed those punches as love taps. He cherished every painful blow because for so long he hadn't felt her at all. Even absorbing her hate felt like love.

This wasn't about the slap. This was for it all. This was an outpouring of all the hurt he had left her with.

"I NEEDED YOU!"

"Morgan!" Ethic shouted, moving to intercept her.

"Nah, O.G. Let her get this off," Messiah said as Ethic stood between them, bear hugging Morgan.

Morgan lunged for Messiah, but Ethic's hold was too strong. She grabbed the remote control off the bed and tossed it at him. "Get the fuck out!" Everything in her reach flew across the room.

"Morgan!" Ethic barked.

"Do you know what you did?!" she cried. She picked up the blood pressure monitor and tossed it. It crashed into pieces at Messiah's feet. The pillows. The box of gloves that sat on the stand by the bed, the IV. Everything within reach became bullets that she wanted to send his way. Morgan wanted to kill him.

Messiah dodged all the items, stepping back, then placing both hands on top of his head in despair. He didn't know how to stop this. How to control it. She was so damn mad.

"Shorty! Let me just get a word. I'm sorry. Baby I'm sorry. Let me—"

"GET OUT!" Morgan yelled. "That's all you're good for anyway!"

Ethic could barely contain Morgan. He had witnessed a lot of meltdowns by Morgan, but he had never seen her like this.

Messiah was dejected. His heart fucking split. "Shorty, please man—"

A nurse entered the room. "Sir, I'm going to have to ask you to leave."

"I can't man! She's mine. She belongs to me. Shorty, you belong to me. Mo, baby."

Morgan's face was buried in Ethic's chest and she was sobbing so badly that Messiah's eyes filled.

"Sir, don't make us call security."

"Bitch, I'll put a bullet through your skull. She here. This where I'ma be."

Messiah refused to leave, and Morgan refused to look at him. He focused on Morgan. On Morgan in Ethic's arms. Why couldn't she run to him like that? Why couldn't she seek comfort in him just like fucking that? He wanted to kill Ethic just so he could take his place. He wanted to be her security. Instead, he was her turmoil.

"Messiah," Ethic stated.

Messiah swiped a hand down his face, clearing tears he didn't even know had fallen. She was gutting him. This reunion was going so much differently than what he had imagined in his mind.

"Ethic, please, man, I just want her. She's my Shorty."

"Messiah." Ethic's voice held a tone that was forceful but empathetic. So much heartbreak in the room. Grief. Angst. Regret. Messiah had been gone for too long. Too much had changed, and that change was terrifying him.

Messiah knew there was no bargaining. Ethic didn't need to say more. He had already repeated the order twice.

"A nigga love you with his whole heart. That mu'fucka beat the fuck up and it don't always work how it's supposed to, Shorty but it's yours. I'm sorry, Mo."

Security came into the room.

"Sir, we have to escort you off the premises," the uniformed officer said. He made the mistake of touching Messiah and he spazzed, slapping the officer's hand so violently that he reached for his gun.

Ethic reached for his.

"I promise you I'm a quicker draw. They gon' be asking if white lives matter if you don't get your hand off that gun," Ethic stated.

The officer lifted four fingers off the gun but kept his hand ready. So did Ethic. Tension thickened the air in the room, and Messiah's eyes burned into Morgan's, pleading with her.

"He's leaving. He doesn't need to be escorted out. Won't be no handcuffs. No guns drawn. He's a man. He's going to walk out on his own two," Ethic stated.

"Let me get right with you Shorty," Messiah signed. "I want to come home."

"No! I don't want to be half-loved. I'm too full of life for that, Messiah! You don't commit. You say that you will and then you pull out. You lie and you deceive and you disappear!" she signed. "I begged you!"

"I love you, Mo."

"Fuck you. Fuck your love. Fuck what you did. I loved you all the way and you left me. You spit on what we had, and you LEFT ME!" Morgan was signing the words so hard that her entire body rocked as she cried. "Then you come back, and you act like I owe you something. You want to raise hell and make a scene because I'm with Ahmeek, like HE owes you something. We don't owe you shit. You've been dead to us for two years! He's good to me Messiah. Before it was anything else, before it turned into anything else he was my friend. I owe you nothing. You destroyed me."

She turned her head toward the window and Messiah lifted his gaze to Ethic.

"Please man." It didn't even sound like his voice. His heart was in his stomach and he wanted to stay but he couldn't. Not yet because hearing her talk about Ahmeek like she loved him, defending him, praising him, it made a fire kindle inside his chest. He didn't want to love her wrong. He didn't want to hurt her more and he feared what he would do if he stayed. Ethic was right. He had to get right for her. He had to grow up. He had to learn self-control. He had never possessed that but if he wanted to ever gain her adoration again he would have to learn it. "I'll be better for her, man. I'll do whatever it takes."

Messiah was breaking, and Ethic's heart was torn down the middle. Messiah was like a son to him in a lot of ways. They shared this hurt.

"Just tell her to give me a chance. To listen to me, O.G."

Ethic turned to Mo, taking her trembling chin in his hand and forcing her to look at him.

"I know it hurts," he signed. "But this is a second chance, Mo. You got to think about everybody, not just you. About your family, Morgan. Hear him out."

Morgan pierced Messiah with her stare. Those pretty ass eyes, eyes he had stared into for hours now marked him. He felt so privileged.

"I can't hear you, Messiah," she signed to him, chest heaving, tears flowing. "You take everything. Took my heart. My life, Messiah. You hit me so hard I can't hear. You took my hearing, Messiah. You took my soul! I was lost without you, and I waited for you to come find me! To come help me! I needed so much help and you never looked back! You didn't come back for me! Ain't no home here. Not anymore. Get the fuck out my room."

Messiah took a step forward.

"Messiah!"

His name halted him. Ethic's voice boomed holding enough weight to keep Messiah from pressing the issue further. Ethic shook his head. "She needs some time."

Ethic's bark was close to becoming a bite and Messiah had to grit his teeth to stop his chin from quivering. They were his family. His people. Ethic and Morgan, and they were putting him out.

Walking out of the hospital took great effort. He wanted to be selfish. He wanted to force his way back into her life, but he couldn't. She was home, but she had changed the locks and Messiah would have to figure out a new way to get inside her heart.

21

Pullllll uppppp
Boy pull down on me
And go downnnn on meeee

Aria laid under Isa's arm, one thigh wrapped around his thin torso, as he placed the blunt to her lips. Ann Marie's voice whispered to them in the background, thumping through the speakers so low that they almost couldn't hear the music. He looked down at her as she inhaled. She closed her eyes and held the smoke for a beat before lifting her chin and filling the room with clouds.

"Morgan is so fucked up," Aria whispered.

"Shit, I'm fucked up," Isa said. "Every mu'fucking hair on the back of my neck stood up when I heard my nigga voice."

"What happens now?" Aria asked.

"We mind our business, Ali," Isa said. "And you suck a little dick for a nigga."

Aria climbed on top of him. "You talk so much." She snickered as she moved to the top of the bed, hovering over his face. She placed hands on the headboard. "Put something in your mouth so you can say less."

"Hmm," he groaned. He lifted the blunt with one hand, passing it off to her then planted both hands on her ass, lifting her a little. Aria hit the blunt, causing her head to spin as Isa captured her peach. Her back arched as she rode his face to the beat.

His phone rang, and Isa lifted her with one hand, then pulled his phone out his pocket with the other.

"You stop to answer that phone and see what's going to happen," she threatened.

Isa peered down at the screen. "Yo, it's bro, hol' up," he said.

He put Aria down and she huffed her displeasure, crossing her arms and tilting her head to the side.

"Casper the friendly ghost ass nigga," Isa answered. Aria popped him upside his head.

"Damn Ali!" he shouted, wincing as he turned to her, light eyes burning into her. A warning. His large hand wrapped around her neck. "You want me to fuck you up," he said.

Aria's brow raised in challenge. "That's exactly what I want, now get off the phone."

Isa snickered and shook his head as he put Messiah on speaker phone.

"My bad bruh, what up? You got a lot of fucking explaining to do, G," Isa said.

"Yeah I know man. Meet me at the spot," Messiah's voice entered the bedroom.

"Yup," Isa replied and then hung up. He leaned over to Aria. "I gotta go. Wait up for me."

Aria rolled her eyes as Isa rolled up from the bed, still pinching the blunt in her fingers.

"Fuck you, I'm going to sleep."

Isa reached for a fresh shirt and slid it over his head, then retrieved his gun from the night stand, tucking it in behind him. "Yo, that wedding shit. I want to get on top of that. Get that shit together. Messiah put his toy down for a little while and now it ain't his no more. I want my name on my toy," Isa stated.

"So I'm an object?" she asked, brow lifted in challenge.

"Here you go putting words in my mouth, man," Isa said. He walked over to her as she stood on her knees in the bed. He gripped her chin, pursing her lips then kissed her so hard it felt like her lips would bruise. "Annoying little ass." He pushed her back onto the bed and then turned for the door. "Start planning nigga. White dress, stupid ass suits, all'at!"

She heard the door slam and she shook her head. She knew marrying a man like Isa was unwise. The life he led was dangerous. It was reckless but damn he was electric. Every time he looked at her Aria felt a challenge in his stare, like she couldn't blink because the nigga would win her over. Everything about them was a power struggle and she loved it. Rock, paper, scissors over her heart. He always put law down when he saw her. Didn't matter if it had been days or a few hours, he reminded her who she belonged too. It felt amazing to be coveted so dearly. She looked at her wrists and fingered the marks on them. Bruises. From the ties. Her skin was so soft that evidence of his preferences had been left behind. Aria wondered if they would last, if she could handle him forever. If she could take the pain he got off on forever. She had given him her body. She had taken his mind in return, but she was nervous about combining their souls. Isa had the ability to shatter her. He already had once before. As she looked down at the ring on her finger she took a deep breath. Nahvid hated Isa. If she went through with this wedding she knew her brother would never support it. Isa was an acquired taste and he wasn't the type of man to put on a show to gain favor. There would be no sucking up to earn acceptance and Aria feared losing her brother. She didn't want to have to sacrifice her relationship with her brother for the sake of love. Aria was terrified to merge her world with Isa's, but it was inevitable. She only hoped that she wasn't making a huge mistake.

22

The hours that passed on the clock filled Ethic with a canyon-sized hole as he paced the hallways of the hospital. Morgan had been taken into surgery hours ago and he had gotten no word of progress yet. He was conflicted. He wanted to be there for Morgan. He wanted to support her decisions, but he felt like he was abandoning his son. Messiah's heartbreak resonated through Ethic like he was experiencing it himself. Ethic reached into his pocket and retrieved his wallet, pulling out a few loose dollar bills as he made his way down the hall toward the waiting room. He steeled when he stepped into the small room. Ahmeek sat alone, elbows to knees, head bowed, hands moving down his waves. He looked up over his brow, then arose placing one hand on his thigh, leaning back.

Ethic stared at him, jaw tense, temple throbbing. He was too mentally exhausted to even fight this battle.

"She's still in surgery," he said. He stepped up to the vending machine and put the money inside. The room was silent. The sound of the chip bag resounded loudly as it hit the bottom. Then Ethic inserted more money. The second item fell, and Ethic retrieved both. He tossed one to Ahmeek who caught it out of thin air.

Ethic sat across from Ahmeek, leaning over onto his knees, keen eyes on Meek.

"Messiah's back," Ethic stated.

"I'm aware," Ahmeek answered.

"And what does that mean for you?" Ethic asked.

"Means I'ma have to let go," he stated.

Ethic sat back, shocked by Ahmeek's answer. Not many people surprised Ezra Okafor. He had mastered the art of summation long ago and normally his first impression of a person was the right one. His first impression of Ahmeek had been wrong however.

"I could hold on. Mo would let me. I think she feels strongly enough to hold onto me on one side, but he's got a hold on her too. If we both pulling at her, it'll break her. So I'ma let her go."

It was the first time Ethic felt something other than disdain for Ahmeek. It was what every father wanted for his daughter . . . for her to find a man who would put her needs before his own. The magnitude of Messiah's fuck ups filled the waiting room. Ethic was a man who always knew how to react. Here and now, he was speechless. Meek stood.

"Tell her I was here," Ahmeek said as he walked toward the door.

"Tell her yourself," Ethic stated. "You waited all this time. Might as well see her open her eyes. They're removing the implant and inserting the new one all at the same time, so it will be a while."

Ahmeek stalled and Ethic shook his head. "Sit down, man. Morgan ain't gon' worry me with you lovesick mu'fuckas," he grumbled.

They sat in there for hours and when a woman walked into the waiting room Ethic looked up in shock.

"Meekie baby, have you heard anything yet?"

Ethic looked at the woman.

"Not yet, Ma," Ahmeek answered.

Ethic's mind was blown. He had no idea how deeply Morgan had infiltrated Ahmeek's life. For his mother to show up at the hospital spoke volumes. Ethic hated that a part of him wanted Morgan to have a man who had a sense of normalcy to him. A mother like this, willing to come to the hospital, to sit with her son while he waited on a woman he cared for, meant Ahmeek had been raised well. It meant Morgan wouldn't be doing the raising of a grown man.

"Ma, this is Morgan's father, Ethic," Ahmeek introduced.

"Ezra," Ethic corrected as he extended his hand. Marilyn shook it.

"Marilyn," the woman introduced. "Now which one of you want to tell me what happened?"

The corner of Ethic's mouth lifted in amusement. Marilyn was indeed a real mother, coming in taking over, demanding answers.

"Did you do this boy? You said there was a fight on the phone and that she was hit. I know damn well . . ."

"Messiah's back Ma," Ahmeek stated. He doubled, and Marilyn placed a hand on her son's back as Ethic sat back absorbing the entire scene. "He's not dead. I don't know where he's been all this time, but he's back and he showed up at Mo's place and I was there and things got out of hand." He paused, glancing up at Ethic because he wouldn't speak the sequence of events after that. He wouldn't sell Messiah out to Ethic. Ethic respected it.

"I already know what happened next," Ethic answered.

"He hit her?" she asked.

"It wasn't intentional. We came to blows and she was just in the way," Ahmeek said. It wasn't exactly how it had gone down, but close enough.

"Did you win?" Marilyn asked.

Ethic lost his cool and released a stubborn chuckle. "I like you a whole lot more than I like your son," Ethic stated.

"Ain't no liking me without liking my son," Marilyn stated frankly, staring Ethic in the eyes.

"Understood," Ethic answered with the nod of his head. Yeah, she was a real mother. She was someone Morgan needed. He was willing to bet that Morgan had enjoyed whatever time she had spent in this woman's presence.

"She's a lovely girl," Marilyn added.

Morgan's doctor came to the waiting room, interrupting them and all three of them stood.

"She's in recovery. The surgery went well. There was bleeding in her inner ear that was draining into her sinuses. She'll be in some pain this time around because we had to go deeper to repair that, but after she heals she'll be good as new. You can follow me if you'd like to sit with her until she awakens."

Ethic extended his hand for Marilyn to pass first and then watched as Ahmeek and his mother followed the doctor to Mo's room. He stood near the door as Ahmeek and Marilyn entered. It disturbed him that Ahmeek loved Morgan. He could see it. His affection for Morgan was obvious. He wore it on his being like it was an accessory . . . one he couldn't take off. When Marilyn placed her hands around one of Morgan's and began to pray Ethic had to turn toward the hall. It reminded him of the love Alani gave. It tore him up inside because Messiah couldn't give Morgan this. There was no doubt in his mind that Messiah loved Morgan more, but he didn't love her better. Ahmeek had perfected his love for Morgan. Ahmeek came with a family that could become Mo's family. He came with a mother that would hold her son accountable. A mother that could become a grandmother to children they might have. Ahmeek was putting an entire life on the table for Morgan. All Messiah could offer was himself. It hardly seemed like a fair fight. Ahmeek's love was potent and Ethic was forced to respect it.

Ahmeek leaned down and whispered in her ear. "I'm sorry, Mo. You ever need me, all you got to do is drop that location. I'm coming to you every time, love." He planted a kiss to her forehead and then forced himself to leave her there.

"You don't want to stay until she wakes up?" Marilyn asked.

"She asked me to leave. I just wanted to make sure she pulled through the surgery," Ahmeek stated. His voice was solemn. Ethic felt that shit. He had lived it. The burden of being without the woman you loved was unbearable to a man and Ethic knew that pain well. *Damn*, he thought. Both Messiah and Ahmeek loved Morgan Atkins but she could only choose one. He had a feeling she cared for them both and as he watched Meek and his mother disappear onto the elevator a part of him rooted for the young king. Another part of him, the part that had raised the underdog, the part that loved Messiah like family, wanted Mo to choose Messiah. Ethic knew the demons Messiah came with however and he was terrified to hand Morgan over to him. He had no idea how things would shake out. Life was complicated, and Morgan's heart was on the line. He had a nagging feeling that the best man might not win.

23

Messiah stood in the middle of the basketball court, dribbling lazily, between his legs, playing with the rock like it was attached to a string. The ball went where he wanted it to go. Pure skill. In another life he could have been a ball player, but in this one he was a killer. Nike hoop shorts, a wife beater, and retro Jordans. The sound of the rubber bouncing off the hardwood floors echoed in the vast gym. He hadn't been here in a long time. The last time he had left a man's teeth in the stands and caused a brawl. The metal doors clanged loudly, announcing Isa's arrival.

"Bruh bruh," Isa greeted as he swaggered into the gym, a Styrofoam cup resting in his hands. He tipped it to his lips, coming in so casually, it was like he and Messiah had been meeting on Saturday every week. It had been years since Isa had been face to face with Messiah but their ebb and flow was undisturbed.

"What up, G?" Messiah greeted, slapping Isa's hand and then leaning in to tap shoulders with Isa.

"Yo' ass," Isa said, pausing to sip then smirking. "You been in the cut nigga? Got niggas out here thinking we laid you down and shit."

"I had to disappear for a minute. Put my ducks in a row. You understand?"

"I feel that," Isa answered.

"A lot of shit done changed I see. Not you though. Real nigga didn't switch up," Messiah noted. They fell into their normal routine. Handshakes. The gangster kind with details they'd made up as boys. Messiah pulled back and threw up a jump shot.

"That jumper still wet, nigga," Isa snickered.

"I ain't missing no shots. Buckets or bullets," Messiah said. "I'm in the mood to shoot. Ya' man got me fucked up."

Isa knew it was coming. A reunion wasn't the only reason Messiah had summoned him. He wanted information.

"Yeah that's rough, G. Real rough to see your girl be his girl, but no lie bro, that's *his* girl. They been on it heavy and it ain't even Meek style to fuck with one bitch like that, but he's fucking with Mo the long way. Because you asked him to. You told him to, G. You got ghost and that's your business. You had to move how you had to move, but you left niggas behind with a hole to fill. Everybody needed somebody bro. We ain't know what to do besides kill shit. Lit so many mu'fuckas up behind what we was feeling because the shit hurt like a mu'fucka. Then that between them happened and shit you gave the okay so as fucked as it is, it is what it is. That nigga in deep with Mo. Same way you used to be, but you left her behind bruh. You knew niggas wasn't gon' let Mo rot on the shelf. At least you know she's been taken care of. Cuz one thing bro gon' do is take care of her. Same as you. You could have come back to some bum ass nigga laying hands on her or you could have found her fucked up and being passed from nigga to nigga because she was lost after you. Shit could be worse, G.

I know the shit got to burn but it ain't all black and white. You niggas need to have a conversation."

"I ain't got shit to say to Meek. If my gun ain't barking what we talking bout? I'm home now. He got to run Shorty back my way. If he ain't trying to talk about that I want smoke and that don't require talking. I'm with that action," Messiah said, his temple throbbing in rage.

"Fuck you talking about, G? We don't bring no smoke over no pussy. That nigga fed you before we were on. Snuck you in his mama crib so you wouldn't have to sleep on the streets before you started getting money—"

"So I'm supposed to just let shit ride?" Messiah bit back. "Fuck that."

"Let me ask you something, bruh? Where's Mo, right now?" Isa asked.

Messiah's stomach hollowed because he knew if Isa was asking then he knew her location.

"It ain't up to you, G. It ain't up to Meek neither, low key. That's why I don't choose females like Mo. She'll fuck up a nigga soul with the bullshit. My bitch keep ten toes in the sand and if a nigga send me up out of here, she ain't gon' fold. She ain't gon' need another nigga to see her through the shit cuz she's a soldier. A fucking goon on her own. Mo's soft. She fell apart and she needed strength. You told him to give her some of his. Now here we are," Isa said. "It ain't right and it ain't wrong because they thought you were gone, G. It's just fucked up for everybody. I ain't falling out with my brothers over pussy that I ain't hitting, so you niggas got to come to terms with what it's going to be."

Messiah hated to hear it, but he knew Isa was right. It still didn't ease the burn. It still seared him. He had only given his blessing because he was supposed to die. What was a man to do when the woman he loved deserted him and his friend became her safe haven? Messiah had never felt so stripped. He had walked away from Mo and the space between them felt monumental. It felt like an ocean lay between them and Messiah had no boat to cross it.

"She gon' drown me, bro," Messiah whispered. "All this air around me and it don't even reach my lungs without Shorty."

Isa remained quiet and Messiah shook his head, then stubbornly flicked his nose before standing. "I'm out of here, man. I got to go grocery shopping and shit."

Isa burst into laughter, balling a fist up in front of his mouth as his eyes danced with humor. "Your ass don't cook. Fuck you going grocery shopping for? Ol' domesticated ass nigga."

Messiah grinned and shook his head. "Condition of me coming back I guess. Ethic's ol' lady is pregnant. Need help carrying the bags and shit," Messiah snickered. "Get with me, man."

Messiah made it halfway across the gym when Isa beckoned him.

"Yo, bruh!"

Messiah turned to him. "You look like an ol' R&B ass nigga with the fade, G. Trey Songz ass nigga," Isa cracked, laughing before sipping from his cup.

Messiah snickered. "Fuck you, man."

"I'm glad you're home bro. My motherfucking nigga. I ain't on no sucka shit, but it feel real good, G."

Messiah nodded and threw up a hand in salute before walking out.

Messiah pulled up to the Flint Farmer's Market and blew out a breath of frustration. The marketplace of vendors was thriving with energy as local businesses put their goods on display for the passersby.

"All these fucking people, man," he muttered as he picked up his phone. He put it on speaker and placed a call.

"Hello?"

The pretty voice filled the interior of his car. Alani sounded like an angel. Her voice was so soft and peaceful that he almost felt disrespectful even tainting her space. Everything about this meet up made him uncomfortable. She had a way of getting him to say more than he wanted to, and Messiah hated it. In just their one interaction she had opened his soul, like a window she was lifting to air out a dank room.

"Yo, I just pulled up," he announced.

"Is that Messiah?" He heard Eazy's excitement and a smile pulled at the corners of his lips.

"Yeah, it's Messiah. He's here. Go out front and get him," Alani instructed Eazy. "He'll meet you up front."

Messiah hung up the phone and lifted from the car. He swaggered across the parking lot, gripping his dick, and neck on a swivel as his eyes swept over the crowd.

"Messiah over here!"

Eazy stood with his hand stretched in the air and jumping to get Messiah's attention. Messiah smirked, his heavy heart lightening at first sight. Eazy was always welcoming of Messiah. He was always happy to see him, and Messiah felt a bit of comfort that at least one person reacted to him the same.

"Big man with the master plan, what's good?" Messiah greeted. He slapped hands with Eazy like he was dapping up a grown man and then ruffled the top of his head. "You done got big, man. Strong. Probably got a fly lil' girlfriend you hiding and everything, huh?"

Eazy's face dipped in discomfort as he blushed, turning red. "No way. Ma would annihilate me!"

"Annihilate huh?" Messiah chuckled. "That's a big word man. You still smart as shit, I see." Messiah was shocked that

Eazy was referring to Alani as "Ma." It was a huge step. It was just one more indication that time had passed him by. That these people he once knew well had evolved and he was stuck in their routine of two years ago. It compounded his regret. Like interest the remorse of leaving a world he knew behind was overwhelming.

"Dad told me you died. How did you come back?" Eazy asked.

"Cuz I'm a super hero man," Messiah said, flexing his muscle.

"Super heroes aren't real!" Eazy shouted.

"Now I know you tripping. You live with one. Yo' pops is a super hero like a mu'fucka," Messiah countered. The perplexity on Eazy's face made Messiah snicker.

"Hey guys over here!"

Messiah looked up and Alani stood there, hand on hip, belly extending out of the long summer sundress she wore. Her hair was middle parted and hung long down her back and white Chuck Taylors graced her feet. She hadn't tried at all, yet she was stunning. Messiah held his breath as he took her in. He and Eazy made their way to Alani and Messiah frowned as he rubbed the back of his neck sheepishly.

"Big crowd."

"You'll be fine," Alani replied, smiling. "Can you grab that basket for me?"

Messiah grabbed one of the red handheld baskets and Eazy did as well.

"I got it covered," Messiah stated.

"She'll need both. She goes crazzyyy here," Eazy said.

Messiah laughed and followed Alani back into the market.

"Grab me some of those peaches," Alani instructed as she stopped at a farmer's booth. She focused on the elderly black man behind the table. "Hey Mr. Clemons, you order my fresh mint seeds yet?"

"Yes ma'am. Ordered and planted 'em already just for you. They'll bloom in a few weeks and I'll bring 'em then," the man answered. "This here the lucky bastard that get to call you his wife?"

Eazy laughed. "Mr. Clemons this is just Messiah!"

"He's family," Alani explained. "Messiah this is Mr. Clemons."

Messiah nodded but didn't say more as he grabbed a few peaches.

Alani reached into her handbag to pay but Messiah slid the man a twenty-dollar bill before she could pull out her wallet.

Alani smiled. "Thank you."

"It's no problem," he answered.

"So are you happy to be home?" Alani asked.

"Happy isn't the word I'd use," Messiah answered.

Eazy ran ahead of them and Messiah smirked at the way the nine-year-old maneuvered through the market. All the vendors spoke to him and Messiah knew this was a routine that Alani did with him often. It was consistent, dependable. It was something that seemed simple or even cumbersome at first glance but it was love through interaction. It was habitual. A shared experience between mother and son. Messiah's gut filled with angst. He'd never had that.

"I think its dope what you did with Ethic and his family," Messiah said. "Being there with them, I mean. Forgiving how you do."

"They're my family too, Messiah. I don't know you very well but I think it's pretty safe to say that they're your family too," Alani said. She turned to a woman who sold natural honey. "Hi Linda. It's really good to see you."

"You too, Lenika!" the woman answered jovially. "You keep a big, strong man with you I see!" The woman smiled as she looked at Messiah. "They take real good care of you too!"

Alani laughed. "I think I'm the one doing the taking care of. I'm loved well however. I can't complain," she said as she picked up two bottles of the golden elixir on display. "I'll take these. This is Messiah. Messiah meet Linda."

"Oh, he's a heartbreaker," Linda said.

"He's been known to break a heart or two. We're working on fixing that," Alani said, smiling.

Alani set the honey inside the basket Messiah carried and when they stepped away from the booth Alani turned to him. "You said you were sick when you left? Sick with what?"

"Cancer," Messiah answered.

Alani stopped walking and turned eyes of surprise up to him. "Messiah . . ."

"I wouldn't leave her for nothing," Messiah said.

"Morgan needs to know that Messiah. The key to her heart is information Messiah. You can't decide what she deserves to be privy to. She'll come back to you if you just tell her where you were and why you left."

"Nah," Messiah declined. "If all she got is sympathy love, I don't want that shit. I'll never let her think I'm weak. Ever. I've always been strong for Mo. I'ma always be strong for her. She don't need to know that."

"You two are more alike than you know," Alani said sadly. "So many secrets Messiah. You and Mo won't ever heal if you don't have transparency. She can't love lies Messiah. What if she forgives you and the cancer comes back? What if you get sick again? Will you leave again? What if you die Messiah? She's mourned you once. You're going to make her lose you all over again? That sounds cruel doesn't it?"

Messiah's brow bent in confusion and he blew out a sharp breath.

"I don't know how to love her right, man. Every time I think I'm doing something for her, it ends up being for me and

I'm just lost on all this shit. Feels like I should have just stayed gone," Messiah griped.

"No Messiah. You should have never left. Morgan is your family. You have an entire group of people here who love you. You don't have to give up on them before they give up on you, because one thing about those Okafors is they don't leave. Even when you've hurt them, they love you anyway," Alani said, speaking from experience. "You take care of the ones you love, and they'll take care of you. We're all here for you. We're kind of all we have. I don't know you well, but my husband loves you. Mo loves you too no matter what she says. My entire family is smitten with you. No more running Messiah. From the past or the present. We're here for you, okay?"

Messiah felt empty inside like Alani was snatching out everything he had put there to keep him tough. All the bricks of anger and aggression he had built up to stop people from getting to the core of him. Alani was moving all the bricks around. He felt open. Like she had come through with an emotional gun and aired the whole damn farmer's market out.

He nodded and gritted his teeth, his temple throbbing.

"Love is a weapon if you don't use it right," Alani said. "Disarm yourself, Messiah."

Alani moved onto the next booth where Eazy's busy hands were picking up every item. She left Messiah reeling with thoughts of all the ways he had used his love against Morgan. He had so much making up to do. He prayed she gave him the chance to make things right.

24

Morgan lay in her old room at Ethic's. It felt good to be there. The sound of her babies running through the huge house and the smell of breakfast floating through the air made these walls sing in contentment. It was a home. A loud one, because Eazy's game blared in the background, mixing with the sounds of old school 90's R&B that Alani was playing. She was happy to hear the noise at all. Three weeks had passed since her surgery and recovery had been excruciating. She still had some time to go before the pain went away. She wasn't even supposed to have the transmitters on at all, but she needed her ears. She needed them turned back on. She had been desperate to hear . . . to see if she would be able to hear again so they had turned them on and every single sound in this house was blaring. She reached for her phone.

Three texts.

- Aria
- Bash
- 810-785-1325

The number that hadn't been assigned was Messiah's. She didn't even want to store his name.

Her heart sank. Nothing from Ahmeek.

Morgan deleted Messiah's message without reading it. There was nothing to say. No communication to be had. He was hoping her anger had waned. It hadn't. She was leaving no room for him in her life.

A knock at the door pulled her attention away from her phone.

"Come in," she called. Her voice was soft, as low as she could speak because even her own voice bounced around in her head like a bowling ball colliding with pins. The headache was loud.

Alani walked in, a large floral arrangement and a box in her hands.

"I don't want them," Morgan said.

"They're just flowers, Mo," Alani replied, smiling sympathetically. "They're beautiful."

Alani placed the arrangement on Mo's nightstand. Morgan reached for the card.

To my Shorty,
I'm sorry.
Messiah

Morgan shook her head and placed the card facedown on the nightstand.

"Something else came," Alani said, handing her the box. Morgan frowned. It was addressed to her, but no return address was written on it. She peeled back the tape and opened the box and her heart ached. It was so tender. Bruised. Because the sender of this package had shot an arrow right through it.

She removed the framed picture. It was small, but it was

perfect. The day at the zoo. A sticky note was inside the frame as well.

> You're my fucking person, love.
> —Ahmeek

Morgan's eyes betrayed her. The sticky note might have been better than the picture. A *Grey's Anatomy* reference that only they would understand. The part she cried on no matter how many times she watched the show. Her favorite episode. Derek and Meredith. Ahmeek and Morgan. Ahmeek made Morgan Atkins feel like she had a person. The unbelievable urge to see him filled her as Alani picked up the frame.

"It's a beautiful picture, Mo," she said.

"Is it bad that I still want him?" Morgan whispered.

"No," Alani answered. "It's not, Mo, but I think you should take some time to figure out what you really want."

The door was pushed open and Yara ran in.

"Yolly Pop!" Morgan signed. "Come here, big girl!"

Yara bounced all the way to her mother and Morgan picked her up.

"Is it a possibility that you might let Messiah into their lives?" Alani asked, looking at Yara sadly. "He's their father, Mo."

"And what if he hurts them?" Morgan asked. "What if he's back to hurt Ethic or you or me?"

"Do you really think that?" Alani asked.

"I don't know what to think when it comes to Messiah," she said. "When I saw him at my party, I forgot everything. I forgot what he did and the things he said. I just wanted to touch him . . . to make sure he was real. I'm glad he's okay. I've never felt relief like that. Seeing him—" Morgan paused and wiped away a stray tear. "If he was alive all this time it meant he chose to leave me. He chose to stay away. I was here dying and where was he?" Morgan shook her head. "I don't know. I just want to feel safe. I don't feel safe with him anymore. It's like I don't even know him. The man I knew would have never deserted me."

"He's their father. At some point you will have to try to get to know him. Even if you never be with him again. They have a right to know their dad and he has a right to know his kids. He would never hurt them. I honestly don't think Messiah could ever hurt you, Mo. I'll take her downstairs with her brother. I'll send Bella up with something for the pain." Alani stood. "Come on Yolly Pop." Alani walked out of the room and Morgan's mind spun.

Morgan dropped her location to Ahmeek. She wondered if she had dreamt the words. She had heard them clear as day while she was in the hospital. How, she didn't know because her transmitters hadn't been turned on yet. She hoped he called, hoped he just showed up. She held her phone, staring as anxiety bubbled in her gut. Her eyes glistened. He wasn't calling, and the sadness that consumed her was overwhelming. This thing with Ahmeek had transformed overnight into something she could have never seen coming. Something real. How had this happened?

She showered and dressed, pulling her wet hair into a sleek top knot.

"Morgan!"

Bella's voice echoed up the stairs and she made her way out.

"Why are you yelling, B? You know my ears . . ."

She stopped walking when she saw him. Ahmeek stood by the door talking to Ethic, hands in his pocket, head nodding as Ethic spoke sternly to him. Why was he this fine? Casual in denim and a blue and white Dodgers jersey. Shining in a gold Cuban link chain around his neck and a matching one on his wrist. Watch game always official, a Rolex rested on the other. When he lifted eyes to her, hers misted. Yara came running at Ahmeek full speed and he bent to scoop her.

"This is who I want to see," he said. "Princess Yolly!"

"Meek!" Messari shouted as he too ran to the door.

Ethic looked at her in surprise. The more Ethic saw, the more he realized how much Ahmeek had been around.

Ahmeek bent down so that he was eye level with Messari. "My homie," he greeted, chuckling. "Yo, you think I can borrow your mommy for a little while? She belongs to you, so I got to get clearance."

Messari nodded as Yara rested her head on his shoulder. Ethic and Alani stood at the bottom of the steps. She felt like she was going to prom. Like they were waiting for her to descend in her fancy dress and take pictures with her date.

"What you think, love? You feel good enough to come take a ride with me for a minute?" he asked.

Morgan wanted to say yes, but she truly didn't feel good at all. "I'm in a little pain." She could barely choke out the words. She wanted to say, FUCK THAT PAIN, but even her footsteps against the wooden floors seemed to reverberate in her head, like bombs going off. It was just too soon to be out.

"Why don't you just stay for a while, Ahmeek?" Alani invited.

"Why don't he what?" Ethic chimed in.

"Ezra." Alani's tone changed, and Ethic knew he should quit while he was ahead. Ethic blew out a sharp breath. "Help me get these babies outside. They've been cooped up all day." Alani took Yara from Ahmeek and nodded to Messari. "Get him," Alani said. "Bella, Eazy! Come to the backyard. We're going to work on the garden while Daddy gets the grill going." She was a marvel of a woman. She had domesticated a beast.

Morgan finally descended the steps when they were alone.

"The sticky note," she said, smiling.

He leaned against the front door, finessing his beard.

"A little lame. I'm embarrassed as fuck, love. Let's not bring that up again," he said, smirking. "Can't believe you got me hooked on that girlie ass show."

"It's not lame," Morgan whispered. "Not even a little. I miss you."

"Ditto, love," he answered, rubbing his hand down his waves, dark eyes sparkling at her.

"I'm sorry you're hurting, Mo. I know it's in more ways than one. I can't lie, shit been real off not talking to you."

She looked at her feet and Ahmeek lifted her chin with a finger. "In my eyes, Mo."

"Facetime," she reminded. He nodded.

"Why aren't we speaking again?" she asked.

"You got a lot of niggas on your line right now," Ahmeek answered. "I'm a little possessive with it. You got some choices to make."

"I don't know what I'm supposed to do," she said. Head down. His finger. Chin up. Her crown was slipping. Morgan was forced to face him. Forced to woman up.

"I miss you," she repeated. Shit, she meant it. His absence was felt in her life. She had been with Bash for two years and she felt no vacancy in the place he used to be. Ahmeek, however, left her heart hollow. Messiah. He left her conflicted. Three different emotions from three different men.

"Yeah?" he asked.

"Yeah," she confirmed.

"Well you know how to find me when you're ready. You know where I'm at with it, Mo. I want you with me. All the time. In my bed. Toys and shit all over my crib. I want you to move in. You got the key. You'll get there one day," he said.

"We had plans," she said, sighing. Morgan was so overwhelmed. "I'm so sorry Meek."

"Look, love. Me with you even for a day was enough, Mo. If all we get is what we've already done, I'm still grateful as fuck because none of this was even supposed to happen. We both know this ain't what it was supposed to be," Meek answered.

"Don't say that. I hate that," she said. "The thought of that makes me want to cry."

"Come here." His deep baritone was the only sound that didn't hurt. Or maybe it did, and she just didn't care, but she ended up in his arms. His embrace felt like love. He smelled like love. Dressed like it. Walked like it. Fucked like it. Talked like it. Everything about this man screamed affection. She rested her head on his chest as he held her close.

"I'm really afraid to let you go. Even for a minute," she stated, honestly. "It's like you're not going to be here when I'm ready."

"I'ma be here, Mo," he promised.

He placed a hand on the nape of her neck and massaged there. Morgan's eyes lowered. It felt so good. His touch.

"I'ma get out of here, love. I just came to check on you."

She lifted sad eyes to him and stood on her tiptoes as she kissed him.

She felt like she was floating. Like a magic carpet was under her feet and it had lifted to take her to some faraway land where she and Meek could love freely. A fairy tale. Ahmeek Harris was the happily ever after she'd wished for her entire life.

"If you walk out of here without me, my heart won't take it, Meekie," she whispered.

"Go ahead, Morgan."

The two of them focused their attention on Alani. It was

like she had appeared out of nowhere. "The twins are fine. Go settle your heart," Alani said.

"And Ethic?" Morgan asked.

Alani smiled. "I'm pretty good at settling his."

Morgan slipped into flip flops, grabbed her handbag, and followed Ahmeek out the house.

He turned down the music when they were inside the safety of his car.

"What we doing, Mo?" he asked.

"I don't know, but I'm going to do it anyway." She shot his words back at him. Words he had told her before and he pulled off. Morgan lifted a hand, stretching it across the front seat to massage the back of his neck.

"You haven't been sleeping?" she asked.

"I'm good, love. You ain't got to worry about me," he stated.

"It's just I haven't slept much either," she admitted. "I'm used to sleeping next to you and at Ethic's I can't even smell you. At Ethic's I feel like Messiah is close by and is lurking somewhere. What if he's back for the wrong reasons?"

"He wouldn't hurt you, Mo," Ahmeek said. "His beef ain't with you."

"If he hurts you, that will hurt me."

"That ain't never happening," Ahmeek stated. "I've known Messiah almost my whole life. We gon' talk. Man to man and you ain't got to worry about when or how that's going to go down."

"I want to go to the loft," she said. "It's ours. I want to go there, and I want to sleep. Is that okay? If we just sleep?"

"No lie, love, that shit sounds legit," he answered.

The hour-long ride was quiet. Morgan lived in her thoughts. This was terrifying to her. It was one thing to be with Ahmeek after Messiah, but suddenly it felt like she was cheating on him . . . like she was committed to Messiah and she and Ahmeek were in the middle of an affair. It hadn't even felt this scandalous when she was cheating on Bash. Somehow even after all this time, Messiah had some type of ownership over her that made this feel wrong.

She followed him inside and he pulled her by the tip of her fingers toward the master bedroom. Her head was pounding.

"Ahmeek I'm a little dizzy. The surgery . . ."

"Let me take care of you, Mo," he said. He pulled her shirt over her head and then bent down to lower her pants, lifting her feet so she could step out of them. Then he stood and removed his shirt, leaving his sweatpants on. He pulled back the duvet on his bed and pulled her into his body as he sank into the oversized, king mattress.

"Damn you feel good, love," he mumbled.

His fingers lived in her scalp, rubbing gently until he heard her breathing go heavy and felt her relax.

"I missed you," he whispered. After three weeks of little sleep he finally found peace now that she was underneath him.

A full night passed. It was a rest they both needed. It was a connection they both craved. When Morgan finally awoke she reached for his beard, pulling him to her face. He groaned as she led him out of his dreams. It didn't matter. She was in his head, in those dreams, but the reality of her was better. He gave in, opening his eyes as she slid into his space.

"In a perfect world you would ask me to marry you, I'd say yes, and things would be easy for the rest of our lives. Your love is easy, Meekie," she whispered. "It feels so good."

"Mo, you're twenty-one years old," he said. "In a perfect world, I'd be picking you up for the movies on a Friday night, taking you to Miami for the weekend or something, not forcing marriage down your throat. I'd date you. We'd get to know one another. You'd probably break up with a nigga a few times, but I ain't crazy, I know your worth, so I'd work like a mu'fucka to get you back," he chuckled. "And then when you're older. When you've become a woman that can make a decision that affects the rest of your life, I'd ask you. I wouldn't do it before that. I wouldn't do it now because it ain't fair to you. I've had my fun. I've made hella mistakes. Been with other women, been in the clubs, on the scene, took trips, fucked around, been wild. You're just starting. I wouldn't put the expectation of marriage on you."

Morgan didn't know if she should feel happy or a little disappointed. She wouldn't mind him putting that expectation on her at all. Bash already had.

"If you ever asked. Like one day down the line, if you ever think about asking, and you're nervous about what I'd say. Ask anyway. I'd say yes," she murmured, her eyes closing as tears stung them. She was crying because she feared it may not be true. With Messiah back it changed so much. She didn't know if they would ever even make it to a future where the two of them could exist. She remembered when Messiah had given her his ring. When he had expressed his need to marry her one day. She had been so different back then. She would have never imagined being with anyone else. Now she couldn't imagine being with him again. The sight of him hurt worse than his absence because she had to face the malice behind his decision to leave.

"You honestly need to be alone for a while, love," he said.

Morgan pushed off his chest, sitting up and looking at him with dismay.

"What does that even mean?" she asked, frowning.

"The fact that you don't know what it means speaks volumes," he stated.

"What are you saying?" she asked. "So you don't want to be with me?"

"I'm not saying that at all," he replied. He came up on one

elbow, his deep brow squinting as he inspected her. Her eyes glistened and the look on her face gutted him. "Why are you crying, love?"

"I'm not fucking crying," she snapped as she climbed out of bed. "Can you take me home?"

She began to put on her clothes, turning away from him so he wouldn't see her distress.

"Morgan—"

"I got it Ahmeek. Be without you. Be alone. Yup. I hear you. Loud and clear," she said.

He sat up in bed, planting feet to the floor and pulled her down onto his lap.

"Hey? That's not what I'm saying," he said, kissing the back of her neck. "I'm going to be here, Morgan." He kissed her shoulder. Once. Then twice.

"Now, it's Morgan? That's all I am to you now?" she whispered as she turned to him. "Meekie, I don't want to be that."

"And you should want to be that, Mo. You don't know who you are. Are you his Shorty? My love? Your fiancé's future wife? Who are you? Without niggas telling you who they want to turn you into?" Ahmeek asked.

"You're going to find somebody else," she whispered. Worry laced every word. "I'm going to lose you."

Ahmeek tilted her chin, pinching it between his fingertips. "You're going to find you, Mo. That's worth losing anybody." Her chin quivered, and he took her lips. His kisses felt like hope. Like she had just found a wish flower and put a sentiment into the air, filling her chest with pride and wistfulness. Her heart melted. Every time she was with him, this was all she felt. The languor of love. There was no effort required to be in love with him. It just was what it was. "I'ma be here for you, Mo. I'm not going anywhere. When you're ready, I'm right here."

Kisses between them were magical and Morgan wanted to stay. She wanted to just say fuck Messiah. Fuck Bash too, but she had to deal with her past. She had to speak to Messiah if there was any chance of moving on . . . of healing because she hadn't even done that yet.

"What if I never make it back to you?" she asked.

"Let me ask you something, Mo and I want you to answer me honestly," he said.

She felt anxiety build in her because she knew what his next words would be. He didn't even have to speak them.

"Do you still love Messiah?" he asked.

Morgan's mind took a trip down memory lane. She saw her entire history with Messiah and her eyes closed all on their own. Her lashes dampened as one tear rolled out of her left eye.

"He hurt me," she cried. "Bad, Meek."

His lips to the tear. It was gone.

"He loved you too, Mo," Meek said. "Let me get you home."

Morgan kissed him again. "Feels like goodbye, Meekie and I don't like it. I don't want to go home. I don't want to leave this loft. It's our bubble."

"Nah love, it's not. I want you to remember me everywhere. All over everything you touch. If you go to that raggedy little liquor store by your apartment I want you to think about the time . . ."

"We knocked over a whole shelf from kissing in the aisle," Morgan finished. "I remember. Every time I go in there." She chuckled. "I thought the owner was going to ban me from coming in there."

"And the twenty-four-hour laundromat by your school, when . . ." Ahmeek started but Morgan finished.

"You helped me wash all my clothes at midnight. It took us hours, but we were the only ones there and we watched *Grey's* on my phone while the cycle ran," she scoffed.

"See. Shit like that. I don't want to have you in a bubble. I want to experience you everywhere, Mo."

"I promise I'ma get right back to you," she said.

Kisses. Long and deep. Passionate and slow. Like they were stealing the last of a batch that couldn't be made again. Limited editions. The Meek and Mo era circa 2020.

"I'm not leaving. I'm not leaving until I have to."

They made love all day and then stayed up all night, scouring the internet on Meek's laptop looking at images of dresses Mo would wear one day at their wedding. He was patient. He entertained it but they both knew that the elephant in the room was looming. The day wouldn't ever come. All they would have was this night of fake planning as they lay beneath the white duvet, tucked up under one another. It was their long goodbye and although they were both pretending otherwise, the tender feeling in both their hearts told them that Messiah's return was bringing whatever it was they shared to an end.

25

"She hates me, B," Messiah said as he walked into Saviour's bedroom. Bleu sat against the headboard as Saviour leaned against her chest. Her son was fading, eyes closing slowly as Bleu held an open book in her hands. Bleu held up one finger to Messiah as she continued to read. Messiah sauntered over to the bed, laying across the foot of it and closing his eyes as he listened to her words. The sound of her voice made his heart still. Bleu looked up over her book and shook her head as Messiah sat there, silently, his eyes might have closed more quickly than Saviour's. When they were both asleep she stood, pulled the covers over Saviour and clicked out the light. She grabbed an extra cover from the closet and placed it over Messiah before retreating to her room.

Bleu sat back in her bed and before she could get comfortable Messiah was standing in the threshold of her door.

"Yo, Saviour's bed is comfortable as fuck," he snickered.

"I see." She smiled. "So, she hates you?"

"Did you know she was fucking with Ahmeek?" he asked.

"I can't say that I did," Bleu answered. "But isn't that what you wanted? You kind of gave him the green light."

"I was supposed to be gone," Messiah said as he walked over to the bed and sat on the edge. "Not sitting back watching him with my girl."

"Morgan loves you Messiah," Bleu said.

"Nah, Shorty hate me, but she love that nigga. I see it," Messiah said, sadly. "Any other nigga I would have wrapped his ass. Duct tape around his neck and ankles. Put that nigga in the bottom of Devil's Lake—"

"Messiah," Bleu interrupted. "Stop. I hate when you do that. When you act like you're the worst person on the planet. The toughest. Like you don't feel anything but rage. If you want to be sad, be sad, but don't hide the shit behind rage."

"Shorty's fucking me up." His voice cracked, and he hung his head.

"See," Bleu said. "Doesn't that feel better than all that anger? Just let the shit out when you feel it Messiah. Maybe if you showed her more than that fake tough guy routine, she'd be open to at least talking to you."

Messiah turned his head to her. "Ain't nothing fake about me, B. Nigga I'm a beast," he said. He turned and reached for her foot, snatching her across the mattress.

"Messiah!" she shouted. Bleu squealed as he picked her up, tossing her over his shoulder and carrying her out the room. Bleu laughed as his fingers danced over her back, tickling her. "Messiah put me down!" He carried her downstairs to the first floor and placed her on the kitchen island. "A nigga stomach touching his back, B. I need nourishment," he said, backpedaling until he got to the table. He pulled out a chair.

"You need god damn help is what you need," she said, smiling. "Crazy ass."

Bleu hopped off the countertop and walked over to the

refrigerator. She pulled out ingredients for breakfast because breakfast at night was the best. "So, what are you going to do about Ahmeek? He's your friend Messiah. You need to talk to him. I know you love Mo, but you love Meek too."

"Fuck that, nigga," Messiah said. There was hurt in his tone. "Tie that nigga mama up."

"Don't make me call Ms. Marilyn and let her know you talking shit. She'd beat you and me," Bleu said, lifting brows.

Messiah blew out a frustrated breath. "You're probably right. I just hoped it would be different when I got back. I worked hard to get back to her and she . . ."

"Messiah," Bleu cut him off. "We thought you were gone. We thought . . ." She paused and took a breath. "It's not simple. You have to show a little understanding if you want her back."

"It just kind of feel like Shorty don't need me no more," Messiah admitted. "Like I went away, and life went on. Like nobody missed me."

"I missed you every day, Messiah. I cried for months. Lost weight. My hair fucking fell out because I couldn't eat. Sometimes I feel like I'm the reason my baby didn't make it. I was sick when you went away Messiah. I didn't take care of myself or my child. Isa AND Ahmeek waged war on half the city just to let some of that hurt out. I can't even imagine what Mo went through. By the time I could bring myself to face her she was gone. We missed you, Messiah. Missed your ass like crazy." Bleu's words were angry and pained as she busied herself with the meal.

"I'm sorry, B. I should have been here for you. For her, man. I'm sorry for not telling you. For leaving like I did," he mumbled. She sniffed and then used her shoulder to clear the refugee tears that slid down her face. Her hands were a mess and Messiah lifted out the chair. He stood on one side of the island and Bleu stood on the other. "Come here," he said. She leaned toward him and he swiped the wetness away.

"Asshole," she spat, then sniffed some more, then shook her head.

"Forgive me, B," Messiah said.

"Save the begging for Mo. You're good in my hood," she assured him.

Messiah's smile spread across his face so wide that it made her laugh.

"A-One since day one, B. You're the shit."

Meek pulled up to the one-story home and leaned forward, retrieving the pistol from beneath his seat. He eyed the two matching BMWs that sat curbside, announcing Isa's and Messiah's presence. It should have felt like old times. It should have been a joyous reunion, but one woman had caused a great divide. He climbed out of the car, placing black Cole Haans to the pavement.

"What up, Murder Meek?" one of the youngin's on the block called out from the hoop game. He trotted over to Meek, dribbling the ball with so much expertise it looked like it was attached to a string, coming back to him effortlessly.

"What up, Henny?" Meek said, acknowledging the seventeen-year-old kid.

"Crazy shit about Messiah," Henny stated. Meek didn't respond as he lifted eyes to the trap house. "Yo that thing? Escorting the armored trucks. I appreciate the opportunity, big homie, but I still want in on everything else too. I'm moving through product like crazy. I'm ready for the re-up."

Isa had put Henny on in a major way. He was running up and down the highway guarding Hak's trucks a few times a week and also hustling the grabs from the semis. Ahmeek felt it was too much for a seventeen-year-old kid. He would have preferred to build Henny's weight up slowly, as a matter of fact he would have preferred for Henny not to do it at all, but such was life. They all had a reason why they had chosen the life.

"Already?" Ahmeek answered, brows lifting. "You out?"

Hendrix pulled down the brim of his hat. "Yeah, me and my team just waiting. We getting money out this bitch. I got a girl to save for, man, so I'm trying to get this fast money and get out even quicker," Hendrix stated.

"Hustling for pussy ain't the move lil' Henny?" Ahmeek chuckled.

"Nah, I'm hustling for something else. My girl going to college in two years. She up out of here and I know I ain't college bound, but I ain't trying to be dead weight either. She looking at them south schools. I need my bread right, so I can make that trip with her. Maybe get in trade school or something near her school. I don't know I just know I got to do more than this to keep her when the time comes, but I can't go nowhere broke. I need to have my paper right. So whatever you got moving, I want in on it."

Ahmeek respected the dream. It was a plan. It was more than he had done at Hendrix's age. Without an exit plan the game was just unending. There were no winners and Ahmeek admired the foresight of the young bull in front of him. "You a smart kid, Henny," Ahmeek stated. "Next time Isa set you up on a run turn the shit down. This game don't love nobody. Get back in Ethic's shops. I know he got you working at his funeral home and garages and shit. Do that. Keep your hands clean and stack your bread. When your girl ready to go away to school, I'll match what you got saved up and pay for your trade school," Ahmeek stated.

Ahmeek could see Hendrix weighing the options in his mind. The game had already tainted young Henny. The heavy bands of cash he could get with just a little muscle in the streets was outweighing the legit offer Ahmeek had put on the table. "Your choice, man," Ahmeek stated. He headed toward the house, removed his key from his pocket and pushed into the house.

Isa and Messiah sat on the couch. Conversation ceased when Ahmeek walked into the room.

Isa stood extending his hand to Ahmeek. "What's goodie, bruh?" Isa greeted, pulling Ahmeek in for a hug.

Messiah didn't move. Didn't speak.

"Yo, G, let me holla at this nigga, man. Ain't no need for a middle man," Ahmeek stated.

Isa's brow lifted, and he nodded. "Hit me later, bruh," Isa said to Ahmeek. "I'ma get with you brody." The last sentiment was for Messiah. "You niggas try not to kill each other. Love sick ass niggas. Mo light skinned ass a witch or something. Casting spells and shit, blowing my mu'fuckin' high," Isa cracked, shaking his head. The door slammed behind Isa as he departed and then silence engulfed the room.

Ahmeek sat in the chair across from Messiah, leaned forward, elbows to knees. Forehead knitted as tension ate up the room.

"How you want to play it, bro? We gon' box it out? Shoot it out? Mob it out on different teams? Or we gon' sit here and chop it up like men? I can be as gangster or grown about it as you want to be. You tell me which way we going with it. I'm with whatever," Ahmeek stated.

Messiah lifted his head, marking Ahmeek with his stare. "If I could kill you, you would already be dead," Messiah said. "She's my fucking everything nigga. You know that. You got everything else, my nigga. I'm telling you right now I pressed pause on my murder game to wait on this conversation. I'ma press play over her, Meek. You know bro. You already know how it's laying over Shorty."

"I'm invested. If Morgan want me to walk away I'm cool with that. If that's what SHE about, I'm about it. But if she want a nigga . . . if she call me . . . I'm coming to her every time. I ain't never slipping when it come to her, for you or nobody else. You been gone a long time Messiah. You asked me to do exactly what I'm doing with her. I didn't for a long time. She lived her life a little, I did me. For two years we didn't even speak, but then we did and now we're here. Now you're here and it's fucked up, but she's under my skin. She's . . ." Meek paused because he didn't even know how to describe what he felt for Morgan. "It ain't casual."

"It ain't casual but she wearing another nigga ring, though? She's light weight to you, nigga. I'm home. All that's dead. Him and her. You and her. Him. Just you, if that's how it got to be. Everything that's in the way is dead. I'm just giving you fair warning."

"I ain't never needed it before. A warning ain't necessary. Like I said, I don't slip. With her and for damn sure not with my life so it's gon' be what it's gon' be. You know how I move with it." There was no guarantee who would walk out of a gun fight alive between the two. Deadly. Cunning. Unremorseful about extinguishing life. They were at an impasse. A declaration of war between brothers. "I love you bro, but I'll put you in a grave if you ever send bullets my way. You know I don't play with it."

Messiah's head hung as conflict swirled in his chest. "I ain't asking over Shorty. I own that."

Ahmeek stood. "That's where you're fucking up, G. She ain't a thing that can be possessed. She's a moment. You live in the moment of Mo. Your moment with her has passed. If she wants to press rewind that's up to her and I'll respect that, but if there's even a chance that she wants to be in the moment with me . . ." Meek shook his head. "I'll see you around, bro.

You've already said what it is. Ain't how I want it, but I can't walk away."

"You won't have to walk away. Niggas gon' have to carry you out," Messiah said. "Better kiss Ms. Marilyn next time you see her, G."

Ahmeek bit into his bottom lip so hard he drew blood. He sucked it into his mouth, using all his restraint to stop himself from escalating this conversation. A man had never mentioned his mother with malice in his heart and lived to tell about it.

"I'ma just kiss my lady instead," Ahmeek stated. He knew it was a low blow. He was objectifying what was pure, but Messiah had dug into him so deeply that it had slipped off his tongue before he could stop it. "Be careful with me, bro."

"Fuck you, nigga."

Ahmeek pushed out of the house with so much aggression that the bottom spring broke, leaving the screen door hanging halfway off. Messiah didn't move. His heart was split open. Ahmeek was his brother. This discord between them felt just as bad as the distance between him and Mo. No matter what he did he was losing but he wasn't selfless enough to do nothing, if he had to sacrifice Meek to get Morgan back.

So be it, he thought.

He would do anything for her. What he had underestimated was Meek's willingness to do the same.

26

Messiah sat on the side of the highway, gripping the throttle of Isa's bike. He only had ten minutes to change his mind. He knew he wouldn't. He had lost too much. He had come back to town anticipating a much different reunion. The welcome he'd received was laced with change. Ahmeek was now the owner of all things that used to belong to him. Ahmeek had not only taken his girl but he now ran I-75 from Bay City all the way to Canada. Over a hundred miles of interstate meant millions. The product that floated between the Michigan cities either belonged to or was being protected by Meek and Messiah was livid. It was like Ahmeek was living his life. Like Ahmeek had laced up Messiah's boots and they fit him better.

Messiah's temple throbbed as he waited. He knew he shouldn't do this, but he was going to. In a situation where Messiah felt powerless, he needed to take a little back. This was his highway. He didn't care who had paid for Meek's protection. He didn't care whose product was being moved up and down this stretch. It was no longer safe. He was taking it. He had planned to keep his hands clean. Legitimate money would give him a legitimate chance to get Mo back. Ethic had convinced him. To focus on bettering himself. On growing into a man Mo would be safe with. He wanted to be that, but Mo with Meek, the thought alone sent Messiah spiraling in the opposite direction of right. It made him want to do so much bad . . . so much wrong. It made him murderous.

Killing Ahmeek proved challenging. They were equal beasts. That's what Messiah told himself. The true reason Messiah couldn't just eliminate his problem was because he loved Ahmeek like a brother. Any other man would have already been delegated to memory because he would no longer exist. Not Ahmeek however. The love and history clouded the circumstance. Messiah hated it. The need to piece his life back together was heavy. He had missed so much time that it felt like he had never belonged in the picture in the first place. Mo with Bash. Mo with Meek. Isa with Aria. Ethic and Alani happy and expecting. Bleu, grieving a child he hadn't even known existed. These people used to be his people, but they felt distant now, like strangers. Like he was being introduced to them all over again. He wanted to show up as a new man for Mo, but he had to get this old shit out of his system. This gangster shit. This "that nigga ain't snatching my bitch" shit. Once Messiah had something set in his mind, he couldn't let it go. His soul wouldn't let him curl a trigger on Ahmeek, but it didn't mean he had to stop the next man from doing so. The shipment coming up the highway belonged to someone who wouldn't take a loss on the chin. If those trucks disappeared under Ahmeek's watch it would spark war. Messiah heard the acceleration of the semi coming. The window of opportunity to walk away with his honor was dwindling and he didn't give a fuck. If Meek wouldn't bow out gracefully Messiah would force him out. Better yet, an enemy of thine enemy was considered a friend. He kicked off the stand of the bike and eased into traffic as the semi passed him. Messiah was in a mood. There would be no sparing of lives today. Kendrick blared through the Bluetooth in his helmet as he maxed out the throttle.

Me and my nigga tryna get it ya bish
Hit this house lick, tell me is you with it ya bish
Money trees is the perfect place for shade and that's just
how I feel

Messiah hit the back tires first.

Four shots took out the double row of tires before he sped up.

BANG! BANG! BANG! BANG!

Back tires gone the truck spun as the driver hit the brakes too hard. The truck fishtailed sending the bed skidding horizontally across the highway. Messiah panicked as the truck wildly spun. He leaned the bike sideways, almost to the concrete as he went beneath the belly of the semi, riding so low to the ground that the denim of his jeans shredded against the concrete.

"Fuck!" Messiah shouted as the ground burned through his skin. He barely kept control of the bike as he brought it back vertical, clearing the opposite side. Ignoring the pain, he accelerated to the side of the semi and fired again. Screeching tires filled the air as the semi came to a stop in the middle of the highway, turned sideways, blocking all four lanes. Messiah barely let the motorcycle stop before hopping off and advancing on the driver.

The door opened, and the handle of a shotgun greeted him first, but the driver never had the chance to fire. Messiah ended him without thinking twice. Hollow tips lifted the man out of his seat and sent him into the passenger side as Messiah climbed aboard. He was a marksman, so the first bullet had killed the man, the one he put in the center of his forehead sent him to hell. Messiah pulled the keys out and rushed to open the bed of the truck. He lifted the bike onto the back, locked it back then climbed into the driver's seat. He pulled off into the night with a dead body and enough heroin in the bed of the truck to send him away for life. He didn't care. He didn't even stop to think of the consequences that would occur if this play went wrong. All he could focus on was the rage coursing through him. The feeling of betrayal no matter how complicated kept him from being cautious. This lick knocked out two birds with one stone. It solved his money problems and put a target on Ahmeek's back. He was supposed to keep his hands clean. He was supposed to be a better man so that he could win the girl fair and square but all's fair in love and war. Over Morgan Atkins it was war and Messiah would remove anyone that blocked him from reaching her heart.

27

"Are you sure you can do this? You're grimacing through the entire routine, Mo," Aria said. "You don't have to rush your healing. If you need more time, you need more time."

Messari and Yara sat against the wall of the dance studio, in front of the mirror, coloring.

"I don't need more time. I have to get this right. I'm fine," Morgan answered lifting fingers to her ears and plugging them for a few seconds. Healing this time around was much more painful than she remembered.

"Mo, you really don't have to perform with us. It's just a club show. You're not missing anything," Aria said.

"I'm not sitting it out. I have to perform. I have to see if I still move the same to the beat . . . if I hear music the same," Morgan whispered passionately. "It's not for another couple weeks. The pain will be gone by then." She turned from the mirror. "It has to be," she whispered.

Morgan snatched a towel from the shelf and wiped the sweat from her brow. "I'm just trying to get back to me. My life's all over the place. I'm just lost right now. You know?"

Morgan and Aria walked over to the twins and sat on the floor.

"You heard from Ahmeek?" Aria asked.

"He came to see me a few days ago. Not since then," Morgan said as she pulled Yara into her arms.

"Come on, boyfriend," Aria said, motioning for Messari who climbed into her lap without protest. Morgan reached for their bag and removed sandwiches she had prepared. Cut in fours, no crust. She handed a square to Messari. Messari lifted it to Aria's lips.

"You eat some," he said. His words were forming perfectly, and Aria laughed and took a small bite.

"Your turn," she said.

Mo smiled and handed another piece to Yara.

"What about Messiah?" Aria asked.

"He sends flowers. Every day. I toss them out, every day," she stated. "Alani digs them out the trash. Tries to keep some around the house. She's trying to indirectly convince me to talk to him. She's the most forgiving person I know. I'm not like her though. I can't ever see me forgiving him."

Aria shrugged. "Can't avoid him forever. And where the hell is Bash?"

"He stopped calling and texting a few days ago," Morgan said. "But I have to see him when I go pick up my cap and gown. I did him so wrong, Aria. I don't even know what I'll say to him."

"Yeah you carried that man bold," Aria stated. "But he has to take some of the blame, Mo. He jumped on you as soon as you were done with Messiah. You were pregnant and open as fuck. Any man could have slid in to fill that hole Messiah dug in you and Bash knew that. He caught you slipping, and you ended up stuck even though that wasn't where you really wanted to be. He can't really say he expected to keep you forever."

Morgan stood and placed Yara on her feet.

"You want to run it back again?" Mo asked.

Before Aria could answer the sound of glass shattering and gunshots blasting filled Morgan's ears.

RAT TAT TAT TAT TAT TAT TAT TAT TAT TAT

Morgan would never forget the sound. Gunshots. A semi-automatic. More than one. More than three because Morgan knew what three sounded like from her days of practicing with Bella and Ethic. This sounded like a firing squad. Like that day at the park all those years ago when Raven had been gunned down. The sound froze her where she stood.

"Mo!"

Morgan heard Aria's voice shrieking . . . calling her . . . it was like everything was moving in slow motion and she fell to the floor, scrambling across the hardwood toward her son.

"Messari!" Morgan cried. Yara was beneath Aria, on the floor and wailing at the top of her lungs because Aria was restricting her from moving. The firing stopped. Only briefly. Only for a moment then started again.

RAT TAT TAT TAT TAT TAT TAT TAT

Why the hell were they still firing? Who was firing? What was this about? Morgan couldn't make it across the room fast enough. The mirrors on the wall were shattering around her baby and he was wailing. He was bleeding. Was he hit?

Morgan scrambled, running as quickly and staying as low as she could until she was within arm's reach of her son. She snatched him so hard that she was sure she had hurt him, but she didn't care. She held him to her chest and turned him to the floor, caging him in with her body then covering her ears as bullets tore the building apart.

Her ears ached as the bullets sounded off like bombs.

Morgan stretched her arm out, reaching for the twins' bag. She pulled out the 9mm handgun. The one Ethic had been insistent that she carry. The one she had never used outside a gun range. Morgan had never shot anyone. Only paper, but those gunshots weren't going away. These men were firing, then reloading, then firing over and over again. She shook so badly she could barely load the clip. She waited as tears ran down her face. They would have to reload. They would eventually run out again. When it ceased again Morgan ran. "Get in the office!" she shouted. "Hurry Aria! Get them in the office and call Ethic!"

"I don't have your phone!" Aria shouted.

"Then call Isa! Aria go!" Morgan shouted.

Morgan's heart ached in fear as she positioned her body against the same wall as the entrance. She was terrified.

Morgan screamed as she ducked, placing hands to her ears as she gripped the gun in her hands and bent down. Those gunshots were so loud that the sound was ripping through her brain. All she felt was pain. It was too loud. It felt like she was being hit but she knew if she didn't do something the pain would hit her tenfold when those bullets began penetrating. She didn't want to die in this dance studio. She didn't want her babies to die. No way could she let these men get through the door. *Why is this happening?*

Morgan thought of her sister. Raven had died before she'd even gotten a chance to live. The man she'd chosen had led her to the grave and Morgan couldn't fathom the thought of following behind her. Someone was responsible for bringing this mayhem to her door. Was it Messiah? Ahmeek? Maybe Isa? It couldn't be Ethic. Ethic had kept her safe all these years. No, these shooters were consequences of being affiliated with the crew. Morgan heard the shots stop and then heard footsteps crunch against the shattered glass of the front door as one of the shooters stepped over the threshold.

This was not a warning. This was meant to be an execution. Morgan lifted the gun and waited. Her heart thundered. She was sure she was having a heart attack. The shooter led with the long nose of his assault rifle and Morgan's lip trembled. She let that gun come through the door first until the side of the shooter's head was in her line of sight.

BOOM!

Morgan slid down the wall because she knew what was coming next. Bullets. Through the plaster from the second shooter. He came through the door aiming for where her head should have been, but Morgan filled his torso, pulling the trigger until she emptied her chamber. No more shots. Hers or theirs. Only the sound of tires as the remaining gunmen drove away from the scene of the crime and the sound of sirens as the police neared.

Morgan ran to the office and slid to her knees.

"Are they okay? Are they hurt?!" she cried. Her hands moved all over Yara's body first. She was fine. Then Messari. He was cut from the glass and bleeding, but Morgan would take care of that. She pulled her twins into her arms and cried as she rocked them.

"Are they gone?" Aria asked.

Morgan nodded as her lips pulled tight in emotion. She sobbed over her babies as she rocked back and forth.

Aria reached for the door and Morgan grabbed her arm.

"Don't. Just stay in here until someone comes," Morgan said, voice shaking in absolute fear. Black mascara ran down Aria's face and her lip trembled, but she nodded. They huddled around the twins, holding hands, praying that help arrived before danger doubled back for them.

Morgan emerged from the building in a trance. The red, blue, and white police lights were everywhere. She held Yara in her arms and Aria held Messari. A crowd stood behind the yellow police tape, but she couldn't focus on anyone behind her tears.

"Morgan!"

She turned and bawled when she saw Bash lift up the police tape.

She took a step in his direction, but Aria's hand to her forearm stopped her.

"Mo . . ."

Morgan turned back around to the other side of the crowd and she saw three white BMWs pull onto the scene.

Ahmeek, Messiah, and Isa hopped out. The expressions on their faces told her they were seconds away from curling triggers. Her lip quivered. She felt safest with them.

Her crew.

The crew.

Morgan didn't know who to run to. Even Isa gave her a sense of security. Like he would light shit up as a consequence of what had occurred.

"Morgan—"

Bash was by her side, pulling Yara from her arms. "Are you good? Are you hurt?" he asked.

Morgan nodded distractedly as she watched Messiah, Meek, and Isa walk toward her. She was in shock, speechless, as she tried to process what had happened. She felt everyone's eyes on her.

Messiah fought against the officers securing the crime scene, trying to get to her. Ahmeek just stood there, looking at her. He was halfway across the parking lot, behind the tape, but she felt his gaze on her. She wanted to run to him but then there was Messiah. She wanted to run to him too. She didn't know which side of her heart to choose so instead she stood stagnant. Stuck in the middle between her past and her future. She could feel them. Both of them. From a parking lot away. Her eyes prickled. She wanted them so badly. Not one of them. Both of them.

"Mo?" Aria called.

Messari reached for his mother. She was almost sure he felt her distress and she tore her eyes away from Ahmeek as the police approached.

"We're going to get you two and the kids to the hospital to make sure you're all okay, then my officers will need to take statements," a plainclothes detective said.

"I'm going to ride with you," Bash said. "My attorney is on the way."

"That won't be necessary," the detective stated.

"It's always necessary when a person of color talks to the police," he stated. Morgan and Aria were ushered to separate ambulances. Morgan heard the commotion of Messiah fighting to get to her and she stopped walking. She turned toward the crowd.

"Morgan, we've got to go," Bash said.

"They're going to arrest him if he doesn't calm down, Bash," she answered. She pushed through the officers on scene. Messiah was like a stick of dynamite and the thought of Morgan being a target had lit his fuse.

"Messiah."

Messiah's rage stilled. It was like she had snapped her fingers. It amazed her that after all this time, it still worked. She was still the only one who could calm his storm. Problem was she was sick of it raining, tired of the downpour. Ahmeek had brought a little sunshine to her life and now all she wanted to do was grow.

He stared at her and it was like the entire crowd disappeared. Her lip quivered.

"Everybody's dying, Mo. Whoever did this is out of here," Messiah said, not caring that a uniformed police officer was standing between them.

"Red means dead," she said. She was in a state of shock,

mind still spinning, body still shaking. The blasts from those bullets setting off titanic plates in her head. Her headache was immeasurable.

"Yeah, Shorty. You did good," he said. "Let me come with you, Mo. Let me be here."

She shook her head, sniffling. "Just get Ethic. Please get him," she said. She turned, and a paramedic led her into the bed of the ambulance. She looked at Bash who had calmed Yara. The paramedics were working on Messari's cuts.

"Is he okay?" she asked. "Are they bad?"

"He'll be just fine. A few stitches on this one above his eye," the woman said.

Morgan's eyes misted. "This could have been so bad," she whispered. "My big boy." She admired Messari who sat completely still as they bandaged him.

"You got them around gangsters and thugs and you're surprised, Mo?" Bash asked.

Morgan's body stiffened as her spine aligned, sitting her upright. He had put the truth right in front of her and it was an ugly one. The type of men she chose would always come with this type of risk. It didn't matter what illusion of safety Messiah or Meek provided, danger could come interrupt it on any given day. Today was proof of that.

Morgan was lost in thought the entire way to the hospital. Even as she watched her son be stitched up her mind was back at the dance studio. Even while she was answering the questions from the detective, she was half-present. She had killed two people today and she couldn't stop seeing it. Couldn't stop hearing it.

RAT TAT TAT TAT TAT TAT TAT

Gunshots were on repeat in her head. They were all fine. Physically everyone was okay, but inside, Morgan was a mess.

"We've given him some Tylenol for the pain and numbed

the area with the stitches. We've also given him a little something to help him sleep through the night. He can rest here for the night and you can take him in the morning," the doctor said.

Morgan nodded.

"Thank you," she said.

"I'm going to give you some privacy," the doctor said before exiting. Bash placed a sleeping Yara in the hospital bed next to Messari and then turned to Morgan.

"Have you told Messiah about the twins? I assume you haven't. He isn't here," Bash stated.

"He's here. Somewhere in this hospital. I can feel him," she said. "I've always felt him. I should have known he wasn't dead." She shook her head in regret. She had spent so much time trying to stifle his memory and his energy that she had missed the fact that his heart was still beating somewhere out there. She should have known.

"He's dangerous, Mo. Meek too. What we had was good. You keep playing with fire and you're going to get burnt. You're going to burn these babies because you can't stop chasing the streets. Didn't you tell me your sister died doing that?"

His words felt like a blow to the stomach.

"My mother has rescinded the credits you earned while in London. You no longer qualify for graduation," Bash said. "You come home. You cut everybody else off and your credits will go back to normal. Otherwise, you'll be put under academic investigation for cheating."

"You're blackmailing me?" she said. "Love you or you'll play with my future? I earned those grades Bash. I went to every class, I took every test."

"And we made sure you passed. We made sure you leveled up. If you leave me, you'll go right back to where you started. The bottom, Morgan. I don't want to do it this way, but since I now know this isn't about love for you . . . I'll play it your way.

You never loved me. You used me. I've built you up in my world and now I need you to play your part. Or don't. It's up to you. I do love you. I do love those kids, but the games are over, Mo. You'll wear my ring and my last name, and you'll wear them well or I'll ruin your life. I don't want to, but I will. I'll play with your emotions the same way you've enjoyed playing with mine and that thing you told me about Ethic—"

Morgan held her breath because she knew what he would say next. She hoped he didn't take it there. She hoped he had limits, but the look of disdain in his eyes told her that he didn't and that he wouldn't hold back.

"About him killing Alani's brother for you . . . that can become a huge problem for you too. The inconvenience I could cause. The freedoms I could take. He wouldn't be so powerful behind steel bars. A cage does something to a man. Confining him. Trapping him. He'd likely die before enduring it."

Morgan's chest locked. She had shared that with him in a moment of weakness and he hadn't mentioned it ever again, until now. "I'll send a car for you tomorrow morning," he said. He kissed her forehead and Morgan felt like it was the kiss of death. Men like Bash didn't need street influence or guns or aggression to control. He had power. His name was deadlier than any bullet ever could be and Morgan was trapped. She felt numb. She felt dead. Morgan ran every decision she had made in the past two years over again in her mind. They had led her here. To this trap, to this emotional prison. He had put her in invisible shackles.

"Bash, I don't want to be here. I don't love you and I don't want this. I don't want to do this anymore. Please just let me go, I—"

SLAP!

Her face stung, and her eyes filled with disbelief and her lip throbbed. It wasn't a hard blow. She was more stunned than hurt but the anger that built up in Mo's soul caused her to tremble.

"You're going to stop talking crazy because you make me act crazy, Mo. Your stupid decisions are putting my kids at risk. You think because he's back that changes anything? They belong to me just as much as they belong to you. Fix your face, grab those babies and stop acting like a bird brain so we can get on with the rest of our lives. If you think I'm letting you take two babies that I raised, two beautiful kids, my kids, and leave like I didn't contribute to them . . . like I didn't contribute to you, you're mistaken, Mo. This is the life you chose so this is the life you live." He kissed the side of her head. "I'll send a car to bring you back home in the morning."

He walked out, and Morgan had to place a hand over her mouth to stop from crying. She thought about calling for help. Ethic would come. Messiah too. Ahmeek would rescue her and never leave her side. She had three hitters. A gang of killers but she felt obligated to keep them safe. She felt like if she called it would be too much. If she asked for help, they would judge her. The world would know that she had messed up her entire life and Morgan was tired of being the one with problems. She was tired of being the one that needed fixing. She could never let Ethic know that she had told Bash what he had done. Morgan had no choice but to play the game by Bash's rules. What if Bash told what he knew? What if she left him and he used the information she had given him to put Ethic in jail? All these things ran through Mo's mind in an instant and then her sister, Raven Atkins plagued her thoughts. She had never understood how she could be so weak for a man who hit her. She couldn't understand because she was looking up at Raven from her childish vantage point. She couldn't identify the manipulation or the mental bondage that Mizan had trapped her in. It wasn't until this very moment that she understood because somehow against her will she had become just like Raven. She had become trapped by a man and she had an inkling in her gut that these instances of confrontation with Bash were the beginnings of abuse. Morgan wanted out, but she would remain silent because there was so much at stake. She wondered what factors had stopped Raven from asking for help. Morgan let her tears fall and she prayed that her silence didn't lead to her death. She didn't want to follow her sister to an early grave. She just had to figure out how to free herself without putting her entire family at risk.

28

"Isa, please just stay." Aria didn't even sound like herself. Her voice was so delicate that Isa turned to her in surprise, brow furrowed as he loaded the clip to his pistol. He placed it in his shoulder holster and then slid into a jean graffiti jacket.

"Niggas got appointments to make tonight, Ali. I got to make sure they on time for that," he said. Aria's eyes landed on the arsenal of guns that he had placed on the bed. Assault rifles. He pulled the cover over the artillery and then turned his back to her. "You could have died in that dance studio. Everybody meeting they maker over that. Meek already outside. I can't babysit you tonight. I need you to be a big girl."

She could feel the tension in the air. She hugged herself, hands rubbing up and down her upper arms. She shivered.

"I can't get the blood out of my head, Isa. I see it." The way her words broke made Isa simmer. He flicked his nose. He wished he knew how to console her. He wished he had it in him to comfort her when things terrified her. He wasn't like Ahmeek. He didn't go soft for the one he loved. Even Messiah had allowed Mo to be a weakness for him. He was the opposite.

He went harder. Loving Ali made him deadly. Somebody had disrespected her. Had put her at risk and he wouldn't be able to sleep until that person paid with their life. He had a debt to collect. Whomever had called the play that led to shooters coming to the studio had to pay a tax. The cost would be heavy. A life for the attempt on her life. God should have never given Isa someone to love because when his emotions were involved it was dangerous.

"Get over here, man."

The order was one she would have usually protested but this day Aria's feet moved. Other people might think he was cold hearted. Many called Isa crass. His crazy had a reputation all on its own, but Aria called him, hers. She didn't need sweet nothings in her ear. Her name in ink on his body, the ring on her finger, and good dick was more than enough. He took care of her in his own way. Showed affection in a rough way, and she endured. She rode the wave because it was exhilarating. He sat on the edge of the bed and he pulled her into his lap.

"A little blood can't scare you killer. Man the fuck up, Ali cuz you about to marry a nigga that's going to put blood at your feet by the gallon. I'm leaving niggas leaking out here over you. How you afraid of a little red when ya' man make 'em bleed? Huh?" he asked. Aria was so mad that tears were sliding down her face because as tough as she was, the events that had transpired had shaken her. He lifted her chin, gripping it, forcing her stare to meet his. "I need you strong, baby. If you weak, what you think my mind gon' be on when I'm out there? You, right?"

She nodded, and he stole a kiss. "Everybody's dying, Ali. I'm lining up caskets, baby. Niggas think it's a game out here. You're off fucking limits. If they didn't know before they'll know by the time I'm done. Blood red got to be your new favorite color. You hear me? I want to see the shit everywhere. Paint your toes red, your lips red, paint this whole motherfucking house red as a matter of fact, every wall . . . until you're used to the color cuz you're marrying a fucking murderer Ali. I can't have you afraid."

It took every bit of her courage to stifle the fear that consumed her. Her hand shook as she placed it on his face. The tip of a stiletto nail traced the tattooed gun against his hairline. "Make them hurt," she whispered.

"I'ma make it hurt real bad, Ali."

She pressed her forehead to his. "I hate you so much." She sniffed as her hand caressed the side of his face, then moved to the back of his head.

"I hate you most Ali. No nigga ever hating you more than me. Nobody. You got into me, Ali. I don't know how, but I'm infected with your bullshit," Isa stated.

"Make me hurt, baby," she said softly.

Isa kissed her aggressively, pulling her lip into his mouth and biting it as he wrapped his large hand around her neck. Isa flipped her, forcing her to the bed. Before she could react, her left ankle was inside the cuff he kept at the end of his bed. Then her right. Aria reached up and bound her right wrist to the top post. Isa moved around the bed to capture her left hand. Isa removed the holster, then his shirt. Skinny nigga. Light skinned–dark skinned type nigga because his skin was yellow, but that heart was dark. Nothing about Isa was a pretty boy. Ink everywhere, even down each finger. Her name A-R-I-A-I-S-M-I-N-E spelled out on each knuckle.

Isa unbuttoned the long men's shirt she chose to sleep in. His shirt. Sprayed with his scent because she was addicted to it.

"Yeah, niggas want to die," Isa said as he admired the view of her body. Her free breasts were perfect, perky and round. The valleys of her toned stomach looked like water should flow through the crevices, and that fucking V-cut that led to her pussy was like a sign leading him home. Isa reached into his night stand and Aria gasped as he removed the leather flogger that rested inside.

Her heart galloped. He'd never used it before. Restraints she had allowed him to, but never the whips or paddles. Certainly not this. Her stomach tensed, revealing a six pack.

"Motherfucking body is amazing, Ali," he said.

The leather swept across her skin, enticing her nipples, making them pucker, and causing goosebumps to rise in protest.

"Is it going to hurt?" she gasped as he wrapped his lips around her breasts.

"Probably," he whispered.

"Bad?"

"You know what to say if it's too much for you, Ali. Let me hear you," he groaned.

"Submit." Her voice skipped out, barely audible, like it was tripping over the fear that tightened her throat. She gulped.

"You say that and I'm gon' stop every time," he said as he hovered over her. So much dick rested on her leg that Aria's breath hitched. This skinny ass nigga was all dick. Dick and burners because he kept a pistol on him. "I'ma free one hand and one leg so you can turn around for me."

She nodded and extended half her rights back. Aria turned over. The arch in her defined dancer's back made Isa's dick jump. He trapped her free wrist to the other one. Her hands steepled in a point above her head as her ass lingered in the air.

He trailed the flogger down her bare skin, making her clench.

"Open up for me, Ali."

Chest to the bed, Aria relaxed.

SWITCH!

She bucked as the leather stung her bare skin. Aria pulled against the leather restraints. They clanged from her resistance. She bit into her lip as her hair fell into her face.

SWITCH!

"Agh!"

"The bruised fruit taste the sweetest, Ali," he moaned as he lowered his face behind her. The way he ran his tongue from her clit to the crack of her ass made Aria close her eyes.

SLURRRRRRP

SWITCH!

"Isa!" she screamed. Calling his name wasn't even a second thought. It was an every night occurrence.

He switched her again and Aria's skin screamed but behind the pain there was a rush. There was a forbiddance that made her grit her teeth instead of using her safe word. He took away her sight next as she felt something silky cover her eyes.

"Isa, I want to see what you're doing," she gasped.

"Trust your man, Ali. Why you got to see if I can see?"

She swallowed down the anxiety building in her. The air conditioning kissed her middle. She was so exposed. Ass up. Face down. Womanhood pulsing, watering. She was so wet she felt it simmering in the creases of her thighs.

POP

"Isa!"

"Stop all that yelling, Ali. If you ain't using the safe word don't say shit. You either want me to stop or keep going. Ain't no bitching up though," Isa said.

The reprimand to her clit. A spanking. Something hard. A quick blow. Her softest parts accepting punishment as Isa tapped it three times with what felt like a leather ruler.

POP

POP

He punished her clit and it was so tender that Aria whimpered. The numb feeling from the injury disappeared when his warm tongue followed up.

He sucked on it like he was trying to shrink an old school jaw breaker.

Aria was delirious. She lost time.

The pain that seared her when he took that flogger to her backside made her cry out and cum at the same time. "Submit!"

Isa gripped her hips, giving up the pain for pleasure and he entered her from behind.

"Damn, Ali. This shit," he groaned.

He fucked her so hard that arch became level.

"Hmmm submit, baby. Submit!" she moaned. The restraints stopped her from doing anything except take it until she came again. "God, this dick is amazing."

Isa hit her with death strokes. One after the other, releasing all of his angst onto the sheet as he pulled out.

He collapsed on top of her, french kissing the nape of her neck. He lifted and reached for the restraints, but even when she was free, she didn't move. She just lay there. He covered her and then her eyes closed. She smelled the soap as he showered. She didn't stir until she felt his lips against her head.

She turned on her side and looked at him. "If you die, I'm gonna kill you."

He snickered and then took her lips.

"Come home to me Isa. I ain't your wife yet. At least die when I'm entitled to some shit. Don't leave me before then okay?"

"Gold digging ass," he said, smiling. "Lock the doors and don't answer for nobody. I might be long, and you might not be able to reach me, but wait for me Ali."

"Forever boy," she answered.

He turned to exit and when he got to the bedroom door she hopped up.

"Isa!"

By the time he turned around she was in his arms. "Be careful," she said as she held onto him.

"Nah, Ali. It's time to get fucking reckless. They should have been careful with you."

He kissed her nose and then pulled back. He was gone before she could miss him.

Aria heard the sound of his BMW's ignition and then the heavy thud of the custom speakers before distance made it disappear.

Aria went to the shower, peeling out of the shirt. The knots of tension that filled her made it feel like she wasn't alone in the house. Aria wasn't a girl who was easily shaken but the shooting had rattled her. She felt safest with Isa at her side. She didn't even want revenge. She just wanted him home. She washed quickly and slid into baggy sweats and a cropped T-shirt before grabbing her keys and her purse. She didn't want to be alone and if she was afraid Morgan had to be afraid too. Aria knew that Isa was going to settle this with the crew. No way was he acting alone. Ahmeek and Messiah would step over Morgan. Even with the elephant in the room between them, no way would they not rectify this on Morgan's behalf. Didn't make sense to wait alone. She sent Morgan a text.

ARIA

Coming to sit with you in the hospital.

Aria didn't wait for a response. She was out the door in seconds. She turned to lock down the house and never even saw it coming. The hand came around her face so quickly that only muffled screams filled the air as she was lifted off her feet.

She dropped her phone and her purse as she fought with all her might. Aria swung and kicked and screamed and bit so much that the man dropped her. She hit the concrete porch face first and her entire brain rattled as stars appeared before her eyes.

"I got her."

It was the last thing she heard before everything went dark.

29

Morgan sat in the town car in silence as she held Messari in her arms. Yara sat with Bash as the city streets passed them by. She had no words. There was nothing to say. Bash had laid out the law for Morgan to follow and she had no choice but to obey.

"I think it's time you start thinking about giving up your apartment." Bash's baritone put so much angst on her soul. She couldn't help but wonder how they had gotten to this place. She knew she was mostly to blame for the rift between them.

"I have a lease, Bash. After the lease is up, we can talk about it, but I don't want to give up my own space right now."

She felt his eyes on her, but instead of fighting she simply looked out her window, falling back into her thoughts. She felt so much despair. Both Messiah and Ahmeek had given her love affairs to remember. They had been filled with passion and unpredictability, with unbelievable yearning and uncontrollable obsession. Bash gave her consistency, but he had hit her . . . twice. She feared there would come a day when she would provoke a third. Morgan had known that she didn't love him when they started. She liked him well enough, but the infatuation that came with something new was only felt by him. She should have pulled out then. She should have taken time after losing Messiah but instead she allowed Bash to fill a seat. She let him lead her, distract her, for the sake of feeling anything else other than the grief that she was going through. Now he was attached, and Morgan wanted nothing more than to detach. The things he knew were damaging however. This game of love and lies had high stakes and if she lost, Ethic would pay the ultimate cost.

When the driver pulled up to her apartment her heart went crazy. It was caught behind a cage that Bash had trapped it in, but it wanted to be freed. Her eyes misted as she popped open the door and stood with her son in her arms.

Ahmeek sat there. On the steps of her building. There was no telling how long he'd been there. His head hung low and he rubbed the top in distress. Morgan almost took off running to him. If it hadn't been for Bash at her side, she would have.

"I thought we discussed this, Mo," Bash said.

"I didn't know he would be here. I didn't ask him to come," Morgan said, under her breath. "I'll get rid of him. I told you. I'm done with all this."

Ahmeek glanced up and faltered a bit before coming to his feet. Morgan could see the disappointment in Meek. The anger. Just at the sight of her standing beside Bash.

"Morgan." Her name rolled off his tongue accompanied by a sigh of relief. He had been worried. She looked at his hands, they were swollen, bloodied, his shirt spattered with blood as well.

"You're hurt?" she asked, a slight panic filling her.

"No, love. A lot of niggas are hurt behind you though. Anybody who I even thought had beef is hurt right now behind what went down yesterday. The shit shouldn't have happened. I don't know who's behind it, but shit gon' be this way until I find out. A lot of curbside vigils out this bitch. I'm sorry, Mo. Tell me you're okay. Your face, love."

Morgan pulled her busted lip into her mouth. "It happened in the shooting," she lied. "When I fell to the floor. I didn't realize it until afterward." Ahmeek reached for her face and Morgan pulled her head back, not wanting him to inspect further. She couldn't let him know Bash had done this.

Morgan turned to Bash. "Can you give me a minute? Take them upstairs?" she asked. Bash's eyes burned into Morgan's and she nodded. "Please, Bash. I know." She tried to hand Yara over, but she resisted, clinging to Morgan's neck. Morgan hoisted Yara up on her hip. "Just take Ssari up. He needs to take more Tylenol soon. I don't want him in pain. I'll handle this."

Bash reluctantly took her key. "Handle it, Mo," he stated. She nodded and he bypassed Ahmeek as he went into the building.

"Handle it? You handling me now, love?" Ahmeek asked.

Yara squirmed in Morgan's hold, reaching out for Ahmeek. He took her like she belonged to him and Morgan's insides ached.

"This has to end, Meek."

Morgan's words were small.

He let silence chew her up and ran a hand down his beard. "Morgan—"

"No, Ahmeek," she interrupted. "No. I can't. It's over. I don't want you!" Every word was breaking her heart.

Morgan's words were like blows to Ahmeek. She may as well have been swinging. "I'm done. You and I never had a chance. It was stupid. I was stupid to ever even start this."

Morgan closed her eyes and the damn tear that slid down her face was all it took for Ahmeek to close the space between them.

Morgan dodged his touch, moving her head and then took Yara from his arms.

"If you don't want me here, why are you crying, love?" he asked. "Do you know how the news of that shooting ate me alive yesterday? Do you know the shit that went through my head?"

Morgan was losing her composure. She sobbed as she looked down at her feet. His finger lifted her chin. "In my eyes," he commanded. "How the fuck we get back here, Mo? You back with this nigga? You playing games again? We been past this stage, Mo. What you doing, love? Just come with me. Come home with me, Morgan."

"Ahmeek!" she gasped. Morgan couldn't breathe. She was falling apart. "I don't love you. It's never been you and we both know that. You were just filling a void. Messiah's back. What do I need you for?"

It was the one thing that she knew would make him hit the brakes on her. The words were so callous that it injured her to speak them, she could only imagine how it felt to be on the receiving end. She saw his eyes change. They went cold in an instant. Ahmeek who was only soft for her had restored his guard. Morgan knew he had turned off his affections for her. She felt it. She had said the only thing that would make him hate her and she immediately wanted to take it back. She wanted to tell Meek that Bash had her in a vulnerable position, but she couldn't. Ethic was at risk because of her. Her future was at risk. One thing Bash was right about was her affiliation with bad boys had come back to haunt her. Her children's safety had been jeopardized and she was lucky they had all walked away with their lives.

"I'm so sorry, Ahmeek," she whispered. Her chin trembled, and her chest filled with emotion. Her wet eyes pleaded with him. He was so close. All she had to do was tell him what was going on. He would handle it. He would keep her safe. He would, and she knew it, but she couldn't take the risk. She had been hesitant to take a chance on him since they had started, and he was done. He was forfeiting the possibility altogether and Morgan just wanted him to look past the outside and read her mind. If he did, he would know that she didn't mean these words she spoke.

He pulled his bottom lip into his mouth, biting it, undoubtedly refraining, showing restraint because she was sure he had so much to say. She could see his frustration. Feel his ire. His eyes flickered with something. A bit of pain. Annoyance. Impatience. Ahmeek nodded then pushed out a breath of disbelief.

He kissed the side of Yara's head and then handed her off to Morgan.

"You want to fuck with niggas that ain't gon' do you right," he said, scoffing and nodding like he was coming to an understanding. "You got it. I'm hands off with it. If you like it, I love it. I'ma fall all the way back."

She wanted to call his name, scream it in fact, as she watched him walk away. If he looked back at her she told herself she wouldn't be able to let him go. He never did. He climbed into his car and pulled away without giving her a second look. Morgan was shattered. She turned toward the building and looked up to find Bash peeking through the blinds. It made her want to run. Dread filled her stomach because Mo was filled with uncertainty. Bash was beginning to show parts of him that proved dangerous. She only hoped that he would think twice before putting hands on her again because Morgan had already told herself that if he did it again, one of them wouldn't walk away with their life. She refused to turn into her sister and she would protect herself and her babies by any means necessary . . .

READ ON FOR AN EXCERPT FROM

Butterfly 3

COMING SOON

DON'T FORGET TO CHECK OUT THE ETHIC SERIES
BOOKS 1–5 ARE AVAILABLE NOW ON AMAZON.

The chime that interrupted commanded their attention to the front door.

Morgan walked down the corridor toward the foyer. "Where did they go anyway?" she yelled.

She pulled open the door and her heart stalled. Ethic was speaking behind her, but she couldn't hear him. She couldn't hear shit.

The scowl that drew wrinkles onto his forehead eased some when he saw her face. Surprise. He was shocked to see her there. Gratefulness. She saw the thought manifest in his mind. He was happy to see her. Messiah. Motherfucking Messiah. Morgan's chest automatically caved around him. It was like he had taken a knife and carved out her heart, every time he was in her space. She hated he had that power. She hated that she would always feel him, be affected by him, love him. Stupid ass.

"Shorty," he greeted. Morgan gripped the wood of the door as her entire body tensed. She hated that her eyes misted. His eyes took her in. "Damn, shorty. You graduating? I missed a lot."

"You missed everything," she whispered. He took two steps and was in her yard, fucking up her grass, trampling all on her flower bed as he trapped her against the wall. Just like Messiah to fuck shit up to get to her. Morgan's breath hitched and her lashes fluttered. Stupid ass nigga. She both adored this feeling and despised it. He just controlled her. Like there was a remote control to her emotions and he was pressing every damn button like a bad ass kid.

"I don't want to miss shit else, Mo," he said. Morgan tried to ease by him, but he placed a hand to the wall, stopping her. She went the other way. Another hand. She blew out a breath and rolled her eyes up to him. Niggas and the traps they captured her in. Trap niggas. Hood niggas. Why the hell did she have to be attracted to that type?

"Hear me, shorty. We gon' get this wrong until we get it right cuz I ain't come back for nothing else but you. I'm not accepting nothing less than you."

"And I'm not accepting nothing less than loyalty. Can you look me in the face and tell me you're done hurting me? That there are no more secrets. Nothing else I don't know. That I'm safe with you?"

Messiah bit into his bottom lip and turned his head as thoughts of Bleu ran through his mind. Thoughts of other things, too.

Morgan scoffed. She could see the secrets he was keeping. She didn't know what they were, but she felt them. She had learned to listen to her intuition. He had taught her to trust it with his deception. She had ignored them before when it came to him. She would never do that again. Ahmeek didn't make her feel this. Like she had to protect herself. He didn't scare her at all. A huge part of her was fearful of Messiah. Like she was alert, on the ready, bracing for emotional impact because he was going to deliver another blow that would devastate her.

"Same Messiah, different day," Morgan said. She lifted his arm and walked away.

She couldn't get away from him fast enough. The fact that she was practically running away from the man she desperately used to pray she could run to bothered her. The change between them unearthed raw emotion.

"How are you okay with him being here?" she asked as soon as Ethic came back into view. Messiah trailed her slowly, coolly. He knew now was not the time to give chase.

"He's trying to make amends, Mo. It's not my place to stop a man from attempting to right his wrongs," Ethic said. "You two have a lot to talk about."

"We have nothing to talk about," Morgan answered. She was adamant in her disdain. Stubborn. Too hurt to let the present heal the wounds of the past.

"Mo, you have every reason to hear him out," Alani reminded as she stood while carrying Messari. Ethic moved to help her. "I've got him, Ezra." She turned back to Mo. "You've got damn good reason, Mo."

"I don't owe him anything . . ."

"Shorty's right. She ain't the one with debts to settle. This is her crib. Y'all her people. I'ma get out of here make it easier on everybody."

Messiah backpedaled. He wasn't trying to upset her. It was like a jab to the chin that his presence upset her so much, but he was willing to baby step his way back into her life.

"You can stay. I was leaving anyway," Mo said.

"You might as well stay and wait for me to hem this gown, Mo. Cut it out," Alani said. She struggled with Messari in her arms. "Messiah, you don't have to leave either. I actually really need your help. Well, Ezra does. He's building me a greenhouse." Alani pointed at Messiah. "Might want to take off that fly ass jacket, playa, because you're helping him."

Messiah licked his bottom lip and debated if he wanted to follow directions. Alani somehow gave them out like a school teacher. No questions. All statements. Messiah didn't particularly like it. He didn't particularly dislike it either. Something about her felt like he was supposed to listen. Like she was the core of everyone in the room and they were to protect her at all costs. It was an odd feeling. He had never felt that before for anyone. Motherly. It was almost motherly. He nodded and then peeled out of the jacket.

The room felt small. Her and Messiah in the same space. The tension. The things floating around in their heads but trapped by sealed lips. Morgan heard her heart racing. She was uncomfortable. Being around him didn't feel the same. He used to fill her with so much confidence. Now all she felt was the insecurity of unfamiliarity eating her alive. Distance and dishonesty had done a number on them. The thought of how much of a stranger he was to her made her sad.

"Let me put Ssari in the hammock outside. Mo, you can come out when you're ready," Alani said. "Grab the sewing kit from the upstairs closet in the master bedroom."

Morgan felt Messiah's eyes robbing her of her courage. Damn outlaw. He stayed stealing shit. She huffed and retreated upstairs leaving him with Ethic and Alani. Morgan quickly located Alani's sewing kit and then she made her way to her old room. It overlooked the backyard. She watched Yara play in the wading pool with Eazy and she smiled as he signed to her. Her eyes drifted to Messiah. Unease filled her but she couldn't deny her relief. Just to lay eyes on him again was a gift. No matter how angry she was with him. Morgan felt like she was staring at a force. Messiah was energy and Morgan could feel his pull. Her heart clenched when she saw Messiah walk over to the pool where Yara played. She sucked in air, forgetting to release it as he squatted. Eye to eye he lingered in front of Yara. The daughter he didn't even know he had, and Morgan froze. Yara retreated, crying as she ran toward Eazy. She didn't know him, and her deaf daughter was an empath. She sensed the wickedness in this gangster. Yara had no idea that the devil inside Messiah would burn an entire city to the ground for her. If he only knew that she was of his loins. Blood of his blood. The combination of what their passion had made. Morgan wasn't sure if it was love anymore. She wasn't sure of anything. What she felt for Ahmeek was different than what she felt for Messiah and she was sure that she loved Meek. Messiah's connection felt like ownership. Like he had purchased her outright and paid in full, all big bills and he was refusing to sign away the title.

Morgan felt exposed when Messiah lifted his attention to the window.

"Let me get that, shorty."

It would have been crass had he spoken the words. It was fucking charming as hell however because he had signed them. Signed them better than ever. Morgan felt her face heat as her fair skin turned scarlet. The arrogant smirk that pulled at the corners of his lips pissed Morgan off so badly she closed the blinds, blocking his view of her.

She wanted to sit in her room, barricade herself inside, but she refused to give Messiah that power. She had cried many tears between these four walls over him. She had prayed to God to bring him back all those years ago. Her prayers had never been answered and Morgan had fallen down a rabbit hole of dysfunction. Morgan was just beginning to feel like herself after losing him and as if he had an alarm that warned him that she was about to move on, he had popped back into her life. It was so overwhelming that Morgan hadn't even taken the time to process his resurrection. She took a deep breath and headed toward the backyard. This was her family. She had every right to be here. Messiah could only make her feel uncomfortable if she let him. She walked downstairs and headed toward the back but as she entered the kitchen Messiah came waltzing through the sliding doors. Her breath hitched and she stopped walking. Messiah stood before her. Fresh fade, white T-shirt, and hoop shorts with fresh J's.

"You good, shorty?" he asked.

"I'm fine."

She didn't even know how she answered him because she was stuck. Stuck in the past, stuck in that kitchen pantry he had devoured her in all those years ago. Stuck between the four walls of her bedroom where she used to grease his scalp. Her memories were like quicksand and although she was standing there calm, she was screaming on the inside.

"After the shooting, I mean. I know how you are with shit like that. You good good?" he asked.

Morgan shrugged and then looked down at her feet.

"You're so fucking pretty, man."

Her eyes shot to his and then they teared. STUPID ASS NIGGA.

"Nah, Mo. No more tears. Not over me. I don't even deserve 'em," Messiah said.

"What do you want Messiah? Why are you here?" Morgan asked. "This is *my* family."

"They're mine too, Mo. I ain't got you. Ethic's all I got."

Morgan felt a bit of guilt because it was true. Messiah had no one. Morgan would have to share her world because for so long he had been a huge part of it too.

"What do you want?" she asked.

"You," he answered. He had never been the one to hold punches. No point in lying. They both knew why he had returned.

"We happened a long time ago, Messiah. It was like living in the clouds back then. You dropped me so hard. You don't make me feel like I'm flying anymore. I sink with you. I just can't let you fill my head with air this time. I've got to keep my feet on the ground."

"Fuck gravity, I want to be high, Mo," Messiah said. He leaned against the wall and lifted one foot as his eyes penetrated hers. She didn't know what to say. She couldn't join him this time. She couldn't let him take her to outer space. There was no oxygen there. She would die this time.

Oddball Dsgns

ASHLEY ANTOINETTE is one of the most successful female writers of her time. The feminine half of the popular married duo Ashley and JaQuavis, she has co-written more than forty novels. Several of her titles have hit the *New York Times* bestsellers list, but she is most widely regarded for her racy series The Prada Plan. Born in Flint, Michigan, she was bred with an innate street sense that she uses as motivation in her crime-filled writings.

 /authorashleyantoinette

@Novelista

 @AshleyAntoinette